MINE

DARK WHY CHOOSE ROMANCE

STRENGTH & HEAT
BOOK 2

T.O. SMITH

Cover Design: Tiff Writes Romance

Editing: Tiff Writes Romance

Proofreading: Kimberly Peterson

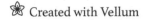 Created with Vellum

For Riley, my reason for everything you do.

My darling girl, may you never know this pain—this suffering—but if you do, I hope you'll find strength in this book.

If you find yourself lost, may you always be like the moon, phasing but always returning to your beautiful glow.

MAY YOU ALWAYS HAVE THE
LIGHT OF THE MOON WHEN
EVERYTHING ELSE IS DARK.

AND MAY IT ALWAYS CRADLE YOU
IN ITS SOOTHING LIGHT.

NOTE FROM THE AUTHOR:

Please note this book contains situations that may be uncomfortable for some readers. Some of these situations include miscarriage, pregnancy, a bisexual male character that continues sleeping with other men with the permission of the FMC, depression, anxiety, PTSD, schizophrenia, neglectful parents, and drug overdose.

If you have any questions about anything in this book before reading, please reach out to me via social media or through my author email (authortosmith@ gmail.com). I will be happy to answer any questions you may have.

1

SPIRALING

Ally

I frowned as I stared down at the textbook in front of me. I hadn't been getting much sleep lately, and it was making it hard to concentrate on my schoolwork.

I had kind of placed my life around school. It kept me grounded, gave me something to focus on. But times like these, when my anxiety started acting up and my depression took a plunge, it was hard for me to do the things that kept me sane.

I shoved my textbook away from me and frowned down at the table, my chest feeling tight. Today was my dad's birthday, and he hadn't spoken to me in three years now.

After I had spiraled to the point that I was hospitalized in a mental health facility, my parents had turned their backs on me. I ruined their perfect little image that they tried so hard to keep up. So, I was shunned, just as my brother was.

All because we didn't fit into their perfect little lifestyle.

My phone began to vibrate on the table, jerking me out of my head. I picked it up when I saw my older brother's name on the screen.

"Axel," I whispered when I answered. I swallowed thickly. "Why is it still so hard?" I asked, my voice shaking.

"You were Dad's little girl, Ally," my brother said softly, understanding in his tone. My chest squeezed. He knew me so well. I didn't even have to elaborate. He instantly knew today would be a hard day for me. "He turned his back on you. It's normal for it to hurt, for it to bother you."

"I didn't ask to be this fucked up," I croaked, my voice breaking. Why did I have to be made out to be the bad guy? If I could be normal, I would.

Axel growled softly. "Ally, don't," he warned me. "Don't do this to yourself. You're not fucked up. You have bipolar depression; you went through hell and back to control that and overcome postpartum psychosis," he reminded me. I rubbed at my chest, that ache never fading. It was just something I was living with. I'd been pregnant when I found my boyfriend cheating on me. I overdosed on my medication. And after finding out I'd lost my baby...well, I sort of lost myself, too. "I know it feels like your loss, but it's Mom and Dad's loss for not wanting to know the amazing, beautiful, young woman you've grown into."

Axel had never lost faith in me. Even when I lost faith in myself, was so lost in my hatred of the world that I self-destructed, he had always believed in me.

"Can I come stay with you guys for a few days?" I asked him. "I feel myself slipping, Axel, and I'm scared," I shakily admitted. "I don't know how to stop it."

"Sis, our home is *always* open to you," Axel reminded me. "I'll let Julian and Meghan know you're coming."

"Thank you, Axel–for never giving up on me," I told him, my voice soft and filled with gratitude.

"I love you, Ally. No matter how bad this shit gets for you, I'm always here for you if you'll let me," he promised. "Come on home."

A little over two years ago when I had been released from the center, I had moved in with my older brother. Since he and his best friend are both with the same woman, I moved in with all of them. Meghan, my brother's wife, had been my rock while I was in the center, and to this day, she was still always there for me when I needed her, even if it was at the drop of a hat.

I honestly didn't know if I would have made it to where I am today without her.

Which is quite hilarious considering I used to hate her guts. I hated her for taking my brother from me. I hated her for having everything I'd ever wanted–unconditional love, a family that gave a damn...

But when my eyes finally opened, I realized she was far from my enemy. Meghan taught me how to swim in treacherous waters.

I quickly packed my bag, but my phone vibrated again as I got ready to zip my bag up. Frowning, I picked it up off the table, my heart beginning to race in my chest when I saw my dad's name on my phone screen.

I squeezed my eyes shut, trying to remember how to breathe, trying to remember how to stop my anxiety attack. Why was he reaching out now after all this time?

I couldn't remember, and I was panicking.

I gasped for air, hot tears sliding down my cheeks as I struggled to breathe. Black spots were dancing in my vision, and my ears were beginning to ring, a sure sign that I was moments away from completely losing my grip and passing out. It happened more often than not.

Large, warm hands grasped my face, pulling my head up. Vibrant green eyes locked on mine, and they were sure and steady as they locked on mine. "Hey, focus on me, okay? Breathe, darlin'," the man in front of me coaxed. He grabbed my shaking hand and pressed it to his large, toned chest. "Breathe. Focus on my steady heart rate; focus on my slow and steady breaths, darlin'."

I whimpered, the pain in my chest intensifying as I tried to breathe like he was. He brushed his thumb over my cheek, his lips tilting up into a sexy, half smile. "There you go. You're doing great. Just breathe, darlin'."

Once the anxiety attack passed, I closed my eyes, drawing in shaky, calming breaths. "Thank you," I whispered, opening my eyes to look at the gorgeous guy in front of me.

He smiled at me as he flicked his dark hair out of his eyes. "I saw you panicking when I walked out of the study room next to this one." He brushed his thumb over the back of my hand. "Does this happen a lot?"

I only shrugged, not wanting to answer him. I was a freak. I knew that. I didn't want him looking at me like I was.

He sat down in one of the chairs at the table. "Are you okay?"

I nodded my head. "Yeah, I um, I'm just on my way to my brother's," I told him.

He stood up and held his hand out to me with a charming, panty-dropping smile. God, he was so fucking gorgeous. It wasn't fair that God made them like this. "Need a lift?" he asked.

"Um, no." I flushed. He'd just seen me have a panic attack, and he wasn't running away. I wasn't sure what to do with that. "But thank you. I can drive myself."

He nodded as I grabbed my bag and stood up from my chair, ignoring the hand he was holding out to me. He casually dropped it back to his side, not the least bit offended. "My name is Christian." He softly smiled at me. "I hope to see you around again," he said, not allowing my hostility to drive him away.

I only gave him a small smile before I quickly walked out of the study room, my cheeks burning hot.

He had to be the hottest guy I had ever laid my eyes on. Of course, he would also be the person to see me at one of my lowest moments.

I swear, I had no fucking luck when it came to guys.

I flinched at that thought, pushing away that dark time of my life. Even if it was currently trying to force itself into my present, I was determined as fuck to keep it in the past where it belonged.

C

Meghan took a seat beside me on the couch and threw a blanket over both of us before she turned her body slightly to face me. "Why did you lie to your brother earlier?" she quietly asked me.

Meghan had taken one look at me when I walked into the house, and she had instantly been able to tell that I'd had an anxiety attack. I couldn't hide anything from her. She knew the signs on me so well. Sometimes, I hated it. But it also helped me breathe a little easier to know I wasn't suffering alone.

I sighed, closing my eyes and leaning my head back. "Axel worries so much already, Meghan. Especially during times like this. I don't want him to freak out. I had an anxiety attack." I shrugged. "It's not a big deal."

She frowned as she ran her pretty green eyes over my face. "How many have you had recently, though?" she asked me softly.

I scrubbed my hands down my face. Meghan was the one person in the world that I could never lie to– especially not after everything she had done for me despite how cruel and hateful I had once been toward her. "This makes the fifth one in two weeks," I told her quietly. "Things are getting hectic at school with exams coming up, and I'm having trouble keeping up with everything." It was only a partial lie.

Meghan grabbed my hand in hers. "You know it's not just that," she gently reminded me. I swallowed thickly. God, why did she have to remember every-thing? "The anniversary is coming up."

I blinked the tears out of my eyes, refusing to cry. I wouldn't cry right now. "He tried to contact me a couple of weeks ago," I confessed. Anger flashed in Meghan's eyes on my behalf. "He's been texting me every other day since then, trying to get me to talk to him."

"Well, that explains your anxiety attacks," Meghan noted. "You need to begin seeing Dr. Gresham again– regularly," she sternly told me when I opened my mouth to remind her that I already saw him once every three months to make sure my medications were still working okay for me. "And you need to tell Axel and Julian what your ex is doing."

I shook my head. "No, Meghan. Not with the kids and everything else you guys have going on–"

Megan sent me a lightly scolding look, shutting me up. I sighed, knowing I was going to lose this argument with her. "You need to talk to them–tonight, Ally," Meghan added, her voice stern. I sighed again. I was just so tired. My anxiety attacks drained me, and I just wanted to sleep. "Trying to deal with this on your own is going to make everything worse, Ally. You need to talk to them and let them handle this."

Julian leaned over the back of the couch and pressed a kiss to Meghan's forehead. My heart ached with that familiar longing for someone to love me as much as Julian and Axel loved Meghan.

"Talk to us about what, babe?" he asked her.

"Go get Axel," she told him.

He frowned down at her, his eyes running over her face for a moment before he went in search of my brother. My heart began to thump wildly in my chest, and nausea swirled in my gut. I wasn't ready to talk about this.

Meghan squeezed my hand, drawing my eyes back to her. "Remember that I'm right here by your side, Ally. You don't have anything to fear. We all love you. Remember that," she soothed.

I drew in a deep, shaky breath. It wasn't that simple because though Axel was sweet and understanding, when it came to family, both he and Julian could become absolute monsters.

C

I watched as Axel took a seat in the recliner in the living room. He still had his slacks and his crisp, white, button-down shirt on, not yet having changed out of his clothes from work. He was a therapist–specifically a trauma therapist. He was damn good at what he did– one of the most highly recommended therapists in the state.

I wanted to be half as good of a person as he was one day.

Julian sat on the loveseat, his body angled toward

us. I nervously looked at Meghan. She gave my hand a reassuring squeeze. "Tell them the truth, Ally–every-thing. You're not burdening them," she promised.

I drew in a deep shaky breath, looking at my older brother. His brown eyes were soft and gentle as he waited on me to speak. I swallowed nervously. "I've had five anxiety attacks in the past two weeks," I informed them, my voice quiet and shaky.

"Jesus Christ," Julian swore as he leaned forward in his chair, his blue eyes intent on mine. "Why the fuck didn't you come to one of us, Ally?" he asked me. Tears burned in my eyes. "You know I would have never judged you." he reminded me, his tone a bit gentler. "I've seen you in some of your weakest moments."

I knew that, too. For years, he kept the secret of me cutting myself with the condition that I promised him I would never cut myself again.

I drew in a shaky breath. "I didn't want to burden you guys," I choked out. "I was trying to deal with it. I can't lean on you three forever."

"Like hell you can't," Axel told me. I turned my eyes to him. "We are your family, Ally. None of us sitting in this room with you are going to turn our backs on you. We love you, Ally. You should have called one of us when you had the *first* anxiety attack."

I looked down at the blanket. "That's not all," I said

quietly. Julian softly growled. "My ex tried contacting me a couple of weeks ago."

"Fucking hell!" Julian snapped as he jumped up from the chair. Axel stood up as well, his eyes murderous.

Almost three years ago, I'd caught my ex cheating on me with a girl from school–and not just any girl, but his stepsister. She and I had actually started becoming really good friends. She had been the first real girl-friend I'd had in a long, long time.

But I wanted to surprise her on her birthday, and instead, I found my boyfriend–her stepbrother–balls deep inside of her.

I'd gone home and swallowed my antidepressants to try to kill myself.

Randall, my ex, had told *everyone* that I had lied, and it had instead been his twin brother. Whereas Randall did have a twin, they weren't identical twins.

I knew what I had seen that day.

Axel, Julian, and Meghan had all believed me when I told them what happened, and after showing them pictures of Randall and his brother, Max, there was no doubt. Randall had been the one sleeping with Heather.

They were together now with a two-year-old little girl and another baby on the way. The text I had received had been of their family, and he had asked me to come to their baby shower so we could all reconnect, claiming Heather missed me.

"What the fuck did he send to you?" Axel demanded.

I silently pulled my phone out of my pocket and unlocked it, handing it over to my brother. Meghan squeezed my hand in hers, reminding me that I wasn't alone. She was still here with me, still supporting me, just as she had promised she always would.

"*What the fuck*?!" Julian roared.

Tears burned at the back of my eyes, and they slowly spilled over onto my cheeks. Meghan quickly hugged me as I drew in a shuddered breath. "I hate that it hurts," I whimpered. "All of this time, and it still hurts that they did that. It shouldn't hurt this much."

Meghan gently brushed some tears off my cheeks. "Ally, one day, someone really fucking amazing will come along, and he'll make you forget about all of the pain you went through. He'll go above and beyond to make sure your every need is met, that you're never unhappy."

The doorbell suddenly rang. Axel cursed as he handed Julian my phone. Julian began to rapidly type on it. I knew he was sending Randall a nasty message, and I knew it would be one that I wouldn't want to read.

Julian was a monster when you fucked with people he cared about.

"I invited one of my interns over for dinner. He wanted to learn more about trauma patients, and unfortunately, school doesn't give him much time," Axel told us. He looked down at me. "If you can't handle visitors tonight, I'll tell him we have to reschedule, Sis. You just say the words."

I shook my head, swiping at my cheeks. "I'll go clean up," I told him. "I'll be out in a few minutes."

I stood up from the couch. My brother wrapped his arms around me, squeezing me to him. I bit back a sob and hugged him back. "I know it was hard coming to us about this, but I'm proud of you, Ally." A lump formed in my throat, and tears burned at my eyes again. "You have no idea how brave and strong you are, Little Sis. Just keep fighting for me, yeah? And when fighting gets to be too hard, come to one of us. We can hold you up."

I nodded, and when he released me, I quickly disappeared down the hall to my room.

2

THE VOICES

Ally

My eyes widened in shock as I stared at Christian. He was sitting beside my usual seat at the dining room table.

Oh, my God–my brother's intern had seen me have a fucking panic attack.

Could my day get any worse?

Christian's eyes brightened at the sight of me, and my body betrayed me by flushing under his gaze. "This is your sister?" he asked Axel, not removing his eyes from me.

I swallowed nervously. Axel stood up from the table and pulled my chair out for me with a warm, brotherly smile. "Yes. Christian, meet Ally, my little sister. Ally,

meet Christian, the intern at my office," Axel introduced us.

Christian gave me a warm smile. My cheeks heated
under the intensity of his dark eyes. His eyes were so
dark, they were almost black. One might think they
would be cold–emotionless–but his eyes were warm
and welcoming, inviting me into his comfort. And God
if I didn't want to seek solace there.

"We met earlier today, actually," he told Axel. My face
paled. Was he going to speak up about my anxiety attack,
about how bad it had gotten by the time he stepped in to
help me? "I was in the study room next to hers, and I
heard her drop all of her books as I was leaving, so I went
in to help her," he informed Axel, turning those mesmer-
izing eyes away from me and to my older brother.

Something warm stirred in my chest.

He'd kept my dark secret.

Julian brought Meghan's hand up to his lips to press
a kiss to her knuckles, but he shot me a knowing smirk.
I rolled my eyes at him, but my cheeks burned red,
giving me away.

Julian knew I liked Christian.

Holden, my nephew, suddenly screeched and threw
his plate of food to the floor. Meghan sighed tiredly,
reaching up to rub her temples. No doubt, the kids had
been giving her a hell of a time today. She normally had

the patience of a saint when it came to them. After losing her first child, she considered both of her children an absolute blessing.

Holden was Julian's son. My brother wanted to give the two of them a second chance at their miracle baby. A lot of people didn't understand it–thought they should all be equal and both of them given equal chances–but what Axel, Julian, and Meghan shared was nothing like I'd ever seen or read about before. Their love was truly one of a kind.

Axel leaned over and lightly brushed his lips with hers, soothing her as Julian got up to clean up Holden's mess.

"You wanted to know more about anxiety attacks?" Axel asked Christian.

My blood chilled in my veins. Meghan caught my eye from across the table. Her eyes flickered to Christian for a moment before they settled back on me. I swallowed thickly.

With that one glance, she knew Christian had witnessed my anxiety attack and that his story about hearing me drop my books was bullshit.

"Yeah," Christian told him. "I was taught in school about the different ways to help coax people out of them, and they taught us coping mechanisms, but not much else," Christian told him. "They just explained there's a lot of triggers. I was wondering if you could explain to me some of the triggers."

I picked at my food, suddenly not even hungry anymore. Julian gently squeezed my shoulder as he walked past me with the broom and dustpan.

"Specific triggers depend on the patient as an individual. But if you're speaking of just in general, some patients have anxiety attacks if they're highly stressed or overwhelmed. Those specific patients would need to learn to control their environments and the amount of stress they get placed under–set boundaries."

Christian took a sip of the sweet tea in front of him, and I couldn't help but stare at his tattooed arms as they flexed. Every bit of his arms were inked, and the designs were intricately woven, one leading into the other. The shark on his hand blended into the waves on his wrist, which blending into a lighthouse. That lighthouse blended into a sky, which then smoothly transitioned to an eagle.

A tiny smirk tilted his lips, but he didn't turn his eyes to me, though I knew he could feel me staring at him. With my cheeks burning, I quickly turned my eyes away from him. My eyes met my brother's across the table. He arched an eyebrow at me, his eyes flickering to Christian for a moment.

I bit my lip, focusing my gaze on my plate again. "Certain events, such as loud noises, smells, or even just

a picture of something, can provoke an anxiety attack."
Axel cleared his throat, drawing my eyes up to his. I
knew he was silently asking if he could use me as an
example. I shook my head at him, not wanting Christian to know that I was so fucked up. He knew enough
as it was.

Meghan reached up and gently used her fingers to
turn Axel's face to her. She gave him a small, reassuring
smile. He frowned at her, but sighed after a moment.
Both he and Julian were extremely protective of her,
and that meant also protecting her trauma from prying
eyes.

"Meghan is allowing me to use her as an example,"
Axel informed Christian. Christian shot Meghan an
encouraging smile. She returned his smile, but there
was nervousness ringing in her eyes.

"Meghan suffers from a combination of anxiety
and depression," Axel informed Christian. Julian
clenched his jaw but focused his attention on feeding
Holden while still listening to the conversation.
"When she begins to hit a low with her depression,
her anxiety levels rise. Something small and insignificant can cause an anxiety attack, but it happens
because she's already feeling down, so she can't find
the positive thoughts to help balance things out, so to
say."

Christian frowned at Meghan. "You have a

wonderful family to lean on," he told her, sincerity ringing in his voice.

Meghan gave him a small, half-smile. "I know, and I'm thankful for it every single day," she told him honestly.

My phone vibrated in my pocket. I pulled it out, my face paling slightly at the message on my screen.

UNKNOWN NUMBER

> You can tell Julian I said to go fuck himself.

I locked my screen, putting my phone back in my pocket. I looked up, surprised to notice Christian had his eyes narrowed at me slightly, a knowing look gleaming in his eyes. I swallowed thickly, turning away from him as I stood up from the table with my plate of uneaten food. "I forgot about an assignment," I blurted. Axel narrowed his eyes at me, not believing me, but he knew I would come to him on my own time about what was bothering me.

"Make sure you eat your dinner at some point tonight," Axel ordered.

Wordlessly, I nodded and took my plate into the kitchen. I covered it with aluminum foil and put it in the fridge, knowing I wouldn't be touching it tonight.

Tonight was too much, and I couldn't deal with more.

I couldn't get feelings for a guy again. I wouldn't allow another guy to rip me apart like Randall had. I was better off alone.

Christian was dangerous for me. I couldn't be in his presence any longer. He drew me in, and I couldn't take that. Not again.

Relationships destroyed people, and my last one almost killed me.

A scream tore from my throat. I was drenched in sweat, and it was making my clothes stick to my body in the most disgusting way. I hadn't even realized I had fallen asleep. I guessed I finally got tired enough. Normally when this date started rolling around, I avoided sleeping as much as possible.

The nightmares and flashbacks always plagued me the worst this time of year.

I picked up my phone, realizing I had actually only left the dinner table thirty minutes ago.

And yet, that fast, I'd had a nightmare.

I was spiraling, and it was a terrifying, blood-chilling fall.

Hot tears slid down my cheeks. Not only had my dad's birthday just passed, but now the anniversary of my miscarriage was coming—and the day I caught Randall and Heather fucking.

I wanted to scream at the world. How could this place be so fucking cruel? Why so much tragedy in such close proximity to each other?

How could I have been so lost in my fucking misery that I decided to take all of my antidepressants, which caused me to miscarry in the first place?

I couldn't even look at my nephew and niece without feeling pain slicing through my heart, cutting me open. I didn't even trust myself around them. Julian, Axel, Meghan–they all encouraged me to, but I just *couldn't*.

I didn't even protect *my own child* inside of me while I was pregnant. How was I meant to be trusted around Holden and Lana?

I couldn't.

I just wanted this fucking pain to go away. I needed some kind of relief.

But there was no relief. No real, true relief from the pain.

You can always cut again.

I hadn't done that since Julian had found me slicing open my thighs. I had promised him I never would again.

But God, the idea was so tempting.

Would it be possible to feel better? One small cut wouldn't hurt, right?

I sobbed, hating that I was so fucked up that I was actually contemplating cutting myself again, contemplating breaking a promise to Julian, who was basically my brother. He'd helped save me from myself numerous times.

Just one time.

"No!" I screeched, reaching up to tug at my hair.

My door burst open. Julian stood in the doorway. I sobbed, curling in on myself.

"Julian, help me," I cried.

Dr. Gresham did something he doesn't normally do that night.

He made a house call.

My bottom lip trembled as I stared up at him. "I'm— there's voices," I choked out. There had never been voices before, and it was terrifying.

He frowned. "What are these voices asking you to do, Ally?" he asked me, his voice kind—not a hint of judgment lingering in his words.

I looked up at Julian and squeezed my eyes shut, terrified to say it out loud. I couldn't let him know I was a hair's breadth away from breaking the most important promise to him.

"I can't," I whimpered.

"Can we have the room to ourselves?" Dr. Gresham asked my family.

Once we were alone in the living room, Dr. Gresham knelt in front of me. "It's just you and I in the room, Ally," Dr. Gresham soothed. "This is a judgment free zone. No anger from anyone, no lashing out. It's just you and me. Tell me what the voices are saying."

"They want me to cut again," I told him, my voice breaking. Tears slid down my face. "I don't want to," I whimpered. "I want the voices to go away."

"I'm going to bring you to the center for a couple of nights," he told me gently. I sobbed. I didn't want to go back. I was always so alone there with nothing but my dark thoughts to occupy my time. "Just so you can be monitored, okay? And we're going to change up your medications. I want to do a further evaluation, but I'm pretty sure you have schizophrenia."

"*Another* disorder?" I asked him. I resisted the urge to wail. Instead, I just sobbed, my chest caving in. "God, I'm so fucked up."

"No," Dr. Gresham said sternly, shaking his head. "You're a strong, young woman who just happens to have it a little rougher than other women your age, and there's nothing wrong with that." He stood up. "I'm going to go get Axel really quick. Stay here."

I watched as he disappeared into the kitchen. A few moments later, he came back with Axel in tow. I started crying harder. I'd failed my family again. I couldn't even stay somewhat sane for them.

"I need to take her to the center for a couple of nights," Dr. Gresham informed him. "She's hearing voices that are telling her to self-harm again." Axel sat beside me on the couch and drew me into his arms. "I just want to keep her supervised until I can get her started on medication, but I'll need to do a further evaluation before I start her on anything new."

"I'm so sorry," I sobbed. They didn't deserve this. How could I expect them to keep trying to hold me together when I was constantly just becoming even more fucked up?

"*Shh*," Axel quieted me. "It's not your fault, Little Sis. I still love you, no matter what," he reminded me. "I'll never give up on you. Remember that. When you feel alone, remember that promise."

I nodded my head. He pressed a kiss to the top of my head. "I need you to be strong, okay? You've overcome worse, and you'll overcome this," he assured me. "Remember there is a light at the end of the tunnel. You just have to find it."

"Tell Julian I'm trying to keep my promise," I whispered. I *needed* Julian to know that.

Axel nodded. "And you're brave for doing that, Sis. It takes real strength to fight those voices. Continue fighting. You didn't come this far to give up." He stood up from the couch. "Come on. Let's go pack you a bag."

I was packing my bag when my phone buzzed on my nightstand. I grabbed it, looking at the message from an unknown number.

UNKNOWN NUMBER

> Your brother was nice enough to give me your number since I want to get to know you better. I know you're having a rough day, but it gets better, beautiful. Just keep fighting. -Christian

Axel gave me a small smile, obviously having read the message over my shoulder. I was too tired and worn out to even be agitated. "Christian likes you, Sis. And I know that's a terrifying thought for you, but he's a good guy. I wouldn't have given him your number otherwise. Go to the center, get evaluated, and get put on new medication. When you come home, we'll ease back into everything." He hugged me, squeezing me tightly. I bit back more tears. I was so tired of crying tonight. "But don't push away people that want to be there for you, Ally. Maybe Christian can be there for you in a way that Julian, Meghan, and I can't."

My phone buzzed again, and Axel released me. I looked down at it to see another message from Christian.

UNKNOWN NUMBER

> Your eyes reminded me of the moon the moment I looked into them. At first glance, they look brown, but there are these beautiful, golden flecks in them, and they shine so prettily when you smile. Be the moon, Ally. I look forward to taking you on a very nice date when you're feeling better. -Christian

My heart swelled in my chest at Christian's sweet words. *Be the moon.*

I hugged Axel one more time before I followed Dr. Gresham out of the house so he could take me to the center. I knew Axel would inform Meghan and Julian of what was going on because I couldn't face them, especially Julian.

You'll break your word soon enough.

I gritted my teeth, tears swimming in my eyes.

Christian's words rang in my head again. *Be the moon, Ally.*

I drew in a deep, steadying breath. It was time to get better once again, and that meant I needed to face my fears.

3

BE THE MOON

Ally

D r. Gresham smiled at me when his eyes landed on where I was sitting out in the garden. I was in front of the late-blooming rose bush Meghan had first pointed out to me when I was determined to get better. It was always the last to bloom, seeming dead for most of the year. And then, within days, it bloomed so beautifully. It always had the most roses and leaves.

It was our symbol of hope and growth.

I had been in the center for three days now. It was my choice to stay a little bit longer, just to be sure I wouldn't do something stupid while I waited on my new medication to do its manipulations in my brain.

"Axel is here," he informed me. "You ready to go?"

I shrugged. I felt safe here. There were nurses here who could keep a close eye on me, make sure I didn't do anything stupid when left to my thoughts. But the voices had stopped, so I didn't think there was any harm in going home now and resuming my mostly normal life.

I was just extremely nervous to do so.

With a deep breath, I stood up from the bench and stuffed my hands into the pockets of my hoodie. The temperature had surprisingly already dropped for fall, and I knew it was going to be a cold, wicked winter this year.

When I stepped into the reception area with my bag, Axel was leaning against one of the walls, his hands shoved into the pockets of his slacks. His eyes instantly found mine, and he offered me a warm smile.

"Hey, Little Sis," he greeted, drawing me into his arms and hugging me.

I sighed, wrapping my own arms around him, thankful to have someone as amazing as him in my life. Axel would always be my rock, and I knew I would always be able to rely on him.

"Come on; let's get you home, yeah? Meghan made blueberry muffins."

I grinned. She really was the best friend a woman

could ask for. We both had a deep, addictive kind of love for blueberry muffins.

"Your woman is amazing."

He laughed. "Trust me, I know. Julian and I are constantly astounded by her. She's the best." His voice was filled with warmth and love for Meghan. The woman was truly blessed to be so deeply and selflessly loved by two men. Most people were lucky to have one devoted man, and she got lucky *twice*.

I slid into my brother's passenger seat. His phone rang as he was backing out of the parking spot. He sighed, the number for his office popping up on the touch screen radio. "This is Axel," he said when he answered.

"Axel, I know you took the day off, but I have a patient here. She's begging to see you. I think you need to come in. She seems scared of something."

"Fuck," Axel swore. He glanced over at me for a moment. "Are you going to be okay if I go to the office for a little while? I can have Meghan come get you from there if you need."

I shook my head. "I'll be okay," I assured him. I could just chill in one of the empty offices like I normally did.

"I'm on my way to the office now," Axel informed his receptionist, quickly hooking a U-turn to head in the other direction. "Please take the patient to my office and have Christian sit with her until I get back. She doesn't need to be alone right now. I'll be at the office in about five minutes. Go ahead and notify the police that I need an undercover."

Christian.

Be the moon.

How many times had I said that in my head while I'd been in the center, clinging to those three words with everything in me?

He hung up the call a moment later after receiving an affirmative from his receptionist. I looked over at him with wide eyes. "Is she going to be okay?" I asked him, trying to get my mind off the man that had been occupying my thoughts lately.

He nodded, giving me a small smile. "She's strong– nothing will keep her down. She just needs to believe in herself," he assured me.

A few minutes later, we pulled into the lot for his office, and he parked in the spot that was designated specifically for him. He slid out of the car, and I stumbled out ungracefully, tripping over my own feet as I tried to stand up to my full height. Axel snorted. "Will you ever grow out of the clumsiness?" he teased me as he pulled his phone from his pocket.

I rushed to his side, knowing he was waiting for me, but he needed to get into the office for his patient. He typed out a quick message, most likely to Meghan to let her know we would be late coming home, before he pocketed his phone.

"You're an asshole," I told him, a scowl on my features.

He flashed me a grin as we began walking toward the door. "I'm not the one that can't walk on my own two feet," he teased.

I picked up a pinecone and threw it at his back. He shot me a warning look over his shoulder, but I only laughed. He rolled his eyes but grinned at me. "Come on, Sis."

I rushed up the stairs to catch up with him as he held the door open for me. "The office in the back is still vacant if you want to chill there while I take care of this," Axel informed me, leading me through the door that separated the therapy rooms from the reception area.

"Sure," I told him. That had been my plan anyway. "Just come get me whenever you get done."

He disappeared into his office, and the sound of someone crying reached my ears before the door shut behind him, bringing silence to the building once more. I walked down the hall to the vacant office at the end. I pulled my phone out of my pocket, getting ready to find a book to read on my phone as I entered the room.

"Ally!" Christian called from behind me.

I spun around to face him, and a squeak of surprise

left my lips when I lost my footing. Christian's eyes widened, and he lunged forward, catching me before I fell on my ass on the floor. My cheeks burned in embarrassment as I stared up at him, my heart hammering in my chest.

God, could I really make a fool of myself around him any further?

He set me on my feet, holding my shoulders until he was sure I was steady. "Sorry," I sheepishly apologized. "I'd say that doesn't happen a lot, but I'd be lying."

He flashed me a grin that I was sure had many women dropping their panties for him. "That's fine, beautiful." My cheeks burned even redder, my blush creeping up my cheeks. "I don't mind catching you."

My heart skipped a beat in my chest.

Was he always so fucking smooth?

I turned away from him–making sure to be more careful this time so I wouldn't slip and bust my face–and turned to sit on one of the couches in the room.

Christian took a seat beside me and reclined back, looking completely at ease–and fucking sexy as hell in a charcoal gray suit that fit him perfectly, as if he'd had it tailored specifically to his body.

I looked down at my phone so I could stop ogling him. "I'm graduating at the end of this semester," he informed me, breaking our silence. I looked back up at his handsome face. There was a light, five-o'clock shadow on his jawline, making him look a tiny bit more rugged. He looked over at me. "Your brother is offering me a position in the office. This will probably be my office." He waved his hand around. "I always preferred this room."

I smiled at him. Gaining a position in my brother's office, that was huge. People were always trying to gain a position here, but my brother always turned them down. Whenever I used to ask him why, his answer was always 'they just don't feel right to me.'

Axel saw something in Christian that he didn't see in other applicants.

Maybe Christian really was a good guy after all.

But it didn't make me any less afraid of the feelings he evoked in me.

"That's great," I told him. "And I really mean that." He smiled at me, but it wasn't a cocky smile. It was warm, and it made me all tingly inside. "My brother–he's never hired anyone else in this office. It's always been him. People have applied, but he always said they didn't feel right to him. So, you really made an impression on him. That's hard to do."

"I'd like to make an impression on his sister, too," he smoothly slipped in, his eyes completely serious, all teasing gone. My breath hitched in my throat, and I tightened my grip on my phone. "There's something about you, Ally–something about you that fucking calls to me." His eyes met mine. "And I want to see these eyes shine–constantly."

"Be the moon," I whispered before I could stop myself, my cheeks burning red right after.

Way to show him you've been thinking about him, Ally.

But he didn't smirk. There was still no teasing in his eyes as he stared at me.

"I know you try to hide it, Ally." I swallowed thickly, my hands trembling. Things had suddenly gotten serious–a little too serious for my liking. "And you hide it well from many people, but I see how much you're hurting." Tears burned at the back of my eyes. How did he see it so easily? "I see all of the pain that you're trying to hide from the rest of the world because you feel like it makes you stronger to ignore it."

My bottom lip trembled. If he didn't stop, I was going to burst into tears and make a complete fool of myself.

"You deserve to glow, just like the moon," he said softly, reaching out to cup my cheek. "I want to help you glow, beautiful. Your brother sees that I would be good for you. Why are you fighting it? I see you fighting it every time you look at me."

A tear slid down my cheek. "I can't," I choked out. If I did, then I would be giving him the power to hurt me. And I had to protect myself at all costs.

He leaned forward, his thumb brushing over my

cheekbone. I closed my eyes, trying to guard myself against the tenderness in his eyes. It didn't take much to undo me. I was so desperate to have the kind of deep love that I saw Meghan receive every day, and yet, I was still so terrified to have it.

"Open those eyes, beautiful."

I shook my head, wishing my brother would walk in and break this moment. I was powerless against Christian and his sweet words already.

"Open them," he coaxed. "Come on, beautiful."

I slowly opened my eyes, locking them on his impossibly darker ones. They drew me in, holding me captive. "Don't give power to whoever hurt you, Ally." I fought the sob that wanted to rip from my throat. "You're denying yourself of all the beautiful things in life all because you're afraid to be hurt again."

I shook my head at him, but he gently gripped my chin, stopping me. "Don't fight me on this," he begged me. "God, I want you, Ally. I've never been drawn to *anyone* the way I am to you. We can take this as slow as you want, but I want to see you glow. That one time you smiled at me—fuck, you ripped the breath from my lungs and took it as your own."

He leaned forward, his lips just barely brushing mine. I sighed softly, losing myself in him, in his sweet words. "Let me breathe life into you, beautiful."

With that, he firmly pressed our lips together in the sweetest kiss I'd ever had.

All of those shattered pieces of my soul? They glowed.

Christian popped back into the back office with a pizza and a bottle of soda. "I ordered food. Axel is probably going to be a while," he informed me. "Hungry?"

My stomach rumbled on cue, answering for me. He grinned. "Thought you would be." He dragged one of the tables over to us and placed the pizza on it. He then went to one of the cabinets and pulled down two plastic cups. I watched as he took a seat back on the couch next to me, pouring soda into both cups. "Here, beautiful," he said, handing me the cup.

I blushed. He ran his eyes over me. "Fucking gorgeous," he whispered more to himself than to me, but I heard nonetheless, and my cheeks burned even hotter.

He opened the pizza box. It was a pepperoni pizza, and I moaned before I could stop myself. "Ooh, my favorite," I whispered to myself as I reached forward for a slice.

Christian smiled at me. "Mine, too. I hate pizza that has all that extra shit on it."

I moaned again as I took a bite of the cheesy slice. Christian adjusted himself, and I almost choked, my heart hammering against my breastbone. "Babe, if you want to take shit slow, you need to stop making all those sexy little sounds," he warned me, his eyes now black.

My breath hitched in my throat. He reached up, and using his thumb, he swiped some sauce from the corner of my mouth. Then, with a sexy smirk, he popped his thumb between his lips, sucking the sauce off his thumb.

My belly tightened as everything down below throbbed for him. My breath hitched in my throat. I couldn't look away from him.

"There it is," he rasped, his eyes locked on mine.

I swallowed thickly. Oh, God, it was going to be so hard to fight the attraction between us. I wanted him–bad.

He finally broke our staring contest, and I sucked a large breath of air into my lungs, my scrambled brain finally resetting itself.

I needed so much help when it came to this man.

Once I had eaten three slices of pizza and drank two cups of soda, I was finally full. Christian managed to eat the rest of the pizza by himself. "Fuck, I was hungry," he groaned as he stood up to throw the pizza box in the trash. "I haven't eaten all day–been busy."

I looked at the time on my phone, frowning. It had

been an hour now since Axel had brought me to the office, and I needed to catch up on schoolwork before class in the morning.

"Something wrong?" Christian asked me.

I sighed. "I need to catch up on some schoolwork. I didn't know this was going to take this long," I told him.

He held his hand out to me. "Come on. I'll take you home." I eyed his hand warily. "Beautiful, you can trust me," he assured me.

I knew I could trust him as a friend, as my brother's employee. My brother wouldn't have offered him a position otherwise. But could I trust him with my heart–my feelings?

I drew in a deep breath, wishing I had Meghan to give me some words of advice at that moment. I was so nervous. I liked Christian–a lot.

Let me breathe life into you.

I placed my hand in his, giving him so much power over me with that single, simple gesture. He gave me a tender smile in return. "So brave, beautiful," he whispered.

My heart skipped a beat as his warm, strong hand wrapped around mine.

4

ALL THE BLOOD

Ally

It had been a week since I'd seen Christian. I'd been focusing on school, playing catch-up, and I'd finally turned in the last late assignment yesterday. Thankfully, after Dr. Gresham's note and Axel's email to all of my professors, I was given a different due date for all of my material to be turned in to them.

Now, I was sitting in the receptionist's chair at my brother's office since his receptionist called out because her son was sick with the flu. He was worried about finding a replacement, but I offered. It wasn't hard. I'd done it before for him.

Honestly, it was so easy that I normally sat there

either reading a book or working on assignments for school.

Like this fucking chemistry assignment that I was stuck on.

I was *really* beginning to regret majoring in pharmacy.

"That textbook is going to catch on fire in a minute," Christian teased.

I jerked my head up, staring at him in shock. I hadn't seen him all day, so I was surprised to see him standing there now. He was wearing a white button-down shirt with the top button undone at his neck. His dark hair was in a messy disarray on the top of his head, looking like he'd run his fingers through it numerous times.

He'd been texting me throughout the week, mostly at night though when I was finally done working on schoolwork. He was honestly so sweet, and he wasn't overbearing. It was...nice to have someone like him that cared.

"What are you working on?" he asked me as he walked around the counter, leaning over to look at the chemistry textbook on my desk. His arm brushed mine, his cologne filling my nostrils. My breath hitched in my throat, my heart pounding in my chest.

Was it normal to be affected so much by someone?

"Ah, chemistry sucks," he commented. He grabbed

another chair and pulled it over next to me. "Here; I'll help. What has you confused?"

I flushed. *Was it that easy to tell that I was lost and frustrated?*

An hour later, my chemistry work was finished. He didn't make any passes at me, keeping everything focused on my schoolwork. I breathed a sigh of relief when I finally closed my textbook. "Thank you," I told him as I pushed it aside, setting my notebook on top of it. I'd have never gotten through it without his help.

He flashed me a heart-melting grin. God, he really had to stop doing this to me. "No problem, beautiful." He grabbed my hand from on top of the desk, linking his fingers with mine. I sucked in a sharp breath, watching the way his hand engulfed mine. But I didn't feel trapped—terrified.

I felt protected.

"I missed you this past week," he told me quietly, his eyes serious. I swallowed nervously. "I'm proud of you for focusing on your schoolwork, though."

I couldn't stop the small smile that slipped onto my lips. He brushed his thumb over the back of my hand. "You're a pharmacy major, right?"

"Yeah," I told him quietly.

"Why?"

I shrugged, looking away from him, my throat closing up, terrified to tell him the exact reason. He gently gripped my chin, turning my head to face him. "Tell me," he coaxed in that low, smooth voice. "I'm not going to judge you, Ally."

I shook my head at him. "I'm sorry," I apologized. "I just—I can't."

A small, reassuring smile tilted his lips. "That's fine," he assured me. "One day, you'll trust me enough," he said, sounding completely confident in that statement.

I frowned slightly. I didn't think I would ever be comfortable enough to tell him how many medications I'd been put on, how many medications I was *still* on.

How I was still so fucked up that I had to have yet *another* medication added to the ones I was already taking.

He dealt with freaks like me on a daily basis. He wouldn't want to be with someone like the people he dealt with all day.

And in a lot of ways, I was worse than them.

"Axel has invited me to dinner again." I arched my brows in surprise. "He said you went back to your place on campus, but will you come?" he asked, sounding hopeful.

"Why?" I asked him.

He leaned forward, his dark eyes running over my face. "Because I like you, Ally. I'm drawn to you. There's something about you that is always pulling me in your direction—like the moon. You're like the moon."

Axel stepped up to the counter. He raised a single eyebrow at us but didn't comment. "Hey, Christian, I need to cancel tonight. Meghan is having a bad night," he explained, worry for his wife in his voice.

I frowned at my brother, worry clenching my chest. "Is she okay?"

He tried to smile at me, but it was more of a grimace. "She will be. I don't have any other appointments today, so I'm closing early. I need to get home to her."

"Go," I told him as I stood from the chair I'd been sitting in, waving him off. "I can close up here. She needs you."

He leaned over the counter to press a kiss to the top of my head before he walked out of the door, pulling his car keys from his pocket. "Does Meghan have a lot of bad days?" Christian asked me as he turned to me, a frown on his lips.

I shook my head. "Not as much as she used to." I sighed softly. "But some things are triggers for her. Axel and Julian will take care of her."

Christian's frown deepened as he gazed at me. I moved out from behind the desk, going to lock the front door so I could begin the closing procedure. "Ally,"

Christian called, making me pause and turn to face him, "who's taking care of you, beautiful?"

My throat closed up. Without responding, I turned around and continued moving to the front door of the office so I could lock it.

Christian

I jerked out of my dream, blinking up at the ceiling, kind of pissed that I was awake. I'd been dreaming of a perfect brunette with brown eyes that had flecks of gold in them standing in front of the moon as she smiled at me.

Ally was under my skin already, and I didn't want her anywhere else.

There was so much pain in her beautiful eyes that she tried to hide from everyone, but she couldn't fool me. And when I spoke to her, there was hope and longing in those eyes, making the gold flecks shine, but she wouldn't let herself go with me.

But I wanted her with me.

I wanted her to stop surviving and fucking start living.

My phone began ringing on my coffee table. With a grunt, I sat up, snatching it up. Ally's name was on the screen. My heart rate picked up speed in my chest, a smile tilting my lips.

She was actually calling me for once.

"Hey, beautiful," I greeted.

"Is this Christian?" a girl's voice asked me, her voice timid and scared.

I tensed, my chest clenching. Why was some random girl calling me from Ally's phone? "It is. How can I help you?"

"Ally, she's—there's something wrong," the girl said, sounding panicked. "There's blood—there's so much. She begged me to call Axel, but he's not answering, and Julian isn't either. I don't know what to do. She won't let me call 9-1-1."

"Fuck," I swore as I jumped up to my feet. I'd fallen asleep in my work clothes, but I didn't give a fuck how much of a rumpled man I looked.

Ally had harmed herself.

"Tell her help is coming, okay? Don't call 9-1-1." Fuck, she could *not* call 9-1-1. They'd commit Ally, and that would make shit so much worse. "Just hold a towel over her cuts to try to stop the bleeding. If she's coherent, then it's not life-threatening," I assured the girl. "What dorm building and room are you in?" I demanded to know.

"We're in Green—room two-oh-four," she told me. "Please hurry. She's scaring me."

I hung up the phone, shoving my feet into my shoes. I shrugged my hoodie on and rushed down the steps of my house toward my car.

Hang on, beautiful. I'm coming.

Ally

"I'm so sorry," I sobbed. The voices had come back. I couldn't stop them.

He doesn't really care about you.

He just sees you as an easy piece of ass, just like your ex.

Go ahead, relieve that pain.

"Julian, I'm so sorry," I wailed.

The door to my dorm room burst open, and Christian rushed in. I stared at him, tears rushing down my cheeks.

He was seeing how weak and fucked up I was.

My roommate quickly moved out of the way as Christian kneeled in front of me. He cupped my face in his hands, forcing my eyes on his. I whimpered. "I'm here, beautiful," he soothed. "I'm here. You're not alone, baby."

My bottom lip trembled. "I'm so fucked up," I cried.

"No." He shook his head. "It's a chemical imbalance in your brain. You're just built a little differently than other people, and that's okay." He brushed his lips over mine. I sobbed, wishing I could cling to him, but I didn't want to spill my blood, my filth, on his clothes and his skin. "Let me see your wrists, beautiful."

He released my face and slowly removed the towels from my arm. I wailed as I looked at my fucked up arms. Christian gripped my face again, forcing my eyes to lock on his. "Stay with me," he coaxed. "Come on, beautiful, don't leave me. Stay with me."

"I'm so sorry," I cried. "I broke my word to Julian. I promised him I wouldn't do this."

Christian kissed me again, and my chest clenched. "Come on, baby; breathe," he soothed. "Breathe me in. It's okay. They're not that deep; they've already stopped bleeding. It's okay."

I whimpered.

"Easy." He kissed me again. "Be my moon," he begged me. "Come on, beautiful, be my moon."

I scooted closer to him, sobs wracking my chest. He sat on his ass on the floor, holding me tightly on his lap. He gently rocked me, his face buried in my hair. "There you go," he praised. "Let it out, beautiful. Be the moon. The moon has dark phases, but it always glows again."

He looked up at my roommate, who was staring at us, her face pale. "Can you pack her a bag that'll last her for a few nights?" he quietly asked my roommate. "I'm going to take her home with me."

My roommate quickly nodded her head and grabbed one of my small duffels, quickly shoving random items of clothing into it. "I'm sorry I'm fucked up," I apologized again, my words sounding strangled.

"Never fucked up, beautiful." My phone rang on the floor next to me. "Your brother is calling you."

My tears came harder. "He can't—I don't want them to know," I cried.

Christian leaned forward, grabbing my phone off the floor. "They have to know, Ally." A pathetic whimper fell past my lips. "I'm here, beautiful. You're not alone. Not ever again," he promised.

He pulled my phone up to his ear. "Axel? Hey, it's Christian." Christian tightened his arm around me. "I'm going to text you my address. You might want to come to my place in about an hour." Christian grunted. "Yes, an hour, Axel. I just need a moment with your sister." He sighed. "She's going to be. Trust me with her."

He hung up a moment later before he easily stood from the floor with me cradled in his arms. "I'll follow you down to your car," my roommate told him. "I have a week's worth of clothes in this bag."

"You did well," Christian told her as he held me tighter to his chest. I couldn't stop crying, and my clothes were stained with blood. "You got her help, and that's one of the most important things you did tonight."

Christian brushed his lips to the top of my head, protecting me from everyone's stares. "Continue being my moon," he coaxed.

Christian carried me into his house, heading straight for a bedroom. "Your brother will be here in about forty-five minutes. You need a shower."

I clung to him. "Don't leave me alone," I begged him. "I'm scared—there's voices," I choked out.

They were silent for right now, but when I was alone, they were cruel and vicious, tearing me down to the girl I'd been before.

"I won't," he promised as he carried me into his bathroom. He set me on the bathroom counter before he walked over to his shower, turning the water on. He walked back over to me a moment later. "Do you trust me?" He reached up to cup my cheek, brushing his thumb over my skin.

I nodded. He'd just seen me at one of my lowest moments, and there was only soothing tenderness in his eyes as he held my broken pieces in his arms. Of course, I trusted him. How could I not?

He gripped the hem of my bloody shirt and pulled it over my head. His nostrils flared as he ran his eyes over me, but he made no move to touch me sexually, instead only doing what he needed to take care of me.

My bra went next. My bottom lip trembled. I knew he could see my old scars there from when I had cut myself. When I had completely spiraled, showed back up at the center bleeding, I had cut everywhere on my body that would bleed the most.

I wanted to kill myself.

He leaned forward and pressed a kiss to one of the jagged scars across my right breast. "Beautiful," he reverently whispered, his dark eyes locking on mine again.

A tear slid down my cheek.

He'd just kissed a damaged part of me, and there had been no hint of disgust in his eyes.

He just wants your pussy.

I squeezed my eyes shut, reaching up to press my hands to my head. Christian gripped my face, pulling my eyes to his. "Stay with me, beautiful," he soothed. "Whatever bullshit those voices are telling you is not true. You mean the fucking world to me."

"You just want my body," I whimpered.

He shook his head. "I do want your body, yes, but when I have this beautiful body beneath me in my bed and eventually on every piece of furniture in this house," my cheeks tinted red, "you'll know how infinitely precious you are to me. Because you are, beautiful. You're my moon."

He helped me down from the counter and pulled my jeans down, my panties following next. I watched as he quickly undressed, my cheeks burning red as he dropped his briefs, his hard cock coming free.

He made no comment as I snapped my eyes up to his. Instead, he grabbed my hand, pulling me to him. "Trust me," he coaxed. "I'll take care of you, beautiful."

I nodded my head, my bottom lip trembling. He stepped back into the shower, gently pulling me behind him. A hiss of pain left my lips as the water ran over the fresh cuts on my arm.

"Turn around," Christian gently ordered.

I slowly turned my back to him. He grabbed his shower nozzle and wet my hair before he hung it back up. I kept my back to him, my body hyper-aware of him moving behind me.

I sighed, my body relaxing as he began to massage his shampoo into my hair. I didn't even care that I would smell like a freshly-showered man after this.

He was taking care of me, just like he promised he would. It silenced the thoughts in my head. I'd never had someone care for me like this before, and *God*, it felt so nice.

Once he began to bathe me, he stopped at my arms,

instead lifting each arm to his lips, pressing a tender kiss to each cut. I sobbed, hot tears rolling down my cheeks. He then drew me to him, pressing his lips to mine. My tears mixed in our kiss, tasting salty on my lips. His hands ran over my body, drawing me closer and closer to him until I couldn't tell where my body ended and his began.

My tears soon stopped, and instead of all of the emotional pain I'd been feeling, I was now consumed by him, desperate for him.

He backed me up against the shower wall, his lips never leaving mine. I ran my hands over his body, imprinting every indentation of his frame to my memory, the way his muscles flexed with every move of his body and quivered beneath my touch.

He softly groaned as my hands ghosted right above his cock, his body shuddering. I gasped in surprise when he lifted me against the wall. The doorbell rang. Christian cursed, his eyes squeezing shut. "Fuck."

"Don't," I begged him, drawing his dark eyes to mine. "Please don't leave me like this."

He must have seen something in my eyes because he ignored the doorbell and lined his cock up with my slit. I cried out his name as he buried himself deep inside of me. Locking my legs around his waist and my arms around his neck, I clung to him as he continued running his hands over my body, whispering about how perfect I was in my ear while he moved in and out of me at a slow, measured pace.

That night, Christian didn't fuck me.

He made the sweetest love to me, showing me with his words and his body that I was more than a quick fuck to him.

He pulled my head from his neck, his dark eyes locking on mine. "Let me see your eyes glow as you come, beautiful."

He continued rocking in and out of me, drawing me closer and closer to that edge. I never ripped my eyes from his. My nails dug into his shoulders, my thighs tightening around his hips as I came hard, my body shuddering with the force of my orgasm.

"Christian!" I cried out.

"There it is—my moon," he growled. And then he released a shout of my name as he came with me.

5

HER BOYFRIEND

Ally

My brother looked a bit pissed as he strode into the living room. All Christian had done was open the front door for him and headed straight for his kitchen to get me a hot cup of coffee.

I was wearing a pair of my leggings that my roommate had packed for me and one of Christian's long-sleeve, button-down shirts since the only shirts my roommate had packed for me were short-sleeved.

"Can someone tell me what the fuck happened?" Axel asked as he ran his eyes over my face. "Sis, have you been crying?"

I squeezed my eyes shut, my lungs feeling like they

were going to cave in—completely deflate. "Ally," Christian called from the kitchen. I slowly ripped my eyes open to look at him. "Breathe," he coaxed. I drew a deep breath into my lungs. He gave me a warm, proud smile before he looked at my brother, the smile dropping from his face. "Let me get this cup of coffee made for her, and then we can talk," Christian told him.

"Goddammit, Christian, I thought something happened," Axel snarled, his nerves on edge.

"Something did happen," Christian told him, not at all fazed by my brother's anger. I swallowed nervously. "Like I said, just give me a damn minute to get this for her, and then we can talk. Your sister needs support; she doesn't need to have this talk with you without me by her side."

Axel dropped onto the chair across from me and closed his eyes, scrubbing his hand down his face. He was in a pair of sweats and an old college shirt with his house slippers on.

He had been taking care of Meghan, and I had ripped him away from doing that. Guilt stirred in my chest. Tears burned in my eyes.

I couldn't ever seem to get this shit right.

"Easy, beautiful." Christian kneeled in front of me. I locked my eyes on his face. He gave me an encouraging smile. "It's hot, but here—hold this. The heat will keep you grounded." He rubbed his hands on my knees. "If you feel an anxiety attack come on, just close your eyes and focus on the heat in your hand."

"Okay," I whispered, so fucking nervous to have this talk with Axel. I had let him down before, and I was terrified to do it again. I couldn't take it if my brother turned his back on me.

Christian sat next to me on the couch and settled his hand on my thigh before drawing in a deep breath. "Alright. I got a call from Ally's roommate a little while ago," Christian began. "She tried calling you and Julian numerous times, but you guys didn't answer." Guilt flashed in Axel's eyes. But they had been taking care of Meghan. I couldn't be angry about that.

Christian looked over at me and gently cupped my cheek. "Be brave—be the moon," he quietly told me. He gently squeezed my thigh. I bit my bottom lip, begging him with my eyes to not tell him. "I have to tell him, beautiful."

I closed my eyes, nodding as I focused on the heat in my hands. I couldn't look at my brother—not right now. Not when Christian was about to tell him how badly I fucked up.

"When I got to Ally's dorm room, there was blood all over her and all over the area surrounding her," Christian told him. Axel sucked in a sharp breath of air. I flinched. "I'm not sure her medication dosage is correct because she's still hearing the voices in her head."

Hot tears slid down my cheeks. I sobbed. I heard my brother move, and suddenly, he was kneeling in front of me, his hands cupping my cheeks. I whimpered. "Ally, Sis, look at me," Axel pleaded.

I shook my head. I couldn't look at him. Not now.

"Beautiful," Christian soothed. His hand slid under the shirt I was wearing, sliding up my spinal cord. "Look at him, baby. He's not mad, I promise."

I slowly opened my eyes, my brother's face blurry through my tears. "Sis, it's okay," he soothed. "I'm not angry. I swear to you that I'm not. You can't help the voices. That's not your fault."

"But I cut so much," I whimpered. A sob ripped from my throat. "I broke my promise to Julian. He's going to hate me."

"No." His voice remained low and soothing— patient, just like always. "Julian could never hate you. We made a promise to you to never turn our backs on you, and we're not. We just need to get Dr. Gresham to come see you, okay?" He pressed a kiss to my forehead. "Let Christian take care of you while I call Dr. Gresham."

I nodded. Christian took the cup of coffee from my hands and pulled me onto his lap before he laid down on his couch, holding me in his arms, turning me so I was snuggled against his chest. He draped his leg over mine, holding me securely to him.

"You're so brave, my moon," Christian praised. "I know it doesn't feel like it, but you're so fucking brave and strong. You're going to get through this, and I'll always be holding your hand as you do. I promise."

"You'll walk away," I choked out, more tears sliding down my cheeks. "We barely know each other. My shit is overwhelming—even for me."

Christian soothed his lips over mine. I whimpered, my chest aching. "The moment our eyes connected in that study room on campus, I've been drawn to you. I don't know why; I can't fucking explain it, but something in my gut tells me that you're it—you're the one for me. I'm not fucking this up. I'm not walking away from you—never. You're a once-in-a-lifetime kind of woman, and I know once we get all of your medications figured out, you'll grow, and you'll thrive, and I'll be there to watch you glow as bright as the moon amidst all of your darkness."

"You're so poetic." I sniffled.

He brushed his nose with mine. "Just for you, beautiful—only for you."

Christian allowed me to roll over onto my other side

when I heard Axel let Dr. Gresham into Christian's house. Dr. Gresham gave me a warm, encouraging smile. "Alright, Ally," he said soothingly as he kneeled in front of me. "You're still hearing the voices?"

I nodded at him. Christian pressed a kiss to the back of my head, his arms squeezing around me for a moment in a silent offer of extra support.

"What did they say this time that triggered you to cut yourself?" he asked me.

I shut my eyes, shaking my head. I didn't want to tell him—didn't want Christian to know that my voices knew I doubted him enough to make me hurt myself like this.

Maybe it'll make him push you away sooner.

You're only a freak, after all.

I whined. "Stop," I whimpered, reaching up to clench my head, as if I squeezed hard enough, they might shut up.

Christian quickly flipped me back over, locking his eyes on mine. "Look at me; focus on me," he gently ordered, his voice stern. "I'm here. I don't give a fuck what those voices in your head may say. I'm here. I'm not fucking going anywhere."

"Ally, can you tell me what they were saying while you're facing Christian?" Dr. Gresham asked me. I bit my bottom lip. Christian ran his hand down my back, soothing me.

"It's okay, beautiful," Christian told me. "I work with patients with schizophrenia," he reminded me. "I know how cruel those voices can be. Tell Dr. Gresham what they say to you." He gave me a tender smile. "I want to prove them wrong, beautiful."

My bottom lip trembled, tears burning in my eyes. "They were saying that Christian doesn't care about me," I said quietly, closing my eyes. "That—that he was just going to use me like my ex had," I whispered.

"And the bit about your ex sent you tumbling over the edge," Dr. Gresham confirmed. I nodded. It always did. That fucker broke me in ways I wasn't sure could ever be repaired. "Can you sit up for me so we can see how badly you hurt yourself?" he asked me.

I looked up at Axel, terrified of him seeing them. Christian sat up, gently pulling me with him. I followed Axel with my eyes as he took a seat next to me on the couch. "I'm here, Sis. This is a judgment-free zone."

Christian nuzzled my neck and pressed a tender kiss below my ear. "Trust me, baby," he soothed. "I'm going to roll your sleeves up. I'm here. Be my moon. I'm in your darkness with you, holding your hand, but I want to see, beautiful."

I swallowed thickly and nodded. As I closed my eyes, Christian unbuttoned the sleeves of his shirt that I was wearing before he gently rolled them up. "I cleaned them up after her shower," Christian informed the other two men in the room. I felt Axel's hand wrap around my right arm, gently running his fingers over the scars, not touching the fresh cuts. I flinched but didn't open my eyes. "They weren't too deep. She wasn't trying to kill herself—probably just trying to relieve some of the pain she was feeling."

I jerked my eyes open, staring at the handsome, perfect man next to me—the man that would always be too good for me and my shit. "How…"

A soft, understanding smile tilted his lips before he held his arms out to me. There were faint, white lines all over his arms. I hadn't ever noticed them before. "You cut?" I asked him.

He shrugged. "When I was younger, yeah. I did to relieve the pain in my head—not to kill myself."

Tears poured down my face. "You understand," I choked out. Oh, God, he actually understood how I felt. That was why he never looked at me with disgust. That was why he was so understanding.

He gently cupped my jaw and brushed my tears off my cheeks. "I do," he murmured. "I'm not talking out of my ass, baby. I know how you're feeling."

I sobbed as I wound my arms around his neck. He gently lifted me onto his lap, and I linked my legs around his torso, clinging to him as I cried.

"I'm going to change her dosing," Dr. Gresham quietly told Axel. I heard the familiar ripping of a prescription paper from his prescription pad. "It's the same medication, but I want her to take it twice a day rather than just once a day. I don't want her to take too much at one time—it'll be too much for her since she's still not completely used to the medication."

"Thank you, Dr. Gresham."

"Ally is my miracle patient, Axel," he told my brother. Christian ran his hands over my back, never stopping their movement as he continued to quietly sooth me. "I want her to continue to live and thrive. Anytime she has an emergency like this, give me a call, and you might want to give her boyfriend my number as well."

I blushed. Christian released a husky laugh. "Boyfriend." He tasted the word on his lips. "I fucking love the sound of that." He gently tipped my chin up so I was looking at his handsome face. "You okay with being mine, my moon?"

My blush darkened. I shyly nodded my head, still not used to how forward he was—wasn't sure if I ever would be. He leaned forward and lightly brushed his lips with mine before he let me rest my head back on his shoulder.

Axel came back into the living room a moment later. "Dr. Gresham is suggesting that we pull you for the semester, Ally," Axel told me. I shook my head at him.

"It's probably a good idea, Ally," Christian told me,

agreeing with Dr. Gresham. "Until we get this under control, it'll be best if you don't have the added stress of classes."

"But—"

"No buts," Axel told me, his tone firm but gentle. "I'm making the decision for you on this one, Little Sis. I'll go do the necessary paperwork tomorrow to get you pulled from classes. They have to medically excuse you. Dr. Gresham will be sending me a formal letter tomorrow that I can take to your school."

School was my normalcy. If they took that away from me, I was going to be one hundred percent lost.

I slowly lifted my head from Christian's shoulder to look over at my brother. He reached forward and brushed a tear off my cheek. "It's going to get better, Ally," he assured me. "I know it's dark right now, but just shine like Christian wants you to, yeah? Don't be afraid to lean on him. He's good for you. Honestly, I don't think he's capable of breaking your heart."

My bottom lip trembled at the mere thought of losing Christian, even though I barely knew him. Axel gave me a small smile. "He's not your ex, Sis. Let him take care of you." He leaned forward and pressed a kiss to my forehead. "I need to get back home to Meghan. I'll talk to Julian. If he calls you, don't be scared. Answer him." He looked at Christian. "I'll give you a week off with pay—let you stay here with her."

"Thanks," Christian told him. "She's in good, safe hands, Axel."

Axel grinned at him. "I know. That's why I gave you her number. She needs someone besides me, Meghan, and Julian that she can lean on—someone that can help her in a way that we can't."

"I'll be everything she needs me to be," Christian told him as he stood up, his arm under my ass to hold me up. "She needs to get some sleep."

"Agreed," Axel said quietly. "I'll make sure your appointments get rescheduled." Axel ran his hand over my hair. My eyelids were already drooping—all of the crying I had done exhausting me. "Goodnight, Little Sis. Sleep well."

"You, too," I told him, my words slurred as I fought sleep. Today had been too long. Too much had happened. I just wanted some rest.

Once Axel left, Christian locked his front door and carried me to his bedroom. He gently laid me on the bed, tugging my leggings off of me afterward. I snuggled into his pillow, breathing in the scent of his cologne and body wash.

My eyes snapped open when the light went off, but then Christian's soothing presence slid into the bed behind me, his front pressing to my back. "I'll purchase a night light tomorrow," he told me quietly. He pressed a kiss to the back of my head. "I'm here all night; I won't let go," he promised.

My heart swelled in my chest as I snuggled further back against him, letting my eyes fall shut as Christian's warmth and safety locked me with him.

6

CONFESSIONS

Ally

I jerked awake, my eyes flying open as I quickly sat up, my heart pounding hard in my chest. Christian sat up as well and quickly turned on a lamp on his nightstand. He gently gripped my chin, turning my eyes to his. "What's wrong?" His voice was husky and groggy since he was still half-asleep.

I shook my head, resisting the urge to press my hand to my belly. The anniversary date of my miscarriage was coming up in three days. How could I even begin to tell Christian that I'd been so selfish that I had destroyed an innocent life?

Tears burned at the back of my eyes, and I couldn't stop them from spilling over onto my cheeks. I sobbed, bringing my hands up to cover my face. Wordlessly, Christian leaned back against his headboard and pulled me onto his lap, holding me tight to him. He didn't say a word—just held me.

How did he know what I needed without me even saying a word to him?

"I don't know what happened, beautiful, but let it out," Christian said softly as he buried his face in my hair, his body wrapped tightly around me, holding all of the broken pieces of me together the best he could.

"I'm a horrible person," I whimpered.

"No, baby; I don't believe that for a second," Christian disagreed as he tightened his arms around me.

I cried harder, my shoulders shaking. "In three days, it will have been three years since I miscarried my first baby," I blurted. I couldn't look at him, even though his soothing touch never stopped. "All because I was selfish and I overdosed on my antidepressant pills."

"Oh, baby," Christian rasped. He gently gripped my chin and pulled my face up to his. "That doesn't make you a horrible person. You were hurting. Mental health —it makes people do stupid shit, but it doesn't make you a horrible person."

"But my baby was innocent," I told him, tears pouring down my red face. He leaned forward and brushed his lips over my cheeks. I sobbed. God, how could he be so sweet right now? I was telling him I was a monster, that I killed an innocent life, and yet he was sitting here treating me as if I were one of the best, most amazing people he'd ever met.

"So were you, beautiful," Christian told me. His dark eyes ran over my face, drinking in every feature of mine.

"I wasn't innocent," I choked out.

"What made you overdose, Ally?" he asked me.

I squeezed my eyes shut. Their betrayal shouldn't hurt so much after almost three years, but it did.

"I found my boyfriend at the time balls deep inside of his step-sister—my best friend," I told him, my voice breaking.

Christian's hands tightened on me. He growled softly. "Are you fucking serious?" he swore. I jerked my eyes open, staring at the gorgeous man in front of me in surprise. "Your mental health was already in a bad place, too, wasn't it?" he asked me, his tone softening. I just looked away from him. He sighed, drawing me back against his upper body. "I want to kick his ass— hers, too," he grumbled. My heart warmed at his words.

"You're not a monster, baby," Christian soothed, his hand running over my hair. "I'll never believe that you are, and one day, I'll make you believe it, too. And when we have a baby together, I know you'll make the most amazing mother."

I jerked back, staring at him with wide eyes. "*When?*" I choked out.

He flashed me a sexy grin. "When," he confirmed. Tingles erupted all over my body. *He knew he wanted that big of a future with me*? "You're it for me, Ally. I'm not letting you go. One day, I'll make you my fiancée, my wife, and the mother of my kids. I want you to be mine in every way that I can think of."

My heart swelled at his words, my soul warming. He leaned forward and brushed his lips over mine. "Be my moon."

I smiled up at him. He grinned. "So fucking perfect," he breathed.

I stumbled out into the living room the next morning, rubbing the sleep from my eyes. I was still in Christian's button-down shirt, and I didn't have my leggings on.

I jerked in surprise, my cheeks tinting red when I saw Julian and Meghan sitting in the living room with Christian. "Sorry," I squeaked before I ducked back into the bedroom, unintentionally slamming the door shut behind me.

I heard Julian bark out a laugh from the living room before Christian slipped into his room with me. He grabbed my leggings from the floor and handed them to me. My cheeks were flaming as I quickly snatched them from him, slipping them on.

"You're so fucking cute when you're embarrassed," Christian said once my leggings were on. He pulled me into his arms, leaning down to kiss me. I pushed against his chest. He quickly pulled back from me with a frown on his perfect lips. "What?"

I covered my mouth with my hand. "Morning breath," I told him.

"*Woman*," he growled. He removed my hand and took my lips in a savage kiss. I moaned, losing myself in him, completely forgetting about my horrible morning breath.

He slowly released me, pecking my lips one more time before he stepped back from me with a sexy, panty-dropping smirk on his lips. "Go brush your teeth and your hair. Then, get your cute ass out in the living room. Meghan and Julian have come over to have breakfast with us."

I frowned, my eyes nervously flickering to the bedroom door. Christian reached up and cupped the side of my neck, using his thumb to angle my head so I was looking up at him. "Neither of them are upset with you. They're worried, yes, but they know you're in good hands with me and that I'll take care of you. They just want to have a light-hearted breakfast with you, and then in a little bit, once we're both showered and dressed, perhaps we can all go out to the local flea market." My eyes brightened. I *loved* going to the flea market. Christian grinned down at me. "There's my moon," he praised. "Go on, baby. I'll be out in the living room."

Christian held my hand in his as he carried on a conversation with Julian over football. He had to leave in a few days for the season. I knew Meghan was sad about it, but with Axel now having his own practice, and Holden and Lana being born, it wasn't practical for them to travel with him like they used to.

"Oh, my God, Ally, look at these!" Meghan exclaimed as she held up a pair of earrings.

They were half-moons—black and simple—but they were so freaking cute. They weren't dangle-y, either, which I preferred. I hated dangle-y earrings. I preferred simple earrings.

Christian pulled his wallet out of his back pocket. "What? Christian, no," I protested, not wanting him to spend money on me. He was already helping me so much as it was.

"Keep your protests to yourself. I'm going to ignore

them anyway," he told me, handing over a ten-dollar bill to the lady working the booth.

I glared at him as he handed me the earrings. He only flashed me one of his perfect smiles, and my glare melted away instantly. I sighed in defeat. Christian leaned forward and gently kissed me. "They'll look perfect on you, my moon. Now, come on." He linked our fingers together and led me in the direction Julian and Meghan went.

"You're a pain in my ass already," I grumbled, but I couldn't deny that the sweet action of buying me a pair of earrings had my soul melting at his feet.

He released a soft, husky laugh. "I can be," he warned me as he looked down at me, his eyes darkening.

My breath hitched in my throat, my cheeks flaming. He leaned down and kissed me again. "Come on before I drag you out to my car."

"That would get us arrested," I hissed at him.

He barked out a laugh, making Julian and Meghan turn to look at us. I swear, my cheeks couldn't get any redder. "It would definitely be worth it," he teased as he flashed me one of his wicked grins.

"Oh, my God," I huffed, but I couldn't deny that my panties were soaked just thinking about him taking me again, even if we would get arrested—especially fucking in his car in broad fucking daylight.

"So sweet and innocent—I love it," Christian whispered in my ear.

Meghan grabbed my other hand in hers, tugging me away from Christian. Christian pouted, but she only shrugged at him. "You're hogging her," she told him, sticking her tongue out.

He rolled his eyes as Julian laughed. "She's my woman, Meghan. I think I have the right to hog her." My entire face turned red.

His woman.

I *really* liked the sound of that.

"Not when she's supposed to be shopping with me," Meghan retorted. "Julian, keep him entertained," she ordered her husband.

"Trust me, bro, it's just best to do as she says," Julian told him. "Meghan and Ally can literally shop until they drop," he warned.

Meghan led me a little further away from them. "I haven't seen you this happy—well, ever," Meghan told me as she smiled at me. I blushed. "He's good for you, Ally. And he doesn't look like the kind of man to give up on you when you lose yourself in your darkness."

I subconsciously rubbed at the scabbed cuts on my arms. "He..." I drew in a deep breath. "He took care of me," I told her quietly. She squeezed my hand in hers. "When he came to my dorm yesterday—God, there was so much blood. On me, on the floor." I looked up at her.

"He didn't freak out. He didn't make me feel like a shitty human being. He just begged me to stay with him, begged me to be his moon."

Meghan gently squeezed my hand again, encouraging me to keep talking. "And then he took me home with him, and he helped me get cleaned up, and he made me forget about all of the pain for a little while." Tears burned in my eyes, but I wouldn't let them fall—not here in front of a bunch of random strangers. "And he didn't judge me when I told Dr. Gresham about the voices in my head." I looked at my best friend. "He understands me, Meghan." I reached up to rub my chest.

"He cares about you—deeply. It's okay to lean on him, Ally. I know you're going to have a lot of days still where it's really dark and you feel like you'll never crawl out of it to see the light again, but he'll be there to hold your hand, to walk you out of that darkness. He'll never let you push him away."

"It feels like it's moving so fast with him—too fast," I told her. "But I can't bring myself to want to slow him down."

"Because he's the one for you," Meghan said with a shrug. "If it gets overwhelming, tell him. I know he'll understand. But otherwise, just hold on to him as you go along for the ride. He won't let you fall off." She glanced over her shoulder at the two men behind us before she looked back at me. "I'm pretty sure that man is already in love with you, even if he doesn't realize it yet. He'll always take care of you, Ally. I can sense it. Let him."

I sighed. "Is it really this easy?" I asked her.

She nodded at me. "I used to always question how easy it was with Axel and Julian," she confessed. I frowned. They always seemed to have it worked out. "I don't know how many times I tried pushing both men away from me. It felt too easy—too simple. Everything in my life had always been so complicated. But they held me with them—didn't let me push them away. They fought to stay with me. They've both helped me out of so many dark holes—like last night. Each time, I try pushing them away. I always feel like I'm too dark, too tainted for them. They're so perfect, and I'm not."

"They love you, Meghan. Julian and Axel have always loved and cared deeply about people that are close to them," I reminded her. "And you're the most important person in their lives besides Holden and Lana."

"I know," she said quietly. She looked at me. "Which is why I'm telling you—urging you—to let Christian take care of you. Because the way that man looks at you? Right now, you're the most important person in his life. Let him hold you with him, Ally. He'll be your light when everything around you is so black and dark that you can't see anything else."

I squeezed her hand in mine. "I'll try," I promised her.

She smiled at me. "That's all I'll ever ask of you, Ally. All women like us can do is just fucking try because, at the end of the day, that means we never gave up."

7

ANNIVERSARY

Ally

I moaned in protest when I felt Christian's arms slide beneath me, gently lifting me from the car. "It's alright," he soothed as he gently closed his car door with his foot. "You fell asleep on the way home."

"I didn't mean to," I mumbled, but I linked my arms around his neck and leaned my head on his shoulder, closing my eyes again with every intention of going back to sleep.

He brushed his lips to my forehead. "I know you didn't, baby. Go back to sleep. I'll put you to bed," he assured me.

"No," I mumbled. "I need to eat something so I can take my medicine."

He brushed his lips to my forehead before he gently set me on the couch. "Let me go see what I can find for you to eat," he told me before he set off for the kitchen.

I stood up from the couch and went into Christian's room where my bag was. I set the small duffel on the bed and rummaged through it until I found my medicine bag. My brother had gotten it for me when I decided to enroll in college. It was a simple, black bag that had the word "Strength" on it in purple, cursive letters. I decided to put my medications in it.

I frowned down at it. When Christian saw all of the medications I had to take on a daily basis, surely he would run from me, wouldn't he?

"What are you thinking so hard about over there?" Christian asked as he walked into the room. "I don't have shit to eat that's quick, so I ordered takeout. I need to go grocery shopping." He glanced down at the bag in my hands. I tightened my grip on it, my heart thumping wildly in my chest.

"Medicine?" he asked me.

I swallowed nervously and nodded my head at him. He cupped the side of my neck and tilted my head back so I was looking directly up at him. "Beautiful, I'm never going to judge you. Stop freaking out so much. I know you have to take medications, and I know that from what I know of you, it's probably quite a few. And that's okay," he soothed. "They help you. I'll always support you in something that helps you and doesn't harm you."

"I take seven different medications," I whispered. I searched his eyes, clinging to every bit of hope that I could that he wouldn't turn his back on me. "You're okay with that?"

He wrapped his arm around my waist and drew me into him, leaning down to softly kiss me. I moaned into the kiss, suddenly wanting him so badly that it hurt. His fingers dug into my sides, his tongue erotically dancing around mine as he deepened the kiss. I clawed at his shirt, my medicine long forgotten. I was desperate for him—a needy mess.

"Fuck," he swore as he forced his lips back from mine. "Food, medicine, and then, I promise, baby, that I will sate every single need that you have."

My cheeks flushed at his words. He flashed me a grin. "That sexy innocence of yours—don't ever fucking lose it, beautiful."

I stared at the picture on my phone through teary eyes. My ex had sent me yet another photo, informing me that they were having a girl, and they really wanted me to come to this baby shower.

He was standing behind Heather with his arms wrapped around her waist. She was wearing a bralette, and his hands were cupping her belly. Their other little girl was pressing a kiss to Heather's swollen bump.

Why did he keep doing this to me? Did he enjoy torturing me with this shit?

I squeezed my eyes shut, a sob ripping from my throat.

Today was the anniversary.

And today, I got another sore, painful reminder that I was not a mom, that I had killed an innocent baby because I was a selfish, destructive bitch.

Christian stepped out of the bathroom. He was still shirtless from our shower, but he had taken longer in the bathroom because he needed to shave. And I was glad he stepped out at that time because I needed someone to hold me together before I started screaming. It was crawling up my throat, begging to be released.

"Ally, baby—" Christian began as he quickly began to move toward me, but I didn't give him a chance to finish before I launched myself into his arms, sob after sob ripping from my chest, each one more painful than the last.

"I'm here, beautiful," Christian soothed as he squeezed his arms around me, holding me to his muscular frame. He slowly walked me back toward his bed. "It's okay, baby. I'm here," he crooned. He peppered kisses all over my face, his hands gripping me like I might disappear right out of his arms if he didn't hold me tight enough.

I knew he had to have seen the text on my phone, but he only quickly lifted it and locked it before he tossed it onto the nightstand. I clung to him, desperate for him to not let me go.

"Easy," he coaxed, his voice soothing but firm. "Breathe."

"I lost her three years ago today," I choked out.

He didn't question that I called my baby *her*. Instead, he just laid down on the bed, pulling me with him. "Baby, I need you to breathe," he said I sobbed again. Breathe? I wasn't sure I knew how to do that anymore. I was crying too hard, my sobs coming too fast.

He gently gripped my face in his hands, his dark, almost black eyes, locking on my own. "Breathe. Come on, baby." He leaned forward and kissed me. "I'm here. Let me share the pain, beautiful. I need you to be my moon."

I whimpered. "I can't," I told him. "Your moon is broken."

He kissed me again, this time deepening it as he rolled me to my back. His hands slid under my shirt, pulling it over my head before he unhooked my bra, tossing it to the floor. His lips never left mine as he hooked his fingers into my leggings and my panties, shoving them down my legs. I kicked them off.

"Let me love you, beautiful," Christian begged as he leaned up on his elbows to look down at me, his eyes meeting mine. "Let me take care of you—breathe life into you. I may not be able to completely heal you, beautiful, but I can damn well try. Let me."

"Okay," I whispered, my voice trembling.

He leaned up on his knees and unsnapped his jeans before he pulled them off. He was completely naked in front of me, and this perfect man was staring at me, running his eyes over my body as if I were the most beautiful thing he had ever seen in his life.

Normally, Christian took his time with my body, learning every curve, every dip, every blemish, and every scar. This time, he leaned back over me, his lips claiming mine again as he eased into me.

I moaned, completely lost in him as he slowly rocked our bodies together. He never sped up or slowed down. It was a slow, steady tempo that I felt through every bit of my soul and my heart.

Christian was making love to me.

And I cried, hot tears sliding down my cheeks as I clutched him to me, allowing him to love me like he'd been trying to do from the very first day he laid his eyes on me.

Dr. Gresham and I walked in silence for a moment as I admired the garden. Fall was settling in for good, and the weather was turning cooler. All of the plants were beginning to lose their leaves.

Honestly, it was my favorite time of year. For me, there was some kind of comfort in the world when everything died to become new again.

"Let's talk about your medications first," Dr. Gresham began. "How are they working for you?" he asked.

"I don't feel like crawling into a hole and dying," I told him with a shrug. "I think my mind is beginning to adjust to them; it's just taking them a moment."

"Any voices?" he asked.

I shook my head at him. "No—no voices since that night. I think the two doses a day is working pretty well."

"Good. Continue taking your medications as I've prescribed," Dr. Gresham instructed me. I shivered when the wind blew and tightened my jacket around me, tucking my hands under my arms. I knew we could talk inside, but I tended to clam up when we were inside. I felt too closed in—too scrutinized.

So, Dr. Gresham and I always did our sessions together outside, no matter how cold it was. He was an amazing therapist and doctor. He wanted his patients to be as comfortable as possible during therapy sessions, no matter what he had to suffer through in the process.

"Let's talk about Christian."

I sighed. I knew this was going to come up, but I wasn't sure I was ready to talk to anyone about him outside of Meghan. Our relationship was still too fresh —too raw. I didn't want to ruin that. And I felt like talking about the two of us out loud would destroy everything.

"What about him?" I grumbled as I paused to look at the rose bush Meghan had pointed out to me on my second round of therapy treatments. It was still blooming, its leaves still green.

It was always so different from all of the other plants out here. It bloomed late, and lost its leaves and petals late, too.

"He seems like a good man, and he understands mental health—has a passion for it that many therapists and doctors lack," he commented. "I had the pleasure of him interning here the first semester of his Master's program. When he graduates, he's going to be an amazing addition to Axel's office."

I nodded. That I did know. Christian was amazing and brilliant, and as Dr. Gresham stated, Christian had a passion for helping people.

"How are you feeling with Christian?" Dr. Gresham

asked me. "You two are together, yes? I remember Meghan mentioning to me that you two are."

"We're together," I confirmed. I drew in a deep breath. "Is it horrible of me to say that sometimes I feel like everything moves so fast with him?" I asked Dr. Gresham, looking up into his kind, aging face. "God, I lose myself in him. He's so good with me. He understands everything, and he's never judged me—not yet, anyway. But he wants *so much*, and I'm terrified that I'm going to fall into him completely, and he's going to end up ripping my heart out." I swallowed thickly, staring at the brick path beneath my feet. "It's already still so broken and bruised," I whispered.

"No, it's not horrible of you to say that, Ally," Dr. Gresham assured me. "It's already a huge step for you to allow him into your life like this. You've always been so guarded, doing your best to protect yourself. But Christian doesn't strike me as the kind of man that will give up on you, Ally. You can push and shove at him, but something in my gut tells me that he'll push back just as hard, forcing you to let him stay." He looked over at me. "And that's not a bad thing, Ally. You've fought so hard these past few years to stay strong for Axel, Meghan, and Julian. You fought so hard to not let them down. Let Christian hold you up while you rest. It's okay to do that."

"Is it really, though?" I asked him. "Christian has a

life outside of me," I reminded him. "He has to go back to work in two days. I'll be stuck at home with nothing but my thoughts to occupy me." A chill raced down my spine at that thought. "They can still be dark," I confessed in a much softer voice.

"I imagine that's due to the fact that your ex is still contacting you, yes? And the anniversary of your miscarriage just passed."

I swallowed thickly as I stared at Dr. Gresham. "How did you know about my ex?" I asked, my voice trembling. I hadn't told anyone about the last message.

"Christian went to Axel about it." My heart thumped crazily in my chest. Axel and Julian never reacted well when I hid shit like this from them. "Axel briefly explained to him that it was your ex texting you, which made a lot of pieces add up in Christian's brain about why you were suddenly so emotional." Dr. Gresham smiled over at me. "From what I understand, Christian had a long and thorough talk with your ex. Maybe you should ask Christian about it, but Axel informed me of what was going on because your brother knows you won't tell me yourself."

I stared back down at the brick path beneath my feet. "Was he angry?" I asked quietly.

"No," Dr. Gresham assured me. "Axel knows you're in good hands with Christian, and he knows Christian will take care of you and help you. Your brother just wishes you would open up more."

"I do," I mumbled. "To Meghan."

"And that's good," Dr. Gresham praised. "It's amazing that you're opening up to her." He looked over at me. "If you're worried about moving forward with Christian, trusting in him completely, talk to Meghan. She went through her own pain and her own torture with another man. You can relate to her in a way because trust me, she didn't want anything to do with Julian either, but like you, she couldn't deny him."

I scuffed my shoe against the ground. "Christian just seems too good for my kind of shit," I told Dr. Gresham.

"Maybe Christian is perfect for your kind of shit, as you put it," Dr. Gresham retorted. I continued staring at the ground. "Stop fighting it. Let Christian decide what he wants to do. And if he wants you, wants to be with you, to help you, then let him do that." Dr. Gresham looked over at me. "Do you want to hurt him?" He asked.

I instantly shook my head no. Pain lanced through my chest at the mere thought of hurting Christian. Dr. Gresham nodded once. "Alright, then. Just let him lead you."

8

UNEXPECTED VISITOR

Ally

I stepped into the house, my eyes instantly landing on Christian. He was standing at the stove, mixing something in a pot. It smelled delicious, and my stomach rumbled in response. It felt a bit weird to actually have my stomach respond to the scent of food again.

Before we ate dinner though, I wanted to discuss something with him—that something being the conversation he apparently had with my ex.

"Hey, baby," he greeted me when he turned to face me, a half-smile tilting his lips. My heart jumped in my chest at the sight of it. *How was one person so damn perfect*? "How did your session with Dr. Gresham go?"

I set my purse on the coffee table before I strode to the kitchen, crossing my arms over my chest. "Actually, I wanted to talk to you about that—well, part of that," I told him. He frowned, running his eyes over my face as he tried to figure out what was going on. "Dr. Gresham informed me that you had a *talk* with my ex."

Christian sighed as he turned the eye off, covering the pot on the stove. He then turned and gave me his full, undivided attention as he shoved his hands into the pockets of his sweats. "Axel must have told him." I nodded. Christian grunted. "I did have a conversation with your ex, and I also blocked him from your phone afterward." My eyes widened a bit in surprise.

He drew in a deep breath. "You can be angry at me for stepping into your personal shit like that if you want, beautiful, but I hate how much he upsets you. He knows about the baby you lost, knows the shit he and his bitch of a wife have put you through, and yet, he still has the fucking audacity to send you pictures of their little family, asking you to come to their baby shower as if they even have a right to ask that of you."

I was rendered speechless.

He thrust his hand through his hair before he dropped it to his side, clenching his fist. But his eyes stayed soft as he held my gaze, not once dropping it. "He tried to claim he wanted to rebuild the relationship between you and Heather, but I wasn't having that shit.

She fucking hurt you. If she truly wanted to have that relationship with you in the first place, she would have never betrayed you like she did. And if she wanted it now, she would be reaching out to you—not him."

"So, what did you do?" I asked him quietly, my hands shaking. I flatted them on the countertop, trying to stop the tremors.

Christian gently laid his hands over mine before he flipped them over, lacing our fingers together. His hands engulfed mine, but instead of feeling trapped, I felt safer than I ever had before. "I told him to lose your fucking number. I'm your man now; I take care of you. And I refuse to let him hurt you anymore. So, I threatened him with a lawsuit for harassment if he dared to contact you again, and I made sure he knew just how powerful I was, not to mention the fact that your brother and Julian would fully back me up on it." He reached up and cupped my cheek. "I'll never let him hurt you again, baby."

Tears burned in my eyes. "You didn't have to do that for me," I choked out.

He moved around the counter and drew me into his arms, holding me tight to him. I quickly wound my arms around his waist, closing my eyes as I sank into him. "As I said, I take care of you. You're my moon. You'll always be my moon, even when you're not shining." He leaned down to kiss me. "And I will always be here to breathe life into you so that you can live for me. Anyone who dares to try to burn out your light, to take away the breath that I'm giving you—I'll fucking protect you from them. You'll never have any reason to doubt that, beautiful."

I leaned up to kiss him. He growled softly and lifted me up onto the counter, quickly stepping between my legs. I moaned when he gripped my hips and yanked me closer to him, his cock pressing between my thighs. Sliding my fingers under his shirt, I glided my fingers over the hard, muscular planes of his abs and over his chest before I pulled back to pull his shirt over his head, revealing his perfect, defined body to my eyes.

"Fuck, I love that needy look in your eyes when you look at me," he growled.

I grabbed his face in my hands, leaning forward to connect our lips again. He muttered a curse against my lips before he slid his hands under my shirt. I moaned into the kiss as his hands slid over my skin, making my body shudder in response. His hands were slightly rough with callouses from working out, and they felt fucking amazing as they glided over my curves.

His doorbell suddenly rang. He tightened his hands on me. "They can fucking wait," he grumbled. "I don't give a fuck how long they have to."

"Christian—oh, fuck, yes." I moaned, quickly forgetting about the door as he nipped lightly at my neck.

The doorbell rang again. Christian lifted his head from my neck and glared at it, almost as if he were trying to make the person on the other side disappear. He looked back down at me. "I'm not stopping until you're taken care of."

"I can wait," I assured him.

He yanked my shirt over my head and quickly unsnapped my bra, tossing them both somewhere on the kitchen floor. His lips ran over my body. I thought I might have heard someone shout Christian's name, but I was too lost in what he was doing to me to pay much attention.

I squeaked in shock when Christian suddenly set me on my feet and spun me around to face the counter. Without having to be asked, I wiggled out of my leggings and panties, kicking them aside with my shoes. My body was quivering in anticipation as I heard him unfastening his jeans behind me.

"Hard and fast. I'm sorry, baby," he apologized.

I didn't care as long as he was inside of me. I bent over, my cheek pressed to the cool countertop, and I cried out his name as he slid inside of me. "Fuck, you are so goddamn tight," Christian growled.

I pushed my hips back, meeting him thrust for thrust. The only things you could hear were my moans and the sound of our bodies smacking together as he fucked me hard and fast from behind, just like he had warned me he would do.

But God, it felt so fucking good.

I tried gripping onto something when I felt myself toppling over the edge, Christian's name falling from my lips. He quickly released my hips and grabbed my hands in his, holding me to the earth as wave after wave of my orgasm washed over me, leaving me weak and spent.

"Always so fucking beautiful," Christian said softly as he pressed a kiss to my shoulder, his hips slowly moving back and forth as he worked my body down from its climax. "I've got you," he soothed when my legs began to shake. His arm wrapped around my waist. "I've always got you, baby."

"I want a nap," I mumbled as I shut my eyes, my heart rate slowly—so slowly—coming down.

He laughed softly before he slowly pulled out of me. A contented sigh left my lips when he gently lifted me into his arms. "Let's clean you up first, and then you can take a nap."

His doorbell rang again. Christian growled. "Jesus Christ," he swore. He eased me onto my feet in the bathroom. "Let me find out who the fuck this is. Take a bath. I'll come in and check on you in a minute."

"M'kay," I mumbled, slowly moving towards the large garden tub in his bathroom, holding onto the wall for support. My legs were trembling something fierce.

He pressed a kiss to my shoulder blade before he slipped from the bedroom, shutting the door behind him.

Christian

I glared at my older brother. He was standing on my front porch with that classic smirk of his on his face. He had been overseas for two years now, and I had no idea he was expected home. He normally stayed with me during his home time.

The surprise was nice, but not while I was in the middle of taking care of my woman.

"You look pissed," he noted, his grin widening. "Did I disturb naughty time?" he teased.

"I'm going to punch you in your jaw," I snapped, but I couldn't fight my smile. It was good to see him again.

He laughed and pulled me into a hug. "Fuck, bro, it feels good to finally be home again after so damn long. Can I come in? Please tell me you have beer."

I laughed. "I have beer," I assured him. "And yeah, but I have someone staying with me." I stepped fully out onto the porch and shut the front door behind me.

"She's it for me, bro, but she's been through some shit. So, just watch yourself, alright?"

He stuffed his hands in the pockets of his uniform pants, regarding me silently for a moment. "Christian, you know you can trust me," he finally said after a moment. "Can I meet her?"

I shrugged, opening the door again. "You will in a bit because she's living here, and I don't plan on her going anywhere else," I informed him. He released a low whistle at that before he stepped into the house behind me and dropped his duffel on the floor by the door. "I just need to check on her. You know your way around."

I slipped into our bedroom. It was quiet—not even the sound of water moving. I slipped into the bathroom, sighing when I saw her asleep with her head resting on the side of the tub, but I couldn't stop the smile that touched my lips.

She was so fucking perfect.

I leaned over the side of the tub and pulled the plug to let the water out. She jerked awake, and I quickly grabbed her shoulders before she made herself slip under the water. "Easy, beautiful," I crooned when she latched those beautiful, brown eyes on mine. "It's just me." I leaned forward and smoothed my lips over hers, enjoying her sigh as she kissed me back. "I have someone I want you to meet. You up to that?"

"Who?" she sleepily asked as she allowed me to help her up from the tub.

I grabbed a towel and began drying her body off, pressing soft kisses to her body as I did so. I groaned when she ran her fingers through my hair, her nails lightly scraping against my scalp. "My brother," I told her. "He's older than me by about a year. He's in the Army, but he's got some home time. Normally, he always stays with me when he comes home." I stood up and wrapped the towel around her body before I drew her into my arms. "His name is Caiden."

She frowned, and nervousness flickered in her eyes. She glanced down at her wrists, at the scars littered there. "I don't know," she whispered.

I grabbed one of her arms and lifted her wrist to my lips, kissing each healing cut. Her bottom lip trembled, her eyes shining with tears, but she didn't let them fall. But there was a slight flicker of beautiful light in her eyes, revealing my moon.

Phases. She was full of beautiful, little phases.

"We can cover these," I assured her. "But he won't judge you. He saved my life when he found me bleeding out on the floor of my bedroom."

Her breath hitched in her throat, and a tear slid down her cheek as pain filled her eyes—pain for me. She reached up and slid her fingers over my cheek. I leaned my face into her touch, my eyes never leaving hers. "What hurt you so bad, Christian?" she asked me quietly.

I reached up to cup her cheek, brushing my thumb over her cheek. "Family," I told her softly. "Family hurt me, baby."

She frowned before she leaned up on her tiptoes to press her lips to mine. I groaned softly, deepening it slightly before I allowed her to pull back from me. "I never want to hurt you, Christian," she said, her words warming my heart.

"Just stay with me, and shine for me, beautiful," I begged her. "You do that, and you'll never truly hurt me, my moon."

The smile she gave me—it fucking lit my soul on fire.

She may not realize it yet, but I completely belonged to her.

9

THE BROTHER

Ally

I clutched the bottom of the sleeves on Christian's shirt I was wearing as I followed him out of his room. Reaching over, he laced his fingers through mine, and he gave my hand a comforting, reassuring squeeze as he led me into the living room where his older brother was at.

"Fucking shit, Christian, when's the last time you went grocery shopping?" a deep voice asked from the kitchen. "All a man wants is a damn home-cooked meal —or something other than damn MREs."

Christian rolled his eyes as he led me into the kitchen. I bit back a giggle. "I know you're not broke, you cheap ass," Christian retorted. "Fucking order something."

A guy that looked almost exactly like Christian popped out of the fridge, his mouth opened to retort something before his eyes landed on me. My cheeks flamed red as I subconsciously stepped closer to Christian. I really didn't do good with strangers.

"Fuck—she is beautiful," his brother said, making my face flame. He flashed me a grin as he closed the fridge and held his hand out to me. "Caiden Greene."

The blush on my cheeks deepened at his words as I placed my hand in his. "Ally Johnson," I shyly introduced myself. Christian pressed his lips to my temple in encouragement. "And, um, thanks, I guess?"

He laughed. "I'm sure my brother tells you enough as it is, but if he isn't, I've always got room in my bed." He winked.

Christian glared at his brother as he pulled me into his arms—a possessive gesture that had me tingling all over. "Get your own, bro. She's mine."

Caiden laughed. "I know. Keep your dick out of your ass." My eyes widened. Jesus, it was like being around Julian. He pulled his phone from his pocket. "Since you're broke and don't have any food," I laughed quietly, "I'm ordering the greasiest, most fattening pizza ever. You guys hungry?" He snorted. "Who the fuck am I kidding? I'm not stupid; of course, you are." He shot me another wink. "I'm not clueless as to why Christian took so long answering the door."

"Oh, my God," I whispered in horror as I buried my face against Christian's chest.

Christian couldn't help himself; he started laughing, his shoulders shaking, the sound vibrating my cheek. "Fuck, baby, you're adorable." He pressed his lips to my forehead. "And yes, dickwad, pizza is fine."

"Better warn your woman I have no fucking filter on my mouth, or she's in for plenty of embarrassment," Caiden warned Christian.

Christian hooked his finger under my chin and tilted my face up to look at him. "If he's bothering you, just say the words, and he'll be sleeping outside."

I placed my hands on his sides, shaking my head at him. "He's fine. It's just—God, he's worse than Julian," I admitted. "And Julian has absolutely *no* filter."

Christian laughed before he leaned down to softly kiss me. I couldn't stop the moan that fell from my lips as I tightened my hands on his sides, pressing myself closer to him. "Fuck, woman," Christian growled as he tightened his arm around me.

"Try not to fuck her in front of me," Caiden interrupted. Christian lifted his lips from mine and shot him a glare over my head.

"Do you ever shut the fuck up?" Christian asked

him. "You're home for less than twenty minutes, and you're already driving me up the fucking wall."

Caiden smirked. "That's what I'm home for, Christian." He walked past us into the living room.

"I swear, I'm already looking forward to you leaving," Christian retorted as my phone went off on the kitchen counter where I had left it earlier.

I picked it up, seeing Julian's name on the screen. Christian gave me a quick kiss before he let me go, going into the living room, continuing to banter back and forth with Caiden.

"Hello?" I asked when I answered, a bit nervous for this phone call.

"Hey," Julian greeted. "I didn't get to see you before I left."

I frowned. I normally made it a priority to see Julian off at the airport, but with everything that had happened, I hadn't had the opportunity.

"I'm sorry," I apologized, instantly feeling guilty for not keeping up with my tradition.

He laughed softly. "I didn't call to make you feel bad. I just wanted to check in—make sure you were okay."

I shrugged as I slipped outside, shivering at the cool air as I slid the sliding glass door back shut behind me. "I'm trying," I told him honestly. That was the best answer I could give him.

"Good," He praised. "Keep doing that. Don't ever

fucking give up, Ally. I know it feels easy to do that, but keep fighting."

"I had a session with Dr. Gresham today," I informed him.

"Oh? How did that go?"

I drew in a deep breath. "My ex has continued bothering me," I began. Julian was quiet, but I knew he was angry that I hadn't come to him or Axel about this. "Christian saw the last text." I drew in a shaky breath, feeling tears burn at the backs of my eyes. "It was on the anniversary," I choked out. I squeezed my eyes shut. "And he sent me a picture of them."

"Easy," Julian soothed, his voice calm. "Take a deep breath, Ally."

I drew in a deep breath as I sank into one of the patio chairs. "Christian—I didn't know—but he, um, he apparently had a long conversation with Randall."

Julian laughed softly. "Good man you've got there, Sis."

"He told Axel about it," I told Julian. Julian grunted, obviously a little peeved at Axel for not telling him about it as soon as he'd found out. "But Christian blocked the number on my phone."

"I blocked it last time you told me," Julian told me, irritation in his tone.

"He just sends it from another number." Tears slid down my cheeks. "Julian, why won't he leave me alone, let me live in peace?" I asked him. "Hasn't he hurt me enough?"

"He fucking keeps on, and he won't have fucking fingers to text you with," Julian snapped. "I want to know if he contacts you again, Ally. He's fucking harassing you, and that shit's not okay. He made his goddamn decision three fucking years ago when he let you find him sleeping with Heather. Don't let him tear you down again. You're stronger than that shit."

"I wish it didn't hurt so much."

Julian released a soft breath. "I know," he soothed. "But everything happens for a reason, remember? And if he hadn't hurt you so badly, you wouldn't have gotten the help you truly needed, and you wouldn't be spending your time with a really good man," he reminded me.

A small smile tilted my lips at the thought of Christian. "He really is good to me," I told Julian.

"Spare me the details." He laughed.

My own laugh fell from my lips. "Julian, I have never, and will never, talk about sex with you."

A breath of relief fell from his lips. "Thank God." I laughed again. "Save that shit for Meghan. I know how much you two women love to gossip."

I cringed. "You and Axel are my brothers," I reminded him. "I *never* want to hear her sex stories."

Julian barked out a laugh, and then the sound of his

coach shouting something in the background reached my ears. "Jesus fuck." Julian swore. "I need to go." He told me. "Call me whenever, okay? And don't forget to have your ass at my place when I have games."

I smiled. "Julian, I still may not understand what the fuck happens in football, but I'll always go watch your games," I promised. "I don't care how shitty of a day I'm having."

"That's my girl," He praised. I smiled. "Alright, love you, Sis. I really have to go."

He hung up before I could respond, but my chest felt a little lighter. It always did after talking to Julian. He had a way of getting me to talk to him—always had.

Christian and Caiden were playing a video game with weird characters, both of them barking instructions into headsets. Christian flashed me a smile before he focused his attention back on the game. "You good, baby?" he asked me.

"Yeah; Julian was just checking in since I didn't go see him off for his flight," I told him.

"Hey, dipshit, shut the fuck up." Caiden snapped into the headset. My eyes widened in alarm. "He's talking to his woman. Some people actually have girl-friends and don't have to use their fucking hands in their momma's basement."

I stared at Caiden with wide eyes. Christian was laughing so hard, he ended up getting killed. Caiden flashed me a grin. "Bro, you can suck my left nut," he snapped into the headset. Christian snatched his headset off his head and reached out to pull me down onto his lap. He then wrapped his arms around me, going back to playing his game.

"Mother fucker, I'm not *gay*. I'm fucking bisexual, dumbass," Caiden retorted.

Christian rolled his eyes. "Tell the fucking world, why don't you?"

Caiden lightly shoved Christian's shoulder with a laugh. "I like dick and pussy. Not a damn thing in the world wrong with that."

My eyes widened in surprise. "Fuck, he's really open," I whispered.

Christian laughed as he pressed a kiss to my shoulder. "He's always been like that," he told me. "It's just something you get used to. He doesn't feel the need to hide from the world."

I looked over my shoulder at him. "Are you used to it yet?" I asked him.

Christian snickered. "No, not really. I've just learned to tune him out."

"Ass," Caiden griped, making me giggle.

The game ended, and Christian set his controller down before he leaned back on the couch, pulling me with him. He rubbed his thumb under my eye. "Did you cry?" he quietly asked me as a slight frown tugged at his lips.

I traced my fingers along his jaw. "Almost," I told him honestly. He brushed his thumb over my bottom lip, pride for me shining in his eyes for me being honest with him. "Julian has a way of getting me to talk." I shrugged. "He always has."

"That your other boyfriend?" Caiden teased.

Christian glared at Caiden as he tightened his hands on my waist. "Gross." I scrunched my face up in disgust as I looked at Caiden. "Julian Markos?" I asked him. Caiden's eyes widened in shock. "He's my brother-in-law, and I've known him since I was a baby."

"Holy shit!" Caiden exclaimed. "Your brother is the quarterback for the Patriots?"

"Yes," I grumbled. I hated when people latched onto that fact. I turned so I was straddling Christian's lap. A low rumble sounded from his chest as he gripped my hips, his eyes darkening, though he knew I wasn't trying to be sexual.

"That's pretty fucking awesome," Caiden admitted as I leaned my head on Christian's shoulder, letting my eyelids shut. He ran his hands up and down my back, easily lulling me to sleep.

"Shut up so she can sleep," Christian grumbled. "She's had a long ass day."

"Pizza will be here in a few," Caiden reminded us.

"I'll eat later," I mumbled, already almost asleep.

Every therapy session I had always made me extremely tired, and then coming home and having hot sex in the kitchen with Christian? I was fucking exhausted.

Christian brushed his lips to my forehead. "Go to sleep, beautiful. I've got you."

"M'kay."

"Fucking perfect," Christian whispered as he pressed his lips to the shell of my ear.

When I woke up the next morning, Christian was gone to do his internship for the day already, but there was a rose on his pillow with a note that told me to have a good day and to call if I needed anything.

I smiled. He really was fucking good to me.

I slipped out of bed and went straight to the bathroom to take my medication. I pulled them all down from the shelf, making a mental note in my head that I really needed to get a pill organizer so I didn't have to open and close all of these damn bottles twice a day.

I frowned at the medication on the counter. I took so many.

I really was a fucked-up mess.

My bottom lip trembled. My head was so fucked up that I took seven different fucking medications every day. How could Christian even stand to look at me like he did?

I was fucking insane, and all of these medications proved that.

Tears slid down my cheeks. I sobbed as I slid down the wall, letting my ass hit the floor with a thump as I dropped my face into my hands. I hated feeling like this. If I had to take all of these damn medications, shouldn't I at least stop having all of these damn lows all the time?

"Hey, I'm making some breakfast—heard you get up —woah!" Caiden exclaimed as he stepped into the bathroom, his eyes on me, not even looking at the medications. I turned my face away from him. "Hey, take it easy," he soothed as he sat on the floor next to me.

"Go away," I cried.

"No," he said softly as he drew me into his arms. "You don't need to be alone—not like this."

I sobbed, my shoulders shaking as I cried. He tightened his arms around me, brushing his lips to the top of my head as I soaked his bare chest with my tears.

One big, fucked-up mess.

10

LOVE

Christian

"What?" I growled into my phone as I picked up Caiden's call. I swear, if he was bothering me again about no milk being in my house, I was going to lose my fucking mind.

"Christian, you need to get home," he told me. There wasn't any teasing in his voice. For once, my brother was completely serious. "Ally needs you, bro."

"Fuck," I swore. I had an appointment in twenty minutes with a patient, but goddammit, I couldn't let Ally suffer by herself. And Caiden—yeah, he was good with me when I was buried deep in my own shit, but he wouldn't know how to handle her.

"What happened?" I demanded as I went in search of Axel. He was free until the afternoon. I needed him to take my next two appointments, and I would get the receptionist to reschedule the rest.

"I don't fucking know, Christian." I heard Ally crying in the background. My fucking heart broke for her, my soul urging me to hurry the fuck up to get to her.

"Axel," I called when I saw him getting ready to disappear into his office. He stopped and turned to face me. "I need to go," I told him. "It's Ally."

He nodded, concern for his little sister washing through his eyes. "I'll handle everything. Go," he ordered. "And fucking let me know what's going on."

I nodded and quickly rushed out of the back door of the office. "Caiden, let me talk to her," I urged him. "I can keep her stabilized. Just let me talk to her."

A moment later, her shaky voice came over the phone. "Christian?" she croaked.

"Hey, beautiful," I soothed as I beeped my car unlocked and slid into the driver's seat. "Talk to me, baby. What's going on?"

She sobbed. "I'm a mess," she cried.

"No, beautiful. You're not." Fuck, she could never be a mess in my eyes. She wasn't perfect by any means, but goddammit, she was perfect for *me*. Every bit of her called to me. The moment I laid my eyes on her, I knew there would never be another woman in my life.

Ally was it for me.

"I am." She hiccuped. "What sane person has to take this many medications?"

"Someone who is trying to be her best self," I gently reminded her as I quickly sped down the street. I thankfully didn't live far—it was normally only a five-minute drive—but since I was speeding, I would be there in a couple of minutes at most. "I need you to fight for me, baby. I'm almost home."

"I'm so tired of fighting all of the time," she whimpered, striking fear in my chest. I would *not* let her give up. Not now.

I quickly turned into the driveway, parking half-assed on the concrete. I quickly jumped out of the car and rushed up to the porch. "Don't say shit like that, Ally. I'm never fucking letting you give up," I swore.

I quickly hung up the phone and rushed into the bathroom where I could hear her crying. Caiden quickly moved out of my way. I leaned down and slid my arms beneath her, lifting her up against my chest. "I'm here, baby," I soothed. I looked at Caiden as I began to carry her to my bed. "Grab her medicine," I told him. "And a bottle of water." He nodded and disappeared to do as I'd asked.

She slept later than usual today. She had a routine

of getting up and going straight to the bathroom to take her medications. Since it was already almost eleven and her medications were still set out on the counter, I knew she hadn't taken them yet.

And since she was used to taking her medications around seven each morning because of school, her not taking them by this point—almost four hours later— was what had messed her up.

"I'm sorry," she whimpered.

I leaned down and soothed my lips over hers. "It's okay," I assured her. Fuck, she looked so broken and tired, and it physically *hurt* to see her like this. "I'm here; let me take care of you." I nodded in thanks to Caiden when he set her meds on the bed with a bottle of water. He slipped out of the room right after, giving us the privacy we needed.

I sat further up on the bed and settled my crying woman between my legs. "Take your meds," I gently ordered.

She reached forward and slowly opened each bottle, putting her medications into her hands until she had a small cluster of pills to swallow down. Once she swallowed them and capped her water again, I quickly knocked everything off the bed with my foot and turned her around, dragging her lips to mine.

"Be my moon," I whispered as I ran my lips over her jaw. She moaned softly, already getting lost in me and what I was making her feel. "Let me help you live, beautiful. All I need is for you to shine for me."

I let her set the pace this time between us, and when she finally slid down on me, her eyes shined.

Always so fucking beautiful.

I encouraged her by running my hands over her body, whispering sweet words about how perfect she was for me. Because she was. And I'd *never* let her believe anything different.

(

Ally

Caiden stepped into the house a couple of hours later. He was holding some groceries in his hands. "I've got a few more bags out in the car," he told Christian. "Can't be letting your girl stay here and starve."

I glowered at Caiden. "I'm not starving," I told him, defending Christian. "I'm capable of cooking. I don't need everything to be microwaveable."

Caiden snorted. "Makes life a hell of a lot easier, though," he retorted. He flashed me a smile. "Glad you're feeling better."

My cheeks darkened, and I shyly looked away from him. Christian tilted my chin up and pressed his lips to mine. "Shine," he whispered against my lips.

I smiled up at him. He grinned before he pressed a kiss to my forehead and stepped back, going to grab the rest of the groceries as Caiden began to put the ones he brought in away. I moved to help, but he shot me a look that quickly rooted me to my seat. "Keep your little ass on the stool," he ordered. "We can handle this."

"I'm not fragile, you know."

He shrugged. "A woman that can cry like that and come out on the other side strong as hell? I know you're not fragile." I blinked back tears at his words. "But you've had a rough as fuck morning."

I sighed. "I have rough as fuck mornings all the time, Caiden. It doesn't mean that I can't help put away groceries."

He shrugged. "Don't care. You're not helping." He looked up as Christian walked into the kitchen. "Tell your stubborn ass woman to stop arguing with me."

Christian grinned at me. "Give him hell, beautiful."

Caiden stood back up to his full height and glowered at Christian. "That's literally the exact opposite of what I just told you to do."

My phone pinged with a text. I slid it across the counter toward me and swiped up on the screen, ignoring Christian and Caiden as they went back and forth with each other.

AXEL

> You good, Sis? Christian said you're alright now, but I'm fucking worried about you.

> I'm fine. Had a rough morning. I didn't wake up on time to take my medicine.

I looked up at Christian, only for his eyes to already be on me. I flushed under his intense gaze. "Everything good?"

I smiled at him and nodded. "Just Axel," I assured him. "He's worried about me."

A smirk tilted Christian's lips suddenly, and before I could ask him what was so amusing, Caiden yanked me off the stool. I squealed in shock when he threw me over his shoulder. "Put me down!" I yelled at Caiden. "You're such a fucking child!"

Christian laughed. "While you were lost in your text with Axel, Caiden and I decided to do something fun with you today." He smiled at me when I glowered at him, Caiden's shoulder digging painfully into my stomach. "How does the zoo sound?"

My eyes brightened. I loved animals. Instantly, I stopped fighting. "Really?" I asked him, momentarily forgetting about the fact that Caiden was purposely bouncing his knees to annoy me further.

Christian's smile softened. "Really, baby."

I slapped my hands on Caiden's back. "Will you stop fucking bouncing?!" I shouted at him.

"Fuck!" Caiden shouted as Christian laughed. "Christ, woman, that hurt!"

"So does your damn shoulder in my gut!" I snapped. I held my hand out to Christian. "Will you *please* save me from this fucking child?"

Christian quickly pulled me from Caiden's shoulder and gently set me on my feet. Then, he then slid his hands around my body and pulled me to him, leaning down to kiss me. I moaned, linking my arms around his neck, our kiss deepening as Christian gripped my ass in his hands, squeezing while he yanked me closer to him.

"Fuck," he swore. He grabbed my hand in his, pulling me toward his bedroom.

"What the fuck?!" Caiden shouted at our backs.

I giggled. Christian flashed me a sexy grin. "Fifteen minutes, bro!" he called over his shoulder before he slammed the bedroom door shut behind us.

I quickly unfastened his belt as he wrapped his hand around my neck, roughly kissing me. I opened my lips under his, allowing him to deepen the kiss. I wanted him so fucking badly.

"Fuck, beautiful," Christian growled when I finally was able to wrap my hand around his cock.

I'd never been so open with anyone before—not even my ex. But Christian had a way of making me lose myself in him. I forgot about everything but him when he and I were like this together.

He yanked my shirt over my head, my bra falling to the floor right after. I quickly kicked my shoes aside and wiggled out of my leggings and panties. He was undressed in record time, and as soon as I kicked my leggings and panties aside, he grabbed the back of my thighs and lifted me up, slamming my back roughly against the wall.

"Christian!" I cried out as he buried himself deep inside of me.

"Yes—fuck," he growled as he began to screw up into me hard and fast.

"Oh, God." I wrapped an arm around my breasts when they began to ache. Somehow knowing without me saying a word, Christian moved me over to the bed and laid me down on it, his body never leaving mine. I wrapped my thick thighs around his hips, my nails digging into his back as he pounded into me.

"You're so fucking perfect," Christian groaned before he took my lips in a savage kiss.

"Please don't stop," I whimpered as I clung to him, my hands losing their grip on his sweaty shoulders.

"Not until you tell me to," he promised.

I arched my back, my pussy clenching around his cock as I came hard. He covered my lips with his, swallowing his name as it burst from me, coming so hard that I momentarily lost my vision.

He dug his fingers into my hip and my shoulder as he spilled inside of me, his lips working aggressively with mine.

"I love you," he rasped, his heart pounding erratically as he continued to slowly thrust, working us both down from that high we were on.

Tears poured down my cheeks as I ran my blurry eyes over his face. "You really mean that?" I choked out.

He nodded, looking down at me with so much love shining in his eyes that I thought my heart might burst out of my chest. "Yes. I fucking love you, Ally. I love every single piece of you."

I brought him back down to me, my lips meeting his. "Fuck the zoo," I grumbled as I linked my ankles behind his back again. "Make love to me, Christian," I begged him.

So, he did. And when I came again, tears slid down my cheeks as I clutched him to me. "I love you, too," I whispered, but I knew he would hear me.

He tightened his arms around me, his lips slowly moving with mine.

And it was all the answer I needed.

We may have been moving fast as fuck, but it felt so right.

11

THE ZOO

Ally

Christian held my hand in his as he led me toward the lions. I hadn't been this excited about anything in a really long time. It was wearing me out, but I was determined to enjoy every bit of this day that I could.

Caiden walked up to us and handed me a soda. "Thank you," I told him. Christian released my hand so I could walk up closer to the glass wall that separated us from the powerful animals. The female lion was asleep on her side in the sunshine, and the male lion was laying in front of her, but he was watching everyone that came up to the glass, and occasionally, he would move closer to his female.

Christian slid his hand along my back as he looked at the lions as well. "He's taking care of his female," he commented.

I nodded. "Watching animals used to make me crave companionship," I blurted, my cheeks burning red after. *Where in the world did my filter go?*

Christian pressed his lips to my temple. "If you ever have to crave that while being with me, then that means I'm not doing my job as your man properly."

I smiled up at him, and he grinned in response, his heart-stopping smile making my chest swell with love. "I love you."

He leaned down and kissed me. "And I love you."

"There are kids around here," a woman griped as she ushered her children along, shooting us both dirty looks. I frowned, quickly looking down at the ground.

"And the fact that you have an issue with two people being open about how much they love each other says a lot about the kind of person you are," Caiden retorted before Christian could open his mouth. "Your poor children will grow up miserable because they're not allowed to see adults love each other."

I gaped at Christian's older brother. "Caiden!" I snapped.

He turned his dark eyes to me with a shrug. "What? It was a simple kiss. It's not like he was making out with you." Caiden shrugged. "Kids today need to see more adults in love. Maybe children will stop growing up to become bitter adults."

I didn't know what to say to that. Christian laced his fingers through mine. "Come on, beautiful," he coaxed, letting the conversation drop. "I think there are tigers in the next little area."

"Tigers are so pretty," I spoke aloud. I suddenly tripped over a raised piece of the sidewalk, and Christian quickly wrapped his arm tightly around my waist, keeping me from falling forward. He shook his head, but I could tell he was trying not to laugh.

"Woman, you are so fucking clumsy," he teased.

I crossed my arms over my chest. "Everything just hates me," I grumbled.

And then, I fucking tripped again.

This time, Christian nor Caiden could contain their laughs. I squeaked in alarm when Christian suddenly stopped in front of me and kneeled down. "Up," he ordered.

"I can walk," I grumbled, crossing my arms over my chest.

"Clearly not." Caiden teased.

I glared at him. He laughed. With a disgruntled face, I got on Christian's back, linking my arms around his shoulders. He hooked his hands under my thighs and began carrying me to the tiger enclosure.

Christian

Ally quietly moaned in protest when I gently reached into the car and lifted her sleeping form out of the backseat. "Easy," I whispered in her ear as I completely lifted her from the car. Caiden quietly closed the back door to the car.

Ally loosely wrapped her arms around my neck and fell back asleep, her head resting awkwardly on my shoulder. "She's worn slap the fuck out, bro," Caiden said quietly as he opened the front door to the house.

I nodded in agreement. "Her mind doesn't exactly know how to handle so much happiness and excitement. So, it wears her out."

I carried Ally into our room and gently laid her on the bed. She had removed her shoes once we got in the car, so I didn't have to bother her anymore. I just pulled the blankets over her and pressed a kiss to her forehead before I slipped out of the room.

I knocked once on Caiden's door before I pushed it open, my eyes widening in horror at what was in front of me. Caiden had his shirt off, and he was removing a bandage from his side. "Caiden, what the fuck?" I growled as I moved forward.

He sighed. "I wasn't ready for you to know about

this," he grumbled as he completely removed the bandage. I stared at the stitched-up wounds on his side in horror. "I got shot—twice. I was trying to protect one of the other guys." He drew in a deep breath as he took a seat on the edge of his bed, staring at the floor. "He was fucking bleeding out in my arms, but I took an oath—I would never leave a fallen comrade."

"Caiden," I said quietly. There was so much pain on his face—so much anguish. I didn't know how to deal with seeing my brother like this. He was *always* the strong one, the one everyone else could rely on.

"I got shot trying to protect him, and he bled out in my arms. I couldn't fucking leave him." Caiden drew in another deep breath, seeming like he was trying to steady the pain he was feeling. He rubbed the heel of his hand over his chest. "I woke up in a hospital. Once I was healed enough, they sent me back here to the states."

I sat beside him. "Are you seeing a therapist?" I asked him.

He nodded. "Yeah. I've got a pretty good one out on base. She's specialized in trauma therapy."

I gripped his shoulder, knowing my next question was going to hurt him, but I already knew the answer. "Your career—it's over, isn't it?"

He swallowed thickly and nodded. "Yeah," he

rasped. He looked over at me. "I'm sorry, bro. I just—fuck, I didn't know how to tell you."

I squeezed his shoulder. "You can stay here as long as you need," I assured him, meaning every word. "I know you get on my nerves a lot," a small laugh spilled from his lips, "but my home is always open to you. Besides, you're good for Ally. You light a fire under her."

He shrugged. "Girl needs someone to aggravate the shit out of her sometimes. She gets too lost in her head."

I nodded in agreement. That she did do. I stood up. "You're making dinner tonight," I told him.

He grunted. "I fucking hate cooking."

I shrugged. "Yeah, well, I need a nap, and I want to cuddle with my woman, so dinner is on you."

He rolled his eyes, and I knew we were okay—that *he* would be okay. Caiden was always the most resilient out of both of us. I had always envied him for it, but I was always the more understanding one of us.

I walked out of the room and headed back for mine. When I slid into bed behind Ally, she snuggled back against me instantly, sighing softly in her sleep. I brushed my lips to the back of her head before I tightly wrapped my arms around her, pulling her securely against me.

"I love you, my moon," I whispered.

Ally

Christian and Caiden were bantering back and forth in the kitchen when I stepped out of the bedroom later that evening. Christian looked up as if he sensed my presence, and a breathtaking smile crossed his lips as he moved toward me.

"Hi, beautiful," he murmured as he drew me into his arms. I sighed softly when he leaned down and soothed his lips over mine. "Medicine?" he asked.

"Already took it," I assured him. I had taken my second dosing of the day as soon as I had woken up from my nap.

"That's my girl," he praised. I beamed up at him. I loved it when he felt proud of me like this.

"And there's my moon," he whispered. He drew me tighter against him, his lips meeting mine again. I moaned as I slid my hands up his chest and linked my arms around his neck, kissing him back as hungrily as he was kissing me.

"I know pornos make people a hell of a lot of money, but don't make one in front of me, please," Caiden interrupted.

Christian glared at his brother. Caiden was smirking at us as he leaned back against the kitchen counter. My cheeks burned. He was leaning on the exact spot where Christian had fucked me at.

And apparently, Christian seemed to realize this, too.

"We already made one in the kitchen," Christian retorted. "Specifically, right where you're standing."

Caiden grunted and moved off the counter. I laughed when he grabbed Lysol wipes. "Fucking disgusting."

Christian pecked my lips before he easily lifted me and set me on the kitchen counter, moving to stand between my legs. "My house. I can have sex with my woman wherever the hell I want to," Christian told him. He nuzzled my neck, and I closed my eyes, biting my lip to keep from moaning. God, he really knew every single spot to have me craving him.

Caiden finished wiping off the counter before he put the Lysol wipes back under the sink. My stomach rumbled, and Christian leaned up to meet my eyes. My cheeks flushed red. "Hungry, baby?"

I shrugged, but my stomach rumbled again, giving him his answer. He laughed before he looked over at Caiden. "Dinner?" he asked.

Caiden grunted before he rolled his eyes. "Yeah, yeah," he mumbled.

I squeaked in shock when Christian suddenly lifted

me from the counter with his hands gripping my ass. I quickly linked my legs behind his back. "Want to watch a movie?" he asked me as he walked into the living room.

"Sure." I shrugged. He sat down on the couch and grabbed his TV remote. I situated myself so I could actually see the television screen, though Christian never let me move off of his lap.

He began flicking through one of his movie apps as he gently squeezed my thigh. I looked over at him. He paused his scrolling. "I know you don't feel like it, but you're one of the strongest women I know, beautiful." A lump formed in my throat. I could feel tears burning at the backs of my eyes. "I know that some days are really fucking dark—like this morning—but every fucking day, I am so proud of you because you force yourself to stand back up, and you shine."

A tear spilled over onto my cheek. "You're too sweet," I choked out, my lips trembling.

He brushed his nose with mine. "I love you." I bit back a sob. "Every time it feels like your darkness is going to swallow you whole, I want you to remember how much I fucking love you, and I want you to search for me. Even if I'm not physically with you, Ally, I will always be there to pull you back into the light. I'll always be there to breathe life into you again so you can shine for me."

With trembling lips, I leaned forward and softly kissed him. "I love you," I whispered.

He hugged me to him. "Forever, baby. I know that seems alarmingly fast to you, but I know it with every fiber of my being. There will *never* be another woman for me."

I shook my head at him. "It does seem really fast, but," I drew in a deep breath, "it feels so right." He grinned at me—that same grin that would always melt my soul. I reached up and trailed my fingers over his face. "This sounds so weak, but I just beg you to stay with me," I told him. "Even when I try to push you away because I *will*. Sometimes, I don't know how to handle the darkness." I swallowed thickly. "I'm terrified of it."

He linked his fingers around my wrist and turned his head to press a kiss to the center of my palm. "I know you are, baby, but don't let it suffocate you. Always look for me. I'll never leave you. I am yours to keep."

12

JULIAN'S GAME

Ally

Meghan wrapped me up in her arms the moment I stepped into the house. I laughed and hugged her back, relaxing for a moment so I could take in the familiar security of my sister-in-law hugging me. "You look so much happier," she said quietly as she leaned back to look me over. "I'm so proud of you for giving him a chance."

"Thank you for pushing me to," I told her honestly. I smiled at Christian over my shoulder, instantly catching his eye. He flashed me his own smile before he turned his attention back to Axel, introducing his brother as he did so. I looked back at Meghan. "He knows exactly how to handle me. I don't feel so lost with him around."

"Just remember to keep fighting for yourself," she reminded me with a stern look. I nodded. "Let him be your light in the darkness, but keep fighting for *you*."

"I will; I promise," I assured her.

Axel wrapped me up in a tight hug, lifting my feet from the ground as he did so. I laughed, squeezing him back. "Dammit, Ally, you've had me worried fucking sick about you." He grumbled into my hair. I frowned, tightening my hold on him. He sighed. "I know he can take care of you. It's just hard for me to let go of the reins for him to do so."

"Auntie Ally!" Holden screamed as he ran down the stairs. Axel let me go, and Holden crashed into my legs, sending me to my ass on the floor. I laughed and wrapped the little monster up in my arms, my throat closing up with tears as I held him.

"Hey, kid," I greeted, forcing my voice to come out normal. "Have you been good for your mom?"

His cheeks darkened. I knew without asking that he had been a little monster. He was so much like Julian, and he always kept Meghan on her toes. Lana was still a baby, so there wasn't much that she could do to freak out her mom, but Holden was damn good at doing everything he could to send her into a panic.

Christian grabbed me under my arms and helped me up from the floor. I leaned down and scooped Holden up into my arms. "I bought cookies, but since you won't be nice to your Mommy, I'm just going to eat them all by myself," I teased.

He pouted. Jesus, he really looked like Julian. I laughed. "If you're good for the rest of the day, and you take your nap without arguing with Mommy and Daddy A, then you can have some cookies later on," I told him.

I set him on his feet, and he rushed over to his mom on his chubby legs. She beamed at him and lifted him up, walking into the kitchen, probably to get him some juice. Caiden and Axel disappeared into the living room, talking animatedly about football. Christian gently turned me to face him, and he settled his hands on the dip in my waist.

"You would have made a really good mom," he told me quietly. I swallowed thickly at his words. He reached up and cupped the side of my neck, brushing his thumb along my jaw. "One of these days, beautiful, I'll give you the opportunity to have that," he promised.

I leaned up and linked my arms around his neck, hugging him. He blew out a soft breath as he wrapped his arms around me as well, holding me to him. "I love you," I told him, my voice thick with emotion.

"You're my moon," he said simply. "I'll do anything in the fucking world that I can for you to keep glowing."

When Julian had a game, their house was madness. And today, it was even more so. Christian, Axel, and Caiden kept yelling at the TV, getting angry when there were penalties and what they called 'dumb moves'. Meghan and I only really knew to yell when Julian had control of the ball, and when the Patriots scored a touchdown. Holden was used to the ruckus by now, so he was just pushing some of his toys across the floor, making weird sounds with his mouth.

A break came on, and I stood up from the couch, heading straight for the kitchen to find something to eat. I heard Lana begin crying upstairs, so I changed my direction, heading for the stairs instead.

"I've got her!" I called.

"Thanks, Sis!" Axel called back. "Hurry up and get your ass back down here, though! Game is getting ready to come back on in a minute!"

I rushed up the stairs and into Lana's room. She was sitting up, her wails echoing around the room. I gagged as soon as I entered, the smell of her diaper making me want to vomit. I barely made it to the toilet across the hall before I began emptying my stomach.

I quickly pushed the door closed and clutched the toilet bowl again as I threw up a second time, my stomach muscles painfully clenching together as I retched.

Lana stopped crying a moment later, and I heard

Axel talking sweetly to her. My stomach was still churning, but I forced myself to hold it down, not wanting to alarm Axel that something was wrong.

I moaned in pain, closing my eyes when I felt it rising again. Tears burned in my eyes. I really hated getting sick.

"Sis, you okay in there?"

I couldn't answer. I clutched the porcelain again, throwing up a third time. Axel quickly stepped into the bathroom and set Lana down on the floor. Tears slid down my cheeks as I gagged, sobs shaking my shoulders.

"Hey, easy, Sis. I'm here," Axel soothed. He gathered my hair and held it out of the way for me, his other hand gently running up and down my back.

"Everything good?!" I heard Christian call from the bottom of the stairs.

I looked up at Axel with fear in my eyes, shaking my head at him. I didn't want Christian to see me like this.

Axel clenched his jaw but opened the door, shouting back down the stairs to Christian that everything was cool and to give us a few minutes. I slowly reached forward and flushed the toilet, sagging back against the wall as I covered my face with my hands, drawing in deep breaths. My stomach was still swirling with nausea, but I didn't feel like I was going to vomit anytime soon.

"How late are you?" Axel asked me quietly as he settled Lana in his lap.

I frowned at him. "What are you talking about?" I asked him.

He sighed. "Your period, Sis. How late is your period?"

I was highly confused. "I'm not late." But then my frown deepened as I thought about it more. My face paled, my heart rate picking up speed. Tears poured down my cheeks. "No," I choked out, shaking my head. I looked up at Axel, my heart breaking, my soul wailing. "I'm on birth control," I sobbed. "This wasn't supposed to happen."

"Fuck," Axel swore. He set Lana back on the floor, letting her explore as he moved closer to me, pulling me into his arms. "It's not the end of the world, Sis. You have family that will support you, and I know Christian won't walk away from you."

"I can't be a mom," I cried. "Axel, I can't. I killed the last baby. I'm so fucked up—"

"Stop—right now," Axel ordered. He gripped my chin, tilting my head back so I was forced to look up at him. "You're not fucked up, Ally. Stop saying that shit. You're going to be a great mom. This is your second chance to do things right. None of us are giving up on you. You have support, and Christian is a really good man. He'll be here for you every step of the way."

I bit my lip hard, resisting the urge to wail. Axel drew me back into his arms, holding me tightly. "I'm so scared," I sobbed. I clutched my brother's shirt in my fists. "Oh, God, Axel, I'm fucking terrified."

"I know," he whispered. "I'm here this time, Ally. I'm never abandoning you again; I promise. Things will be different."

"Things are moving so fast with Christian," I sobbed. "What if he decides this is too much? What if he walks away?"

Axel tightened his arms around me. "Then I'll kick his ass, and when Julian can come home for a little bit, he'll kick his ass, too. You'll move back in here, and we'll help you. But he's not giving up on you, Ally. You know how fucking protective I am of you, but every bit of me tells me that Christian will *never* turn his back on you."

I shook my head, staying quiet for a moment. "I don't know if I can tell him," I whispered.

"Then take some time to come to terms with it," Axel soothed. "Christian will understand why you didn't tell him the moment you figured it out. I don't think that man is capable of ever truly being angry with you."

"He'll notice something is wrong," I quietly told Axel. "He says my eyes shine when I'm happy, when I'm okay." I shook my head. "His moon won't glow," I whispered, hiccuping, more tears burning in my eyes.

"He's such a fucking smooth ass," Axel laughed. I couldn't help it; I laughed with him, though it sounded watery and pained. Axel squeezed me to him. "Do what makes you feel comfortable. Boundaries, Ally," he reminded me. "Even if you might hurt someone else, love yourself enough to put yourself first."

We sat in silence for a minute, the only sound in the room being Lana's coos as she explored what was under the bathroom sink. "It wasn't supposed to happen like this," I said quietly.

"Nothing ever happens the way we plan it to," he gently reminded me.

I yawned, resting my head on his shoulder. "Crying is exhausting," I whispered.

Axel laughed. "Yeah, I know." He looked up when the bathroom door opened, Meghan poking her head in. She frowned at my tear-stained face. "Christian is fucking going nuts with worry down there," she quietly informed us.

My bottom lip trembled, and I squeezed my eyes shut. I hated that he worried so much about me—hated that he even had a reason to, to begin with. "Hey, just breathe," Axel soothed. He looked up at Meghan. "Can you take Lana downstairs? And keep Christian down there—Caiden, too. She needs a nap, and she doesn't need to be disturbed."

Meghan ran her worried eyes over my face but

nodded her head and lifted Lana up into her arms. "Whatever is going on, Ally, you have a family. Don't ever forget that."

I nodded at her as a tear ran down my cheek. Axel stood up from the floor with me cradled in his arms. "I'm going to put you in our room." I scrunched my face up in disgust. He laughed. "We just cleaned the sheets a little while ago, Sis. They're clean."

He gently laid me down on the bed and pulled my shoes off of my feet, setting them by the bed. He pressed a kiss to my forehead. "Get some sleep. You need it."

I nodded. "Axel," I softly called as he was getting ready to close the door; he turned to face me, "thank you."

He gave me a small smile. "Love you, Sis."

I smiled. "Love you, too, Big Bro."

As soon as the door was shut behind him, I cried. And I cried until the only thing I was capable of doing was sleeping.

Christian

Axel stepped outside where I was pacing back and forth on the porch, too anxious to sit down. I knew in my gut something was wrong with Ally, but Meghan asked me to respect her wishes to not come to her.

And that didn't sit right with me. I didn't allow my woman to suffer by herself.

"Don't fucking tell me you left her alone," I growled at him when he stepped outside.

He arched a single eyebrow at me, clearly not appreciating the way I just spoke to him, but I didn't give a shit. "She needs some time to sleep."

I clenched my jaw, my hand fisting at my side. I forced myself to stretch my fingers back out. Punching my girlfriend's brother—my boss—in the face, wouldn't do me any bit of fucking good.

"She's fucking hurting, and you left her alone," I snapped at him. "What fucking sense does that even begin to make in your goddamn head?"

Axel sighed. "Christian—"

I shook my head, moving past him to go into the house to find her. I made a promise that I would always be there for her. She didn't have to tell me what was wrong. I respected her enough to not force her to open up to me when she wasn't ready. But I would *not* let her suffer alone. Even if the only thing I could do was hold her through her pain, then I fucking would.

Axel stepped in front of me, preventing me from entering the house. "Leave her be, Christian."

"Goddammit, Axel!" I barked. "My fucking woman

is upstairs, probably crying her fucking eyes out, and you think you're going to stop me from holding her and reminding her that she's not fucking alone?" I growled. "Get the fuck out of my way. She's scared of the dark, Axel, and I promised her I would always be her goddamn light. So fucking *move*."

I barged my way past him and rushed up the stairs. It was easy to find her since it was the only closed door upstairs. She was asleep, but tears were running down her cheeks. I quickly kicked my shoes off and moved toward the bed, sliding in behind her, my heart bleeding for her.

I drew her into my arms, pressing a soft kiss to her lips. Her eyes slowly fluttered open. They were dim. Her light was gone.

My soul wailed.

"I'm here, my moon," I whispered as I held her tight to me. She sobbed. "You're not alone," I promised.

13

PROMISES

Ally

I groaned in protest when I felt Christian lifting me from the bed. I squinted open my sore, puffy eyes to look up at him. He pressed a soft kiss to my lips. "I'm taking you home," he said quietly. "Go back to sleep, beautiful. I've got you."

I loosely linked my arm around his neck and draped my other arm over my belly, resting my head on his shoulder as I closed my eyes again. I could hear Caiden talking quietly to Axel, but their conversation stopped when Christian stepped down the stairs.

"Christian—" Axel began.

Christian grunted, cutting him off. I kept my eyes

shut. They were too sore to open them. "I'll be at work tomorrow morning. I'm not in the fucking mood."

I lifted my head, opening my eyes despite their soreness, looking between my boyfriend and my brother. Axel frowned, his eyes moving to me. With a sigh, he walked over and pressed a kiss to my forehead. "I'm here if you need me, Sis. Always," my brother promised.

Christian moved past Axel and carried me out of the house before I could respond to him. "Christian, what was that?" I asked him.

He shook his head. "Not right now," he grumbled. "Please, just let me get you home, and then we can talk about what happened."

Caiden came outside and slid into the backseat without a word as Christian set me in the passenger seat. Christian pressed a kiss to my lips before he shut the door and walked around the front of the car. I followed him with worried eyes.

I didn't like the fact that he'd obviously had a disagreement with my brother, and it had fear settling in the pit of my stomach.

C

I watched Christian through the mirror in the bathroom as he closed the bedroom door, giving us some privacy. I turned to face him, crossing my arms over my chest in a defensive gesture. My stomach churned. I was normally uneasy in confrontations, and it sometimes made me nauseated, but now being pregnant was about to make it a hell of a lot worse.

"What happened between you and Axel?" I asked him.

He sighed, pulling his shirt over his head and tossing it into the laundry basket. "We had a disagreement before I came upstairs." I stayed silent, watching him as he toed his shoes off. "He wanted me to leave you alone."

I frowned. "I asked him to be left alone," I told him. Christian shook his head at me.

"I know," he informed me as he somehow managed to toe his socks off as well. He moved toward me, his hands coming up to cup my cheeks. "I promised you I would never leave you alone in the dark," he reminded me. My bottom lip trembled as I fought back tears. "You asked me to stay with you even when you try to push me away. I don't make empty promises, Ally. I will always be your light when everything around you is dark. I don't know what happened, but I will never leave you alone to suffer."

I squeezed my eyes shut as a tear slid down my cheek. "Christian," I whispered, my voice breaking on his name, "please promise me that you won't walk away from me."

He brushed his lips to my cheek, his lips capturing the tear that had fallen from my eye. "You're my moon. I will never leave you. We're forever, beautiful."

I circled my fingers around his wrist and opened my eyes, bravely looking up at him through the tears in my eyes. Slowly, I pulled his hand down and pressed it to my belly. I watched as he tried to figure out what the hell I was doing, but then his eyes widened in shock, his lips slightly parting as his eyes flickered to my belly.

"You're pregnant?" he asked in a whisper, his eyes snapping back up to mine.

I nodded, the tears now pouring down my cheeks. "I'm ninety-nine percent sure," I told him, my voice breaking. "I need to take a test and see a doctor, but I was really sick earlier, and my period is late. Axel put it together before I did."

"Fuck, baby," Christian rasped, his voice rough with emotion as he tugged me into his arms, rocking me gently from side to side. I sobbed as I clutched at his shirt. "I'm here, beautiful. I'm never going anywhere." He pressed his lips to my cheeks, forehead, nose, lips—anywhere on my face that he could reach. "You're not alone, and this won't be like last time," he promised. "I will do everything in my fucking power to ensure you carry our little one to term—to make sure you give birth to a healthy, chubby little baby."

"I'm scared," I cried. God, I was terrified. I wasn't ready for this, but it was happening regardless.

"I know, baby, I know." He tightened his arms around me. "But I'm here. We're going to get through this together."

Christian held my hand in his as we walked down the aisle that held the pregnancy tests at the local pharmacy. He kept me close to him, giving my hand little reassuring squeezes to remind me that he was there, that he wasn't going anywhere.

I had cried for a good hour at least earlier, and he had held me, never letting go. He just continuously promised me that I wasn't alone, that I was it for him, that we were forever.

It all felt too damn good to be true, and that was what had me so terrified.

Because with Randall, it had *always* been too good to be true. But I didn't realize it until I found him fucking my best friend.

I looked up from the floor and jerked to a stop, my heart pounding hard and fast in my chest. My ex-best friend was standing in front of me, staring at me as well. She was glowing, her belly swollen with her second baby, and she was holding her little girl's hand in hers.

Randall turned down the aisle. "Babe, I can't find the damn—"

His words were cut off when he saw me, his jaw dropping slightly. I trembled. Christian brushed his lips to my temple, nothing in his expression as he looked back at the small, happy family in front of us. "Come on," he said softly, his arm going around my waist.

"Ally," Heather called as I got ready to let Christian lead me away from them. I tensed. His hand gently squeezed the dip in my waist. "I'm sorry," she apologized.

"No, you're not," I said, thankful that my voice came out strong despite how weak I felt at that moment. I drew in a deep breath. "I just hope you have everything you've ever wanted."

"But I don't," she said quietly. "You were my best friend. It just all feels so wrong without you."

I shook my head and began to walk away, but Randall's voice drew me to a stop. "Walk away," he taunted. Tears burned in my eyes. "That's what you're good at, right? You either walk away, or you let other people fight your battles for you."

My chest painfully tightened. I didn't want to have a confrontation in a store. I frankly didn't want to have this conversation at all.

"Randall, shut up," Heather snapped at him at the same time Christian spun around to face them.

"Shows what kind of man and father you are that you would publicly hurt and humiliate a person in public," Christian sneered. "And as a matter of fact, for your fucking information, she didn't tell me about the pictures and texts you were sending her. I found the last ones by myself, and *I* took it upon myself to call you. You've both done enough fucking damage. So, shut the hell up." He snatched two pregnancy test boxes off the shelf before he grabbed my hand in his.

"Pregnant again?" Randall snapped. I could hear the hurt in his voice, and I knew he wanted me to feel just like he was. I flinched. "You'll lose this one, too."

Christian spun around. I barely had time to grab him, holding him with me. "Christian," I pleaded. He looked up at me, his dark eyes—black in his rage—looked down at me. "Please," I begged him. "Don't. You'll get arrested."

He cupped the side of my neck and pressed his lips to mine in a hard kiss, but he didn't walk from me. He did, however, narrow his eyes at Randall, looking like a deadly man instead of the sweet guy he always was with me.

"If you're itching for a fight, you know how to find me. I don't hide. But if you're not, then shut your fucking mouth about her. You don't know a goddamn thing about my woman. But I can promise you, starting shit with her is the last fucking thing you want to do."

With that, he grabbed my hand in his and led me down the aisle, heading to the self-checkout lane, leaving Randall speechless behind us. "Ally," Heather called. I looked at her over my shoulder. Tears burned in her eyes. "Congratulations. You'll be an amazing mom."

I turned back around, silent tears sliding down my cheeks. When we got in the car, Christian quickly pulled out of the lot. He turned down a couple of random streets until we were in the dark parking lot of one of the parks near the pharmacy.

I squeaked in alarm when he yanked me out of my seat and settled me on his lap, his lips meeting mine. "You are fucking everything to me," Christian promised. "And I hate that he can still fucking hurt you, but I understand it." He slid his hands under my shirt before he yanked it off. I moaned as his hands slid over my exposed skin. "I'm a hairsbreadth away from going back to that fucking pharmacy and bashing his face into the fucking concrete, so I need you, and I'm sorry ahead of time if I hurt you."

I knew Christian could never hurt me, so with sure, quick movements, I removed my clothes for him, knowing he liked seeing every bit of me when we were together like this. He quickly unsnapped his jeans and tugged them down his legs.

Once I slid down on him, he proceeded to fuck me

like he hadn't touched me in *years*; he fucked me like a man deprived.

And I loved every fucking minute of Christian losing himself in me.

With trembling fingers, I slowly opened the bathroom door to look at my pregnancy tests. Two each came in the box. So, I took two a few minutes ago, and I would take the other two in the morning, regardless of what these two said.

Christian was right behind me, and he wrapped his arms around my waist from behind as I looked down at the tests.

Pregnant.

Pregnant.

"Oh, God," I choked out.

Christian turned me around to face him, and he cupped my face in his hands, kissing me so sweetly—so tenderly—that I felt like my heart might completely fucking burst in my chest.

"I love you. We're forever. I'm not fucking leaving you." He smiled down at me—a smile filled with so much love and adoration for me that it set my soul on fire for him. "I'm going to be a dad."

I nodded as a tear ran down my cheek. He kissed me

again. I vaguely registered him tossing the tests into the trash can before he lifted me onto the counter. He yanked my shirt over my head, tossing it to the floor before he reached behind me and unclasped my bra, my breasts spilling free as he pulled the straps down my shoulders.

His lips moved over my neck, and I released a soft moan as I tilted my head to the side, giving him better access. "Fuck, yes," he growled as he cupped my breasts. I moaned his name, my hands burying themselves in his thick, dark hair as he drew a nipple between his lips.

I gripped the hem of his shirt and pulled it over his head, revealing his perfect, muscular body. Running my fingers through the light dusting of hair on his chest, I drew a deep groan from him in response.

He slid my leggings and panties down my legs, tossing them to the floor before he unsnapped his jeans and dropped them down to the floor with his boxers.

"What—*yes*," I breathed when he kneeled on the floor and buried his face between my thighs. I laced my fingers in his hair, a soft cry falling from my lips. He was a fucking god with his tongue.

I cried out, my thighs shaking as I came. He continued eating me out, taking in everything that I was giving. I barely had time to come down from my orgasm when he stood up and buried himself inside of me. He wrapped one arm around my waist and pressed his other hand to the mirror behind me. Then, he proceeded to make sweet love to me.

"Thank you," he rasped as he drew us closer and closer to the edge of that glorious cliff.

"For?" I moaned, opening my eyes to look up into his dark ones.

"For making me a dad," he rumbled.

I grabbed his face in my hands and kissed him. He growled, taking my lips in a rougher kiss, unleashing the savage inside of him. I clung to him, my lips never leaving his as my body shook in his hold, my world exploding around me.

14

THERAPY

Christian

I flipped through the appointment planner that the receptionist kept for me, knowing I liked having something tangible in my hands to hold. Don't get me wrong, the appointment system on the computer worked great, and it was a lot more efficient, but I couldn't stand the damn thing.

Axel stepped through the door. I didn't spare him a glance as I looked through my morning appointments, writing them down on a sticky note I took from Jhenna's desk.

"Christian," Axel called. I only grunted. I wasn't in the mood to deal with him. Ally's weekend had gone to complete shit on Sunday, and this morning, it had been a struggle to get her to take her medicine. Caiden was with her today, and when I left, she was curled up on the couch, her eyes on the TV screen, but I didn't think she was seeing it.

I wanted to stay with her. Fuck, I really wanted to. She fucking needed me. But unfortunately, bills didn't stop coming in just because I needed to be with her. I had to work.

Caiden had promised to call me if it got worse, but she had an appointment with Dr. Gresham today, so I was hoping he could talk to her.

She wasn't alone. I wasn't giving up on her. I just needed her to realize that.

I would *never* fucking give up on her.

"I'm not in the fucking mood, Axel," I snapped at him.

I was still pissed about what he had done on Sunday —trying to keep me away from her when she needed me. He *knew* Ally didn't need to be alone. My woman hit lows all of the time despite the medications she was on, and when I called Dr. Gresham personally yesterday evening and told him that she needed to come in and see him, and explained to him her situation, he promised to try to adjust her medications.

She opened up to me. She was getting better about doing that, about not trying to hide how she was truly feeling from me. And now was more crucial than ever since she was pregnant. If she lost another baby, I didn't think she would ever recover from it.

"Look, she asked me to not let you up there with her," Axel said anyway. I tightened my grip around the pen in my hand before I forced myself to loosen my grip. My patience was wearing thin. Between Axel and Ally's fucking ex-boyfriend and ex-best-friend at the pharmacy yesterday, I was in a right fucking mood to fight someone.

I glared at him. Jhenna shifted uncomfortably in her seat. "So, in other words, you're fucking telling me that if Meghan begged to be left alone, and you knew she was crying, that she was fucking upset about something, you would leave her alone because she asked?" He sighed, seeing my point. I shook my head and turned back to what I was doing, writing down my last appointment of the morning. "Exactly." I handed Jhenna back the appointment book. "If she doesn't want to talk, I don't force her, Axel. But that doesn't mean that I won't hold her while she cries. Being alone is the worst fucking thing for her, and if I hadn't gone to her yesterday, she would have spiraled."

With that, I turned on my heel and stormed down the hallway to my office. I looked at the couch, a small smile tilting my lips when I remembered kissing Ally there, seeing her smile at me, her eyes glowing.

You'll shine again, my moon, I silently promised.

Ally

I groaned in protest when Caiden gently shook me awake. I blinked up at him, trying to clear my bleary eyes. He gave me a small smile. "You have an appointment with your doctor soon," he said quietly. "I figured you might want to get a shower and maybe eat some lunch before we go."

I wanted to protest. I didn't want to do anything but wallow in my own fucking misery, but I forced myself into a sitting position and scrubbed at my face, feeling really exhausted.

Depression was a bitch.

"Come on," Caiden coaxed. I sighed and stood up from the couch. "Get a nice, hot shower. It'll help you feel a tiny bit better; I promise. I'll whip you up something for lunch."

I nodded at him as I trudged towards the bedroom I now shared with Christian. I knew a shower would help me feel a little bit better, too, but it was the matter of actually getting one that was the issue.

My phone vibrated on the nightstand as I stepped into the bedroom. I slowly walked over to it and picked it up, unlocking the screen to see who had texted me.

CHRISTIAN

> I know today is going to be
> hard, baby, but I'm still with you
> – still lighting your way through
> your darkness. You're going to
> glow again, my moon. Just give
> me the time I need to breathe
> life into you again. I love you.
> Hold me with you.

My bottom lip trembled as tears slid down my cheeks. *Oh, Christian.* My phone vibrated again, and a tear ran down my cheek as I read his next message.

CHRISTIAN

> Get your shower, baby. You're
> so strong.

I dropped down onto the first bench I saw outside, my stomach churning with nausea. It hadn't bothered me all day, but ever since I had eaten the grilled cheese sandwich and bowl of tomato soup that Caiden had put together for lunch, I hadn't been feeling good.

And I really didn't want to throw up. Getting sick always hurt so much.

"Christian called me yesterday evening and informed me of what has been going on," Dr. Gresham said as he took a seat next to me on the bench. "How are you feeling?"

"Sick at the moment," I told him. "I cried a lot yesterday when I figured out what was wrong with me." Dr. Gresham frowned at my choice of words. "I'm not ready for this, Dr. Gresham. I'm not ready to be a mom. I killed the first one because I was selfish. Selfish people don't deserve to be parents."

"First, being pregnant doesn't mean there's something *wrong*," Dr. Gresham told me. "It's your time for your second chance. You have a wonderful man at your side who loves you and just wants to see you happy, to see you prosper, and be great. You have an extremely supportive family." I shook my head, but he kept going. "And Ally, you were hurting. You were young, and you weren't being taken care of properly. You were neglected by your parents. Everything is different this time around."

Tears burned in my eyes. I rubbed at them. I was so tired of crying, but it seemed to be all that I could do. "I don't know if I can do this, Dr. Gresham."

"You can," he assured me. "For the duration of your pregnancy, I want you to come see me on Mondays and Fridays. On Wednesdays, I want to do virtual therapy sessions with you. I'm going to change your dosing a little on your meds—see if it helps your lows a bit."

"A fucked up mess—always," I whispered.

"No," Dr. Gresham disagreed. "You're just different, Ally, and that's okay. Different can be good. It's all about how you look at it, and right now, you're looking at it through negative eyes."

I released a bitter laugh. "I'm bipolar, depressed, and schizophrenic. Not to mention I have fucking anxiety." I shook my head. "On top of that, I'm pregnant. And then I've got an ex who just can't seem to leave me the fuck alone even though he's got the dream I've always wanted."

"Do you still love him?" Dr. Gresham asked me.

I shook my head. "No. That ship sailed long ago," I told him confidently. "But the betrayal still hurts." His words from last night at the pharmacy rang through my mind. "And for whatever reason, he wants to see me suffer."

"I'm proud of you for walking away," he told me.

I looked up at him. "I cried," I told him bluntly. I blinked back tears. I looked back down, squeezing my eyes shut to keep them from falling. "I cry over *everything*."

"Ally, I remember a time when you never cried— when you were just angry, and that's the only emotion you allowed yourself to feel. Do you remember that time?"

I nodded, my mind flashing back to when I had first been admitted into this center. Julian was paying for every bit of treatment I got here, but I just wanted to suffer. I wanted to hurt. So, I did.

And in the process, I hurt everyone around me. Julian was ready to completely give up on me. Axel had walked out on me. And Meghan, so sweet and selfless, had held so much hope for me, and I shit all over it.

I was a bitch back then, and it was a fucking miracle that Julian and Axel ever let me back around her, though I don't think she really gave them much of a choice. Even after everything I had said about her, everything that I did to her, she still held my hand in my darkest moments, proving to me that there was light.

"Crying means you're healing, but that it still hurts," Dr. Gresham told me. "And that's okay. The kind of low you hit, Ally, it's a hard one to come back from. You're still climbing. But as long as you continue to climb, it's okay to cry. It's okay to rest and take a break because it does get exhausting. But don't ever go back down. Sit there in that spot for a moment if you need to, but always remember to keep climbing up."

He gently squeezed my shoulder. "And as for your ex? You're stronger than him, Ally. You have a beautiful soul, and if you allow him, he'll tear it apart. You have to be strong enough to tilt your chin up at him, even if you're crying when you do it. Show him—prove to him —that he will *never* tear you back down again. You have your own small army of people standing behind you, ready to fight for you, and Christian is at the front of your small army. Remember who is backing you— remember that you're not alone."

Julian's face appeared on my phone screen requesting a video call. With a sigh, I pressed the green button to accept it, holding it out in front of my face since I was laying in bed. "What?" I grunted.

He laughed. "I figured you would be a little ray of sunshine today," he sarcastically retorted. I only closed my eyes, my lips not even twitching with a smile. He released a quiet sigh. "Meghan told me about what happened on Sunday. Neither she nor Axel will tell me what the fuck is going on, Little Sis. Talk to me."

Tears slid down my cheeks. "I'm scared," I whimpered.

"Of?" he asked quietly. I looked up as Christian stepped into the room, shrugging off his blazer. He quickly kicked his shoes off and removed his belt. "Ally, come on." Julian coaxed, dragging my eyes back to my phone screen. "I'm the one person you can't hide from."

Christian slid onto the bed behind me and pulled my body back against his, wrapping me up in security and giving me the strength to break the news to Julian.

"I'm pregnant," I told Julian quietly. There was no judgment on his face or in his eyes. "What if I kill it, too?" I cried, the tears I'd been holding in all day finally rolling down my cheeks.

"Easy," Julian soothed. "You're a completely different person now, Ally, and you're so much stronger. You're going to be an amazing mom."

"Every time I close my eyes, I see myself swallowing all of those pills that day," I choked out. Christian tightened his arms around me. I sobbed, my free hand latching onto his arm, holding on to him.

"Ally, darlin', you're one of the strongest people I know," Julian soothed. "You're going to give birth to a healthy, full-term baby, and you're going to be an amazing mom, and you're going to make Christian a fucking happy as hell dad. I plan on spoiling the fuck out of my little niece or nephew." A small smile tilted my lips. He grinned at the sight of it. "You're going to take care of yourself, Ally. Keep pushing forward; don't ever give up. Lean on Christian. He loves you, Sis. Let him love you."

"Okay," I whispered.

He smiled at me. "Get some rest. I need to call Meghan. Call me if you need me," he told me, his voice becoming a bit sterner as he said the last part.

"I will," I assured him.

I set my phone on the nightstand and rolled over to

face Christian. He leaned down and kissed me, his lips wiping everything out of my mind for a moment. He then tucked me close to his body, his chin resting on the top of my head. "I just want to lay here with you for a little while."

"I'm trying," I croaked.

His arms flexed around me. "I know, my moon. Just let me breathe life back into you. We're going to make it through this, and when we do, you're going to shine so fucking beautifully that you'll blind everyone with that perfect as fuck smile."

15

TRUTHS

Ally

C hristian sat beside me at the bar and picked
up a bite of the pancake, holding it up to my
lips. With a small, resigned sigh, I allowed
him to feed me. He gave me a small smile. "You're doing
good, beautiful."

I shook my head as I chewed on the bite of pancake.
"I'm failing at this," I told him once I finished swallowing my food.

He softly kissed me before he leaned back and
picked up another bite of pancake. "You got out of bed
this morning without me having to force you, and you
took your medicine. You even got a shower with me,

baby. You're not failing. You're pushing through; you're climbing. Just keep climbing."

I held my hand out for the fork, my hunger finally making itself known. The proud smile that tilted Christian's lips as he handed me the fork had me smiling back at him. He kissed me. "There's my moon. You're going to glow; I promise."

I drew in a deep breath and began eating. Caiden pressed a kiss to my temple as he moved past me to go into the kitchen. "I rented some movies," Caiden told me as he grabbed the orange juice out of the fridge and poured himself a glass. "I thought a day of movies and junk food sounded like a plan."

Christian shrugged on his blazer as he got ready to leave for work. "What kind of movies?" I asked Caiden after I swallowed my food.

"Sappy ass romance movies." He grinned. "The Notebook is one of my favorites."

"You like romance movies?" I asked him. I hadn't expected that—not from him.

He grinned. "Girly, I *love* romance movies. I used to drive Christian nuts after a break-up watching them."

Christian laughed. "Bro, you always cried like a baby. I kept telling you that you were going out with dicks."

Caiden shot him a deadpan look. "They were men. Of course, they were dicks."

Christian rolled his eyes as he shot me a smile. I returned it. "Not all men are dicks, right, my moon?" My cheeks burned as my smile widened. He kissed me. "Shine, beautiful. I'll be home before you know it."

"I love you," I told him as I reached up to cup his cheeks. I pressed my lips to his again. He growled as he stepped between my legs, pulling me closer to him. "I'm going to do my best," I promised him when I slowly parted our lips.

He gave me another quick kiss. "That's all I ask, beautiful. I have to go. Text me. Call me if you need me."

"I will."

He pointed a finger at Caiden. "Take care of my woman."

Caiden rolled his eyes. "Go to work, Christian."

I giggled. Christian flashed me a sexy smirk before he turned and walked out of the house, shutting and locking the front door behind him. I finished my pancakes, and Caiden talked my ear off about a hot guy he'd flirted with at the supermarket a couple of days ago. When I finished eating, Caiden stuck my plate and fork in the dishwasher. "Movie time!" he cheered.

He grabbed my hand and led me into the living room. I sat down on the couch as he dumped a bag on the coffee table. It had all kinds of chocolate, different candies, and all varieties of popcorn flavors. "Oh, my

God, you didn't have to do this," I said with a small laugh. But I reached forward and grabbed a bag of M&Ms—my favorite candy.

"Oh, I didn't?" Caiden teased. I rolled my eyes. He held up *Mean Girls*. "First movie," he told me.

I grinned. "I *love* that movie." I grabbed the black throw blanket off the back of the couch and covered myself up with it as Caiden got ready to put the movie in. He plopped on the couch with the remote in his hand.

"You don't talk during movies, do you?" he asked me. "Christian likes to annoy me by doing that."

I shook my head at him. He smiled. "Good."

He hit play on the remote and grabbed a bag of Skittles, ripping them open.

☾

I smiled up at Christian when he came into the house later that evening. He quickly returned the smile as he pulled his shoes off and shrugged his blazer off his shoulders. He tossed it over the arm of the recliner before he moved over to me. I leaned up and pressed my lips to his when he cupped my cheeks.

"Hi, beautiful." He looked over at Caiden. He was passed out on the other couch, his mouth hanging open, soft snores leaving his lips. "Let me guess—sugar rush and then a crash?"

I laughed and nodded. "Yeah." I stood up from the couch and stretched. Christian wrapped his arms around my waist. "I need a shower, but then we can order something in for dinner. How have you been feeling?"

"It got a little rough around midday," I told him honestly. "It was a random low. I don't know what triggered it."

Christian pressed his lips to my forehead. "I'm proud of you for pushing through."

"I promised you I would try," I told him. And I would. I didn't like breaking my promises.

He kissed me again. "One day, you'll push through because you want to for yourself, but right now, I'm okay with being your reason." He brushed his hand over my belly. "How's the baby treating you?"

"No nausea yet. I have a gut feeling that it's going to hit this evening, though." I grabbed his hand and led him to the bedroom. "Shower?" I asked him.

He lightly smacked my ass. "Thought you'd never ask, beautiful."

When we stepped into the bathroom, I slowly undid his shirt buttons and pushed his shirt off of his shoulders, revealing his perfect, muscular upper body to my eyes. I ran my lips over his chest. He released a soft sigh, his hands sliding under my shirt to grip my waist.

He pulled my shirt over my head and unclasped my bra. I let it slide down my arms until it fell to the floor at our feet. Taking a couple of steps back, I wiggled out of my leggings, pulling my panties down my legs after. His eyes were almost black as he stared down at me, his nostrils flaring. I lowered myself to my knees, licking my lips as I smiled up at him. He slid his fingers through my hair as I unfastened his belt and let his slacks drop to the floor, his briefs quickly following. Silently, he stepped out of them, kicking them to the side.

Looking up at him from beneath my lashes, I wrapped my hand around the base of his cock. He sharply inhaled, his hand tightening in my hair. "Ally," he growled, his pupils blown as he stared down at me.

I licked his tip before I took him between my lips, taking him deep into the back of my throat. He growled as he lightly thrust, and I moaned. Hollowing out my cheeks, I proceeded to suck him off, watching as he closed his eyes, his head rolling back on his shoulders as he forced himself to stand still.

But I wanted him to lose himself with me.

I gripped his balls. "Fuck," he swore as he began to thrust into my mouth, his hand tightening in my hair.

"Is that what you fucking wanted?" he asked me, his eyes narrowed down at me, his voice rough.

I sucked harder, giving him my silent answer. When he came, I swallowed, though a couple of drops fell from my lips. He slid out of my mouth, his breathing heavy. I brought my hand up and used my thumb to wipe the cum off my lips, sucking it off my thumb after.

I squeaked in shock when he suddenly lifted me off the floor and sat me on the bathroom counter. He kneeled between my legs, and with a wicked smirk thrown up my way, he buried his face between my legs.

I sat between Christian's legs on the couch as I ate yet another slice of pizza. Caiden was blearily staring at the TV, having woken up about two minutes ago.

I was wearing one of Christian's button-down shirts with a pair of his boxers, and he had the last three buttons open to reveal my bloated belly, and he was tracing circles on it with his fingers.

Caiden finally looked over at me. "Sorry I fell asleep," he grumbled, reaching up to rub his eyes.

I shrugged. "It's okay," I assured him. "Thank you for all the junk food and the movies."

He smiled at me. "No problem, Ally." He looked at his phone when it pinged in his hand. "I've got a movie date in two hours." He groaned like it was the end of the world.

"Doesn't sound like you're excited," Christian noted as he lifted his head from the back of the couch.

Caiden shrugged. "Nervous is more like it," he confessed. I frowned. Caiden didn't seem like the kind of guy to get nervous. "It's the guy from the supermarket that I told you about," Caiden said, talking to me. "He's so fucking hot—completely out of my league."

"Caiden, any guy or girl is lucky to have you," I assured him. "Don't be nervous. Just be yourself. You're funny, sweet, and caring. If this guy is really into you, then he'll love your personality."

"And if he's not, and you want me to kick his ass, just let me know," Christian said as he leaned his head on the back of the couch again, closing his eyes. I ran my fingers over his forearm.

Caiden rolled his eyes. "I don't need a protective little brother, Christian," he teased.

Christian shrugged. "Just enjoy yourself, Caiden, and like Ally said, just be yourself. You're one of a kind, and I mean that in the best way."

Caiden blew out a soft breath as he stood up from the couch. "I'm going to steal a couple of slices of pizza, and then I'm going to get a shower and get ready for tonight." He pressed a kiss to the top of my head as he got ready to walk out of the living room. "You did good today, Ally. I'm proud of you."

I blushed. "Thanks," I whispered.

Christian nuzzled my neck as Caiden disappeared from the living room. "You're so much fucking stronger than you give yourself credit for, beautiful."

"You make me feel strong," I told him honestly.

"No," Christian disagreed. I turned my head, frowning at him. "I just make you realize how strong you really are. I'm here to remind you that you're capable of being strong, my moon. You glowed so beautifully today." He pressed a kiss to my jaw. "It's a beautiful sight."

"What happens when it dims again?" I asked him as I turned on his lap to straddle his thighs.

He wrapped his arms around me, bringing me closer to his chest. "Then I take extra care of you until you're glowing again. You're going to have phases, beautiful, but I know you'll always glow again."

"I feel like I just need to grow the fuck up," I told him honestly. "I feel like I'm too old to continuously be going through this."

He shook his head at me. "No. You have mental health disorders, baby. That's not something you just get over. You'll deal with it for the rest of your life. But that's okay."

I drew in a deep breath. "And our baby? How is it

going to feel having a mom who continuously hits lows?"

"I think it'll be proud to have a mom that's so strong, that pushes forward every single day and doesn't give up, no matter how tempting it is." My heart squeezed in my chest at his tender words. He kissed me soft, slow, and deep. I moaned, rocking against him. He stilled my hips, making me whine. "They'll know just like I do that Mom is a moon—always changing, always phasing in and out of her darkness—but she's strong, and she'll always glow again."

I drew in a shaky breath as I cupped his face in my hands. "Why the fuck are you so perfect?" I asked him.

He laughed softly and turned his head to press a kiss to each of my palms before he focused his attention back on me. "I'm not perfect, beautiful. I just try to be everything you need."

"That's perfect in my eyes," I told him.

He smiled up at me. "And you're perfect in mine, my moon. Despite everything you go through, you are perfect—perfect for me."

I leaned forward and kissed him, letting him deepen it before I slowly pulled back. And then, I gagged. I quickly rushed off the couch and ran for our bathroom. Christian was right behind me, his hand pulling my hair out of my way as he rubbed my back.

"Guess the baby felt left out," he lightly teased,

trying to make me feel better once I was finished emptying my stomach of all the food I'd just eaten.

I swiped at the tears on my cheeks. Throwing up always made me cry. "I guess so." I leaned against his side as he handed me some mouthwash. After rinsing my mouth out, I closed my eyes, burrowing against him. "I think I'm ready for bed after that," I said quietly, a yawn falling from my lips.

Christian lifted me up from the floor. "Let's go to bed, then, baby." He brushed his lips over my forehead as he laid me down on the bed. "Let me go check on Caiden, make sure he's not freaking out for his date, and then I'll come lay with you."

"M'kay," I mumbled, sleep already tugging at me.

"So perfect," he whispered before he lightly kissed me.

16

CUPCAKES

Ally

D r. Gresham's aging face appeared on my computer screen, a warm smile tilting his lips, deepening the lines around his aging eyes. "How are you feeling today, Ally?" he asked me, always one to cut straight to the chase.

I shrugged. "Nauseated," I told him honestly. "But despite that, the medication seems to be working better. I don't feel so down all the time now." And that was the truth. I was having more good days.

His smile widened. "That's good. Let's talk about your pregnancy. How do you feel about it?" he asked me.

I frowned. I wasn't sure I was ready to talk about it, but I'd never face it if I wasn't forced to.

It was one of my toxic traits.

"Still conflicted," I blurted. He nodded, no hint of judgment in his kind eyes. "I feel like I'm very slowly beginning to come around to the idea, and Christian helps by being so supportive and happy about the baby, but I'm so terrified that something is going to happen— something that's going to cause me to snap again—and I'll do something careless and stupid to kill this baby, too. I'm terrified of the past repeating itself."

"Alright, Ally. Let's talk about that day," he began. I shook my head, not wanting to dive into those thoughts. I was so tired of crying lately, and I knew if we talked about that horrible day when I turned into a selfish monster, I would cry once again. "No, Ally. We need to talk about this," he sternly told me. "It's something you're not coping with, and you're struggling to move past it. So, let's discuss it."

I swallowed thickly but finally nodded my head. Dr. Gresham had remained my therapist and doctor for years now because he was so good at helping me. I knew everything we did together was for a reason.

It didn't mean it sucked any less, though.

"Okay," I told him quietly.

He steepled his fingers together in front of him. "Let's start with your relationship with Randall," he suggested. My nausea worsened. "How long did you two date?" he asked me. It was things we'd already gone over, but Dr. Gresham believed in continuously bringing things up until I began to heal.

"We were together for three years."

"And when you told Randall that you were pregnant, what was his response? How did he react?"

My mind flitted back to that day. I had stayed over at his place for the night, but I was feeling extremely sick the next morning, and I couldn't keep anything down. So, he insisted that I should go to the doctor, and he came with me because I wasn't in any condition to drive.

He was in the room with me when the doctor told me that I was pregnant.

Randall had frozen up, and he'd been silent all the way home as I silently cried in the passenger seat. He hadn't said a word when he dropped me off at my place —hadn't even kissed me goodbye.

Later that night, he texted me, telling me he was sorry about his shitty reaction to the news, that he was excited. Now that I thought about it, for the little while we remained dating, Randall was distant with me.

"He was never excited," I finally realized. I looked back at my laptop screen, tears blurring my vision. "He put up a front for me, but that had to have been around the time he started sleeping with Heather, because he would hardly touch me anymore."

Dr. Gresham gave me a sad smile. "What happened that day that you found him with your best friend?" he asked.

I drew in a shaky breath. "Heather shrieked when she saw me, but he just—he didn't care," I quietly admitted. "He never stopped—just shouted for me to get the fuck out of his room, that we were done." A tear slid down my cheek. When would their betrayal stop hurting? "And he told *everyone* that I was lying, that it was his twin—not him. Any friends I'd had quickly abandoned me, and then, after I was admitted, everyone began calling me an attention-seeking whore for swallowing those pills, and he made sure to tell everyone that I killed our baby."

"Let me ask you this, Ally," Dr. Gresham requested. I opened my eyes, looking at him through my computer screen. "I'm going to ask you a question. I want you to tell me the very first word that pops into your mind. Don't think about it. Don't hesitate with your answer. The very first thing."

I frowned, then nodded. "Okay."

"How do you feel about this baby?" he asked.

"Love," I blurted, surprised at myself. He smiled at me as I let the word tumble in my brain, the shock of it rendering me speechless. Then, I sobbed, tears rushing down my cheeks. "I love this baby," I croaked, suddenly realizing it.

"I've always known you do, Ally. You just needed to realize it for yourself."

I dropped my face into my hands and cried, but I wasn't upset. I was happy. My last pregnancy, I was so miserable. I didn't know how to cope, how I was going to try to be a good mom. I had no real support from anyone. I hadn't even told my family—just Randall.

Everyone around me now was so supportive—Axel, Julian, Meghan, Caiden.

And Christian. Fuck—Christian had been supportive from the very first second I told him.

"Take a nap," Dr. Gresham suggested. "But you're going to do just fine, Ally. You're going to be a fantastic mother. It's still going to be rough—don't think that it won't. But this baby? Use it for something happy to focus on during your really dark days because when it's born, there's going to be so much love in your heart that you're barely going to be able to breathe past it."

I nodded at him as I swiped at my cheeks, sniffling. He smiled at me. "Remember to call me if you need a session, Ally. But get some rest. Stress isn't good for the baby, and you've been under a lot of it lately."

"Okay," I whispered, my voice cracking. "Thank you, Dr. Gresham."

His smile widened. "Always, Ally."

Caiden shook his head at me from his position at the bar where he was filling out job applications online. I was trying to make dinner, but I had very few cooking skills—just enough to not starve—and this stupid ass cookbook didn't make any damn sense.

"Whisk?" I asked in confusion, looking over at Caiden. "What the fuck is a whisk?" I asked him.

He laughed as he got up from the bar stool and walked around the kitchen island, his patience with me and my cluelessness seemingly endless. Pulling open a drawer, he pulled out a strange, metal kitchen utensil and handed it to me. "This is a whisk." He laughed as he looked in my bowl. "Good luck, woman. Those cupcakes are definitely going to be one of a kind."

I scowled at him. I had baked chicken in the oven. That was the easiest thing to put together. I just sprinkled salt, pepper, soul food seasoning, and season-all seasoning on both sides and stuck them in the oven on three-fifty, letting them bake for an hour and a half. I still had forty-five minutes to go before I needed to start the side and the vegetable, and I wanted to try my hand at baking cupcakes.

Baking was definitely not my forte.

I began stirring the cupcake mix, but it wasn't doing like the book said it was supposed to. I frowned. Caiden started laughing again. "Jesus, woman, poor Christian is apparently going to be the one that always has to bake anything around here," he said as he got up once again and came over to me. He took the whisk from my hand and showed me how to properly use the foreign object. I blushed.

"Oh," I muttered, feeling like a damn idiot.

I took the whisk back from him and mimicked his movements. He leaned against the fridge and crossed his arms over his chest, watching me to make sure I didn't fuck up again.

"Good!" he praised when I finished. I beamed. "Now, do you have cupcake holders?"

My smile fell from my face. "I need cupcake holders?" I asked him.

He shot me a deadpan look. "You thought you were going to make cupcakes without cupcake holders?" he asked me in all seriousness.

Embarrassment colored my cheeks. "Hey! In my defense, this is my first time making cupcakes," I retorted.

He rolled his eyes. "Dufus, it's common sense. Have you ever eaten a cupcake without a fucking wrapper around it?" he asked me.

I planted my hands on my hips, narrowing my eyes at him, now getting annoyed with him. "Yes! They were blueberry."

He ran a hand down his face and heaved a tired sigh before staring down at me, a bit of disbelief in his eyes. "Don't fucking tell me you're talking about muffins," he groaned.

My frown deepened. "Wait—aren't they the same thing?" I asked him.

He drew in a deep breath. "Oh, sweet baby Jesus, you need help, woman."

I clenched my jaw, wanting to do nothing more than smack him. "You're a jackass. You knew I was going to make cupcakes. You could have said something before I did all of this work," I snapped at him.

He threw his arms up into the air in exasperation. "Woman, I thought it was common fucking sense! You make cupcakes—you need wrappers for them!"

I screamed in frustration and threw the entire bowl of cupcake batter at his face right as Christian walked in the door. Caiden released an animalistic kind of growl as I glared at him while I threw the plastic bowl back onto the counter. "You are a fucking asshole," I sneered at him, too angry and upset to even laugh at the mess I made of his face. Cupcake batter dripped from his chin and slowly slid down his cheeks.

"What the fuck is going on?" Christian asked as he stepped into the kitchen, looking between me and his brother.

"Your girlfriend needs a good dick down because

she's pissy as fuck," Caiden snapped as he grabbed a towel to wipe his face so he could see.

I grabbed the whisk and threw it at him next. "What the fuck?!" Caiden barked at me.

"You're such a dick!" I shouted back at him.

"And you obviously need some!" Caiden snapped.

I reached for the measuring cup next, but Christian quickly grabbed me around my waist and pulled me back against him. Before I could throw it, he plucked the cup from my hand and tossed it into the sink. "Alright. Let's all chill the fuck out for a second. What happened?" he asked, releasing me and moving to the side so he could look at both of us.

"He knew I was trying to make cupcakes, but he didn't tell me I needed cupcake wrappers." I glowered at the asshole cleaning batter off his face.

Christian rolled his lips into his mouth, his eyes lighting up with laughter. I shoved myself away from him. "Not you, too!" I shouted.

He laughed softly. "Babe, that is kind of common sense," he told me. I childishly stomped my foot, and his grin widened. He pulled me to him, taking my lips in a soft, slow kiss, his tongue dancing with mine for a moment. I moaned, my anger evaporating as I pressed myself closer to him, running my hands over his chest and broad shoulders.

"See? She needs a fucking dick down."

This time, Christian was the one that threw the measuring cup at his brother. I glared at Caiden. "At least I can get dick," I retorted.

He narrowed his eyes at me, but I only smirked. "Oh, not so cocky when the tables are turned, huh?" I asked him.

"Woman, you're playing with fire," he warned me.

I only smirked at him. "Sometimes, a woman likes to be burned."

Christian growled softly as he nuzzled my neck. "Keep on, woman, and I'll burn you," my man huskily promised as he nipped at my earlobe. A soft moan crawled up my throat, and I closed my eyes.

Caiden groaned. "I'm going to take a shower. Don't forget your food is in the oven, so don't be fucking in the shower for an entire damn hour like you two seem to make a habit of."

With that, Caiden flashed me his trademark smirk and spun on his heel, striding from the kitchen. Christian swung me up into his arms, and I squeaked in shock, but that squeak quickly turned into a needy whimper when his lips took mine in a hard kiss.

17

PAST COMES KNOCKING

Ally

"How did your session with Dr. Gresham go today?" Christian asked me as he slowly ran soap over my body.

"I cried," I told him honestly. He pressed a kiss behind my ear, a small reward for always remaining open and honest with him. "But I realized something during my session today, or rather, Dr. Gresham helped me realize something."

"And what was that?" Christian asked me, gently turning me so he could wash my back.

I rested my hand over my bloated belly. "That I love this baby," I said quietly.

Christian turned me back around to face him as he

dropped the loofa to the floor of the shower. His lips settled over mine, taking them in a slow, sweet kiss that had tears burning in my eyes. "You're going to make an amazing mom, Ally," Christian told me, his voice nothing more than a deep rasp. "And when your world turns dark, you have support—always," he reminded me.

I swallowed thickly, nodding my head. He kneeled down on the shower floor and gripped my hips. A sob ripped from my throat as he pressed light kisses to my belly. Only then did I realize how much he had been holding himself back so I wouldn't be overwhelmed.

Christian was *actually* excited about having a baby with me.

"You've been excited this whole time, haven't you?" I asked him, reaching down to run my fingers through his wet hair.

He pressed another kiss to my belly and nodded his head. "Yeah," he told me honestly. "I just tried to keep my excitement to a minimum because I knew you weren't and because I knew you were struggling to come to terms with it."

"I'm sorry," I whispered. "Please don't ever hide how you're really feeling," I begged him. "It would have helped me so much to know that you were really happy about this."

He stood back up and pulled me into his arms. "I

love you," he softly told me, brushing his lips to my temple.

I smiled up at him. "And I love you."

Christian

Ally glowered at Caiden when he snatched her bag of pretzels from her hand and took a handful. I laughed softly. Ally and Caiden had a weird sort of dynamic. Most of the shit he did, he did on purpose to annoy her, to put that fire in her eyes.

I knew my brother had feelings for Ally. I wasn't blind. But whereas I soothed her, comforted her, held her down, and kept her grounded, kept her from losing herself in her darkness, he put a fight in her.

So, I kept my mouth shut. I just wanted Ally to be happy.

If that meant that sometime down the road, she grew feelings for my brother, then so be it. Menage relationships were becoming more and more common these days, and oftentimes, they worked out really well. I mean, hell, look at Meghan, Julian, and Axel. Their dynamic was beautiful to witness.

I just didn't know if my brother could handle something like that—being in a committed relationship with a woman. I knew my brother well. He was bisexual, but he preferred men over women, though he liked both.

And if he decided he wanted to be with her, too, I didn't know if Ally would be able to handle the fact that Caiden would still explore relationships with other men.

When I first met Ally, first saw those fucking pretty brown eyes, yeah, I might have lost my shit if someone looked at her the way my brother was looking at her right now.

But the way his annoyance made her eyes shine? There was no way in fucking hell I could be angry at him.

He helped my woman glow, and that was more than I could ever ask for.

"Caiden, I'm going to punch you in your jaw," she snapped at him as she snatched her bag of pretzels back.

He smirked at her. "I'd like to see you try," he teased, practically taunting her.

Before she could say something back, she yawned. I wrapped an arm around her, pulling her closer to me. "Sleepy?" I asked her.

She nodded, snuggling closer to me, letting her eyes close. Caiden stood up when she was almost asleep and grabbed her bag of pretzels from her lap. "Thank you," she mumbled as she turned her body so she was draped over my lap, her head resting on my shoulder.

I slid my arms beneath her and stood up from the couch, carrying her to our bedroom. I pressed a kiss to her cheek as I laid her down on the soft mattress. "I'll join you in a little bit," I told her quietly. "Go to sleep, beautiful."

She snuggled into the blankets and nodded her head. I smiled at her.

Fuck, she was so perfect—just like the moon.

I slipped back out of the room, pulling the door closed, but not shutting it completely. Caiden was picking up Ally's trash off the coffee table, dumping it into the trash can he had in his other hand. He glanced up at me before he went back to what he was doing. "Surprised you didn't go to bed with her," he commented.

I stuffed my hands in my pockets. "I wanted to talk to you about something."

He arched an eyebrow at me in question as he walked to the kitchen to put the trash can back. "What's that?" he asked, giving me his undivided attention now that the trashcan was back in its rightful spot.

I stood on the other side of the bar, watching as he began washing his hands. "For exactly how long have you had feelings for Ally?" I asked him.

He stayed quiet, but he continued washing his

hands. I sighed. He did this shit when he didn't want to start a fight. He figured silence was always the best answer.

Which confirmed what I already knew. He had feelings for Ally.

"Caiden, I'm not going to be pissed," I assured him. "I can see the way you look at her." He turned the water off and began drying his hands, still staying quiet. "Bro, fucking look at me," I snapped, getting annoyed.

He finally looked up at me. He tossed the dishtowel in his hands onto the counter, crossing his arms over his chest. "What?" he snapped back at me. "So, I have feelings for her. I know how to ignore them, Christian. She needs you. I'm not intruding on that. You're the best fucking thing for her. I can move on just like I have every other time I've started falling for someone."

"What if I allowed you to be with her, too—if that's what she wants?" I asked him.

He looked at me like I had lost my mind. "And what?" he asked me. "Be in a relationship like Axel and Julian?" he demanded. I shrugged because that was exactly what I'd been thinking. "That's fucking ridiculous, Christian, and you know it. I'm bi. I like men and women—prefer men. If I were to try being with her, too, she wouldn't be able to take it if I decided to have a boyfriend as well. She's too fragile for that shit." He shook his head at me. "I'm good with being her friend, Christian. I'll get over my shit eventually."

I sighed. "I think she likes you, too, Caiden," I told him. He only stared at me, not a hint of what he was thinking or feeling on his face or in his eyes. I fucking hated that he hid his shit so well sometimes. "I don't think she realizes it yet, but the longer you're around, I can see it clearer every day. You spark a fire in her that I've never seen in her."

"I'm not walking away from her, Christian. I'm basically her best friend right now. So, you don't have to worry about that."

"And if she admits one day that she has feelings for you?" I asked him.

He sighed, running his hands down his face. "I'll cross that bridge when I come to it." He grunted and turned on his heel. "I'm done with this conversation, Christian."

"Caiden," I called, making him turn to look at me, "whatever decision you decide to make when the time comes—because it *will* come—don't fucking rip her heart out."

He sighed. "I'll do my best, bro."

☾

Ally

Caiden stepped out of his room wearing a pair of black slacks and a white, button-down shirt. His dark hair was still slightly messy. He always had the most untamable hair. It was curly and unruly now that he was letting it frow out from his military cut.

"Finally landed a job interview?" I asked him.

He nodded as he sat on the couch next to me to pull on his shoes. "Yeah."

I frowned. For the past few days, he had been kind of short with me, lost in his own head most of the time. I grabbed his bicep, swallowing thickly when his arm flexed beneath my hand. He looked over at me, those dark eyes clashing with my brown ones. "Are we okay, Caiden?" I asked him.

He smiled at me—that easy-going Caiden smile—and my worries and fears disappeared. "We're good, Ally," he assured me. "I just have a lot on my mind lately—that's all."

"Want to talk about it?" I asked him. I didn't like the idea of him suffering in silence.

He stood up from the couch and brushed his lips to my forehead. I drew in a deep breath, inhaling the scent of his cologne—something spicy with earthy under-tones. "Maybe later. I need to go. Call me or Christian if you need one of us, okay?"

"Alright." I squeezed his hand as I smiled up at him. "Good luck, Caiden."

He flashed me a grin before he walked out of the house. I stared after him, rubbing my hand against my chest as it began to ache a little.

Why did my heart skip a beat when he kissed my forehead?

I set down the TV remote when the sound of knocking reached my ears. With a frown, I stood up from the couch, moving to go answer the door. We never got visitors. Who in the world would be here knocking? If my brother or Meghan stopped by, they'd call or text first.

I was not expecting to see Randall on the other side of it.

"What are you doing here?" I demanded to know, my heart thumping hard and fast in my chest. I wasn't prepared to face him by myself. "And how in the hell did you find out where I live?"

"Not hard to find out when your little fuck boy works for your brother," Randall retorted. I clenched my jaw. "Are you going to invite me in?" he asked.

I snorted. "No."

I moved to slam the door shut, but he shoved it back open, knocking me on my ass. I shrieked in alarm. He stepped into the house, slamming the front door shut behind him. Fear clawed at my throat, squeezing the air from my lungs.

"Heather fucking left me all because of you," he sneered at me. "You fucking ruined *everything*."

"I didn't do anything!" I exclaimed as I scrambled up from the floor, trying to put distance between us. My heart was hammering fast and hard in my chest, making me dizzy and nauseated. My blood was pumping too fast in my veins.

"She took my kids from me, and she's filing for divorce. You couldn't have it all with me, so you destroyed my marriage. It's just like you. Always a fucking attention-seeking whore. If you're not happy, no one else can be."

"I didn't do anything!" I told him. "Randall, please, I swear I didn't."

"She's been upset for years because she felt like she ruined her friendship with you. She even broke up with me after you ran out of the fucking house!" he shouted at me. "It took me *months* to get her to come back to me, and the second she sees you again, she fucking leaves me again! You're the fucking root of all of my problems! It's a goddamn blessing you murdered our kid."

I slapped him, my chest heaving up and down with rage and hurt, tears streaming down my face.

But that was probably the worst thing I could have done.

He wrapped his hand around my throat and slammed me against the wall, lifting me a couple of inches off the floor. I clawed at his wrist and hand, my lungs screaming for air. I could barely think past the panic clouding my brain.

"You stupid, little bitch," he snarled.

I swung my leg up, kneeing him between his legs. He roared in pain as he dropped me, falling to his knees. I scrambled up from the floor and rushed for Caiden's room, knowing he would have *something* I could use to defend myself with. An ex-military guy had to have *something*, right? If he didn't, I was fucked. Well and truly fucked.

I quickly closed and locked his bedroom door, tears rushing down my face as I called 9-1-1.

Before I could hit the call button, the door burst open behind me, the wood splintering. Randall tackled me down to the floor, and the phone went flying from my hand. I screamed, and the world went black, a flash of pain firing through my skull.

18

NOT YOU

Caiden

The front door was hanging open when I pulled into the driveway. I quickly slammed on my brakes and threw my car in park before I jumped out, leaving the car running. My feet slapped against the concrete as I rushed toward the stairs.

"Ally!" I shouted, rushing inside.

I checked her room first, thinking she might be in there. "Caiden," she whimpered, the sound tearing at my soul.

I quickly changed direction, rushing toward my room where her voice had come from. My door was hanging off of its hinges, and Ally was on the floor. Her face was bloody, her clothes ripped off. She was shaking and trembling, bruises already popping up on her porcelain-like skin.

"No," I whispered hoarsely. Fuck, it was a scene out of a goddamn horror movie. "Fuck, baby, I'm here," I soothed as I snatched my sheet from my bed. I kneeled beside her on the floor and draped the sheet over her. "I'm here. It's going to be okay." Tears tracked down her cheeks, her shaking intensifying.

"It hurts," she whimpered.

"I know," I told her, my voice low and soothing. "I need to wrap you up, okay? It's going to hurt. I'm so fucking sorry."

I didn't know which emotion was stronger—rage or concern. She'd been raped. There was no fucking question in my mind as to what had happened to her. And I would kill whoever the fuck did this to her. No goddamn doubt about that. I'd rip this world apart for her.

She whined, the sound tearing at every fiber of my being as I moved her up, wrapping the sheet around her body before I lifted her from the floor, easily standing up with her in my arms. I rushed out of the house and carried her down the stairs to my car. I brushed my lips to her bloody, bruised cheeks. "We're going to get you help, baby. Just hang on for me, okay?"

"Okay," she whispered, her voice breaking, blood trickling from her split lip.

I gently eased her into my passenger seat and rushed around to my open driver's side door, calling Christian through the Bluetooth system. His phone just rang, but he didn't answer, most likely with a patient.

I called Axel next as I hit the pavement, flying toward the hospital.

"Axel Johnson-Markos," he answered.

I grabbed Ally's hand in mine as she sobbed, the sound making my heart squeeze in my chest. "Axel, it's Caiden. Where's Christian?" I asked him.

"With a patient," he told me, his tone becoming more solemn and worried. "What's going on?"

Ally began to cry—loud, soul-shaking sobs. I brought her hand to my lips, holding them there for a moment. "I'm taking Ally to the hospital," I told him. God, her cries were ripping at the shreds of my sanity. They were so heartbroken, so painful. I drew in a deep breath. "It's bad, Axel."

"Where's my sister?" his voice thundered through the car, making Ally whimper. I gently squeezed her hand, pressing kisses to her bruised knuckles.

"She's with me," I told him. "Something happened. I'm not talking about it over the phone." He growled, but I wasn't intimidated by him. I'd faced men thousands of times more terrifying, pointing a gun in my face. "Fucking get my brother and tell him to get his fucking ass to the hospital."

With that, I hung up. "We're almost there, baby," I soothed. The terms of endearment were slipping out without a second thought, but I didn't care. All the boundaries I'd put in place for myself were now out the fucking window, fluttering down the highway.

"Don't leave me, please," she cried.

I pressed another kiss to her bruised knuckles. Looking at her battered hands, I could tell she had fought back, and for that, I was fucking proud of her. She hadn't laid there and taken it. "I won't," I promised. "I will fight through hell and high water to stay by your side," I swore.

When I pulled into the hospital parking garage, I grabbed the first spot I saw and got out, rushing around to her side. I gently lifted her into my arms, cradling her to my chest. A whimper of pain sounded from her throat. I pressed my lips to her cheeks, whispering soft words of apology as I strode toward the emergency room entrance as fast as I could without jostling her too much.

Everyone stared as I carried her inside, and it took everything in me not to tell them to turn the fuck around and mind their own goddamn business.

I barely made it to the receptionist when two nurses rushed over to me with a gurney. "We can fill out paperwork once she's in a room," a nurse told me. "Just set her on here. We'll take care of her," she promised.

"I'm not leaving her side," I told them.

"Sir—" she started, but Ally gripped my shirt in her fist with surprising strength, though her arm shook.

"Please," she begged the nurse, her tears running down her beautiful face, tearing at my soul.

"Okay," the nurse gave in. I gently laid Ally on the bed, pressing my lips to her forehead. I grabbed her hand in mine, walking with the nurses as they pushed her through a set of steel, double doors to take her into a triage room.

"Her boyfriend, Christian, is on his way here," I told them as they got her bed situated in the room. I stood to the side but kept her hand in mine as they shut the door, giving the four of us privacy. "And her brother is most likely on his way here as well."

They nodded in understanding. One of the nurses held up a hospital gown from a closet. "Alright, sweetheart, can we put this on you?" she asked.

Ally shook her head, her hand tightening around mine as she grasped the sheet in her other hand. I rubbed my thumb over her bruised and swelling knuckles. "How about my shirt?" I asked her. "Will that be more comfortable?" Ally lifted her eyes to mine and slowly nodded.

The nurse began to protest, but I shot her a dark

look, shutting her up. Ally had just gone through something extremely traumatic. She wanted familiarity. A
hospital gown was foreign.

I pressed a kiss to her fingers before I gently placed
her hand on the bed and began unbuttoning my shirt,
leaving me in the plain, white t-shirt I had on under it. I
sat down on the edge of her hospital bed and gave her a
small, gentle smile. "Alright, darlin', I need to unravel
you from the sheet, okay? And then I need you to sit up
so I can help you into the shirt."

"Okay," she whispered.

I gently pulled the sheet from around her, keeping
my eyes on her face, not letting them stray to her body.
She moaned in pain a few times, anguish darkening her
normally beautiful, brown eyes. Her body trembled as I
gripped her under her arms and helped her into a
sitting position.

She didn't look at her body. She kept her eyes on
mine as I helped her into my shirt. It swallowed her,
which worked perfectly. "Can we have a blanket?" I
asked the nurses without turning to look at them as I
buttoned the shirt for Ally. She was terrified to look
down at herself. So, I swallowed down every rising
feeling for this woman and focused on taking care
of her.

I was handed a blanket a moment later, and after
having them set her bed up into a more upright posi-

tion, I situated her pillow behind her and draped the blanket over her, grabbing the now bloody sheet and handing it to one of the nurses to dispose of.

Christian burst into the room at that moment, his eyes wild with fear and worry, his hair a fucking mess on his head.

And Ally burst into tears, loud sobs wracking her chest. I grabbed her hands in mine as Christian quickly sat on the bed beside her and wrapped her up in his arms. His eyes met mine over her head, so many questions in his gaze, but I just shook my head at him.

Not now, I mouthed.

I placed my cigarette between my lips and took the coffee from Axel that he was holding out to me. It was well past midnight. Ally was asleep in a room on the third floor. She was suffering from a severe concussion, so she was under observation for the next couple of nights.

Detectives had come in to try to talk to her, but she was unresponsive. And I wouldn't force her to talk—not right now. She was shutting down, but anytime one of the detectives tried to ask her anything, fear—so much fucking fear—was in her eyes, draining the blood from her face.

It made me murderous.

So, as of right now, all the detectives could do was just wait for the lab results to come back to see if there was anything left in her or on her that they could use. They took samples from under her fingernails and from between her legs. Christian had given them permission to turn our home into a crime scene to figure out who the fuck did this until she was able to cooperate.

"I was hoping nothing like this would ever happen to her," Axel said quietly as I stomped out my now-smoked cigarette.

"I'm frankly not in the mood to talk about it," I told him bluntly. "Christian is your best bet for that conversation. Right now, I just want to find this son of a bitch and fucking beat him to death."

He was quiet for a moment. "Julian is coming home," he finally spoke up. I grunted. "I called him—told him what happened. He's on a fucking murder spree. Their season was ending soon anyway, so his coach is letting him come home early—shockingly."

I just stayed quiet. I wasn't in the mood for conversation. My phone vibrated in my back pocket, and I pulled it out, looking at Christian's text.

CHRISTIAN

She's asking for you.

With a sigh, I spun on my heel and quickly moved into the hospital, heading straight for the elevator. When I got to her room, she was awake, staring at nothing in particular until I stepped into the room.

"Hey, baby girl," I said quietly as I moved towards her.

Her bottom lip trembled. Christian brushed his lips to her temple, pain flashing through his eyes for a moment before he smothered it. "I want a shower," she croaked. "I feel dirty." The nurses had given her a sponge bath once the detectives had taken whatever pictures they needed, but I understood what she meant.

She could feel his touch on her.

Christian sat up, ready to go help her shower, but she panicked, shaking her head. "No," she choked out, breaking my fucking heart. Fucking sad as fuck day when she wouldn't allow my brother to help her. "I can't —you can't—"

He swallowed thickly. She didn't want him to see what had happened to her. She didn't want to be ruined in his eyes.

"Let me work with her," I told him quietly.

He gently held Ally's face in his hands, brushing his lips so tenderly with hers that she sobbed, her hands circling his wrists. "I will never, ever look at you as anything other than my perfect moon," he told her quietly. "Breathe for me, beautiful. Just breathe for me," he begged her. Fuck, that was all either of us could ask from her. Because right now, asking her to live might be too much to ask of her.

She closed her eyes, her beautiful face scrunching with pain as she sobbed. He stood up. "I'm going to get some coffee," he told me quietly. I knew it was killing him to leave her like this, but we had to do what was best for her. "Please take care of her."

"Always, bro," I assured him.

"I'm sorry," she blubbered as soon as he walked out of the room, the door shutting behind him. "He—he—"

"I know, baby," I soothed, gently running my hand over her matted hair. I gently uncovered her, looking at the bruises and scratches covering her legs. I sat beside her on the bed, facing her, and I reached forward to slowly unbutton the shirt that she was wearing. "You don't have to explain anything to me, baby girl. I'm here. I'm going to take care of you." I brushed my fingers over her cheek. Even so broken, so sad and scared, she made crying look so fucking pretty. "Just know that Christian will never look at you differently, darlin'. He loves you. My brother loves you so fucking much."

She nodded, though she kept crying. I finished undressing her. Rage—white, hot rage—pulsed through my veins. She had bite marks all over her skin, black and purple bruises, and scratches. She cried harder, her body shaking. I pulled her into my arms, holding her tight to me. "Don't cry, baby," I crooned. "You're still so fucking beautiful," I promised.

I gently lifted her from the bed and carried her into the bathroom. I didn't know how the fuck this was supposed to work. If I showered in my briefs, then I wouldn't have any boxers to wear with my slacks, and that wasn't an option considering my slacks were made to be fitted.

I gently set her on the side of the tub before I stripped my t-shirt over my head and toed my shoes off. "Are you going to be okay if I strip?" I asked her. "If not, I'll shower in my briefs or my slacks. Whatever you're comfortable with."

She swallowed thickly. "I trust you," she whispered. And for her to say those three words to me after what she'd just gone through...*fuck*.

I nodded and continued stripping out of my clothes. I adjusted the water temperature before I stepped into the shower and gently lifted her in with me, helping her stand on her shaky legs. I kept one hand on her hip, holding her to me so she could use my body for support. Blood washed off of her body and out of her hair, turning the floor of the shower crimson.

She wrapped her arms around me, resting her head on my chest. Silently, I wrapped my own arms around her, holding her. I don't know how long we stood like that, but I held her as long as she needed me to. Her body felt amazing against mine, but I pushed aside everything I was feeling.

All that mattered at that moment was taking care of her and giving her whatever she needed to just keep breathing.

19

PHONE CALLS

Christian

When I walked into the hospital room, Caiden was passed out on the hospital bed with Ally draped over his chest. His arms were wrapped around her with one knee bent, his foot flat on the bed, her leg draped over his that was still lying flat.

Julian slipped in behind me. Once he had gotten here, Axel had gone home to help Meghan get the kids ready for daycare so she could come here to see Ally.

"Holy shit," Julian whispered as he ran his eyes over Ally. Her skin was different colors, and her face was swollen. He clenched his jaw, his hands clenching and unclenching at his sides.

Caiden cracked open one eye, looking at us. "Shut the hell up," he whispered. "I just got her to go to sleep about thirty minutes ago."

At that moment, I was more thankful than ever before for my brother and his presence in Ally's life. She wouldn't let me help her. I understood it. It didn't mean it didn't hurt any less. But at least she was being taken care of by someone who deeply cared about her.

I sat down in the chair beside the bed, running my eyes over her face. All the blood was gone, leaving behind my battered woman. I wanted to kill whoever did this to her. And when my eyes met Caiden's, I knew he felt the same way.

Ally moved in her sleep, a whine of pain leaving her lips. Her eyes slid open, her hand fisting on Caiden's bare stomach. Her bottom lip trembled. "It hurts," she whispered.

I covered her hand with mine, squeezing gently. "I know, my moon," I said softly. I'd give anything in the world to make her pain mine so she didn't have to deal with it.

I hated that I hadn't been home to protect her from this shit. I would never forgive myself for this happening to her.

"The baby?" she asked me, looking fearful of the answer.

"You're still pregnant," I assured her. Her body

relaxed slightly. It was the first real question she had asked me about something surrounding her rape.

She slowly turned her head, her eyes locking on Julian, who was standing silently at the end of the bed. Tears burned in her eyes. He swallowed thickly as he moved to kneel in front of her. "I'm so proud of you for fighting," he rasped. "You didn't just lay down and take what he did to you, and I'm so, so fucking proud of you."

She closed her eyes again. "Do you want Christian up here?" Caiden asked her.

She nodded. He moved to get up, but she wrapped her arm around him, holding him to the bed. I just shook my head at him and moved around the bed, sliding onto the tiny, hospital bed behind her, and wrapping my arm around her waist. Julian squeezed her hand. "Keep fighting, darlin'," he told her. "Don't you ever dare fucking give up."

"I won't," she croaked.

"Promise me." A pleading note entered his voice. He was doing his damnest to hide how he felt from her, but we were all afraid this would send her over the edge.

But if there was one thing I knew about Ally, it was that she took her promises seriously. She did her damnest not to break them. So, I knew why Julian was making her promise. One of us would have the opportunity to save her before we lost her if it ever got dark enough for her.

"I promise," she whispered.

I pressed my lips to her hair. "Be my moon," I begged.

She began to cry, breaking my fucking heart. "I'm trying."

"Just keep trying, beautiful," I soothed. "You'll glow again; I promise."

Ally

I was sitting between Christian's legs, my back resting against his chest. Caiden was laying sideways across the bed, playing a random game on his phone. We were staying at Axel and Julian's until the cops were finished at our house and repairs could be done.

My phone vibrated in my hand, a blocked number showing up on my screen. Christian plucked the phone from my hands and answered the call, putting it on speaker.

"How's your pussy feel, bitch?" Randall's voice snarled through the phone.

Axel and Julian had both stepped into the room as soon as Randall's voice came through the phone. All of the blood drained from my face, my body shaking. Tears poured down my cheeks, and I squeezed my eyes shut, my lungs screaming for air as fear clawed at my throat.

I didn't want them to know who did this to me. Randall had promised to do it all over again if I opened my mouth. I couldn't go through this again.

"I'll fucking kill him!" Julian roared at the same time Christian aggressively threw my phone across the room. Caiden jumped off the bed and stormed out of the house. "Did he fucking do this to you, Ally?" Julian barked at me. "Was this fucking Randall's doing?"

I wailed, shaking so hard I could barely think. Despite his rage, Christian wrapped his body around mine, holding me and making me feel safe and protected. "Calm your fucking shit!" Axel roared at Julian. "You're not the only one that's fucking pissed, but taking it out on her isn't going to do shit but make my sister feel worse! So, shut the fuck up!"

Julian stormed out of the room. I sobbed, my body still aching so badly. Axel sat on the bed and grabbed my hands in his. "Baby, breathe," Christian coaxed, gently rocking me side to side. "Come on, baby. I won't ever let him fucking hurt you again," he promised.

"H-he promised to do it a-again," I sobbed. "I'm s-sorry."

"Nothing to be sorry for," Christian soothed, tightening his hold on me. "You're scared. There's nothing wrong with trying to protect yourself."

"Julian, no!" Meghan shouted. "Julian, don't you fucking go after him!"

"Shit," Axel swore, jumping off the bed to go stop Julian from doing something stupid.

"Goddammit," Christian swore as he released me. "Stay here, baby." He rushed after Axel. "Caiden!" Christian roared down the stairs.

I pushed myself off the bed, forcing myself to walk down the stairs despite the pain that flared with every step I took. It was pure fucking agony. "You're really about to stop me from taking care of the asshole that fucking did this to her?!" Caiden shouted at Christian as Axel spoke to Julian in low tones, Meghan standing with her arms wrapped tightly around Julian's waist. I had no doubt she was the only thing keeping him together.

"Yes, because Ally needs you here, not in prison!" Christian barked at him.

I resisted the urge to wail in pain as I forced myself to walk onto the porch. I stepped around Christian and wrapped my arms around Caiden's waist. His body relaxed, his arms instantly wrapping around me as well. "You shouldn't be out of bed," he grumbled, burying his face in my dark, brown hair.

"Orange won't look good on you," I mumbled.

He sighed, adjusting his hold on me so he could support most of my weight. I breathed a sigh of relief. "I wouldn't go to prison, Ally."

I shook my head. "Not risking it," I told him. "Now, carry me back upstairs. Everything hurts."

He leaned down and gently lifted me into his arms. Christian smiled at me before he leaned down to press his lips to mine. When Caiden eased me back down onto the soft mattress in the room we were staying in, I grabbed his hand before he could move away. I wanted him close to me, not only to keep him from doing something stupid but because I felt safe with him around.

He flashed me that easy-going Caiden smile and laid down on the bed beside me. Christian slid on behind me, his arm wrapping around my waist as I held Caiden's hand captive in my own, holding him with me.

I looked up at Caiden. "Don't go," I quietly begged him. He helped keep the fear at bay.

He sighed before he pressed a kiss to my forehead. "I'll stay as long as you want me to," he assured me.

"M'kay," I mumbled, sleep tugging at me.

He gently squeezed my hand. "Sleep, darlin'."

Christian

"She's falling for you," I quietly told my brother once Ally's breathing evened out, her body relaxing into sleep as much as it could.

He grunted. "I know," he responded.

I looked at him over her head. "Where are you at in your head, bro?" I asked him. "When she's ready to make that move with you, you need to know whether she's what you want or not."

He drew in a deep breath before he slowly released it. "I can't walk away from her, Christian. She's got me as long as she needs me, and I'll do everything in my power to always make her happy." He released a soft laugh. "I never thought I would possibly be sharing a woman with my brother." He shook his head.

I shrugged. "Kind of already are," I reminded him.

He brushed his thumb over her bruised knuckles. The swelling in them had gone down, but it had taken quite of bit of ice to get her hands to return to normal. "I know."

Axel poked his head into the room. "Police have just arrested Randall outside of your home," he quietly informed us, taking note of Ally's sleeping form. "They'll be clearing out within the next couple of days, and then you can have someone go in to repair every-thing. Your phones were downstairs," he explained at my confused look. I sighed. Must have forgotten them earlier when we got here.

I tightened my arm around her. "I don't think she's going to want to go back there," I told him. "Not after what happened. For her, it's going to be like walking back into a nightmare."

"You guys can stay here as long as you need," he assured us. "Our home is your home." He pointed his finger at Caiden. "You fucking hurt my little sister, and you'll quickly find out that both Julian and I can become monsters over our family."

Caiden grunted as he shut his eyes, not the least bit bothered by his threat. Axel rolled his eyes. "My sister always had a thing for the moody ones." Caiden flipped Axel his middle finger, and I quietly laughed. "Just take care of her, yeah? It's going to take her a long time to overcome this. She almost completely lost herself when he called her."

Caiden nodded. "I suffer from PTSD. I know."

I clenched my jaw. I hated that Caiden went through shit overseas that fucked with him. He didn't talk about it. I just knew he spoke with a therapist once a week, but I didn't know the depth of his symptoms, nor how badly it affected him.

But I knew if anyone would be able to connect with and help Ally, it would be him. I could ground her, hold her together, but he could be the one that lit that fire in her eyes and gave her a reason to fight.

And for that, he was perfect for her.

Both of us together? With a bit of healing, my moon would shine brightly every single day.

Caiden got a little more comfortable on the bed, bending his right knee up. "I'm going to take a nap," he told me. "If you leave, let me know. She needs someone holding her."

I nodded in agreement before I pressed a kiss to the back of Ally's head. "Just breathe, my moon," I whispered in her ear. She was so deeply asleep that I knew it wouldn't wake her. "One day, you'll shine—just like you're supposed to do."

"Sappy fuck," Caiden grumbled.

I laughed quietly. "Okay, *baby*," I teased, mocking him calling her that in the hospital.

"I'd punch you if she wasn't between us."

I laughed again. "Go the fuck to sleep, asshole."

20

TRUST

Ally

Silent tears fell down my cheeks as I looked down at my body, the tears mixing in with the water from the shower. I covered my mouth to silence the sob that ripped from my throat, my body shaking.

Randall ruined me.

I had scratches and bite marks all over my body that I knew would leave scars behind, forever blemishing my skin and further adding to the scars that I had already inflicted on myself.

"Ally?" Caiden called from the other side of the door. "You've been in there for a while, darlin'. You okay?"

I was terrified to answer for fear that I would just cry harder. I wasn't okay. I was ruined. *How in the hell had Caiden been able to look at me, to hold me, when I looked like this?*

I knew it was bad, but I had no idea it was *this* bad.

I could never let Christian look at me again.

The door opened, and as soon as my eyes met Caiden's through the shower door, my tears came harder. I turned away from him as I covered my face with my hands, my shoulders shaking as I tried not to sob. Suddenly, the shower door opened, and then Caiden was there, his arms wrapping around me.

"Don't do this, baby," he pleaded as he turned me to face him. He pulled my hands down from my face before he reached up to cup my cheeks in his hands. "He didn't ruin you. You're still so perfect, baby. Don't do this to yourself."

"Christian will never look at me the same again," I cried. And that fucking *hurt*. I was going to lose one of the best things to happen to me all because of Randall.

Caiden brushed his thumbs over my cheeks. "Yes, he will. My brother loves the fuck out of you, Ally, and the moment you let him, he's going to replace that fucker's touch with his. You've always been his, but he's going to make you feel like it again."

My lip trembled. I wanted to scream. "How can *you* look at me like this?" I choked out.

He ran his hands down my neck and over my chest until he reached my right breast where a healing bite mark was at. Without a word, he leaned down and pressed a soft kiss there. I trembled, a sob ripping from my lips. "Perfect," he whispered. He moved to the next bite mark, doing the same thing. "Beautiful." Then, the next. "Strong."

He did this all over my body. I was a sobbing mess by the time he had kissed every bite mark, scratch, and bruise on my body. Then, he grabbed my face in his hands and pressed his lips to mine.

I moaned, my eyes closing as I gripped his muscular biceps, feeling them flex under my hands. My lips moved with his, easily losing myself in him. He may have looked a hell of a lot like his younger brother, but Caiden was all himself. He was rough around the edges, blunt, and cocky as fuck.

But it was clear he loved hard.

His hands moved over my body, his lips never leaving mine. He deepened the kiss, his tongue swiping over my bottom lip. With a soft moan, I opened my lips under his, kissing him back just as hungrily. My hands ran over every hard, muscular, defined part of him.

I didn't know where all of these feelings for Caiden had come from, why I was allowing him to do this with me. Maybe it was because despite how much of a mess I always was, he never looked at me differently, instead doing everything in his power to keep a smile on my face. And when I had been raped, there had never been pity in his eyes. He had never looked at me differently as he had taken care of me and helped me bathe for nights on end.

I cried out his name when he slid his hand between my thighs, the heel of his hand pressing against my clit as he slid a finger along my slit. My body shuddered, a moan falling from my lips. He opened his eyes, looking down at my face as he slowly slid a finger inside of me, his hand rubbing against my clit as he did so.

"Oh, fuck," I moaned, my nails digging into his biceps.

"Yes," he growled as he slipped his finger in just a little further. He paused. I dragged in a ragged breath, my body on fire for him. "You good?" he softly asked.

"Yes," I mewled, my body shuddering. He wrapped his other arm around my waist, holding my body up as he nudged my legs further apart with his knee, slipping his finger in all the way. My mouth opened on a silent 'O' when he slowly moved his hand, allowing me the opportunity to tell him to stop.

"Ally, beautiful?" Christian called.

I froze up, my heart hammering hard in my chest. Caiden molded his lips to mine. "Don't," he warned me. "It's okay; I promise."

"Fuck," Christian growled. Caiden quickened his

pace, making me lose myself in this moment with him again. I moaned his name, my breathing quickening as I drew closer and closer to that all-consuming moment.

Suddenly, Christian's lips replaced Caiden's, his hands moving over my body. Caiden tightened his arm around me. "Don't freeze up, baby," Caiden groaned when I tensed, unsure of what was happening. "Let him love you. You deserve this."

I cried out as Caiden sent me over the edge of that cliff. Christian's lips took mine again in a hard kiss, his hand splaying protectively over my belly as he held my chin in his other hand.

My heart was still pounding hard in my chest after Caiden rode me down from my orgasm. I looked up at Christian, nervousness shining in my eyes. "I'm sorry," I blurted. Caiden tensed behind me. "I just—it just—"

"Easy, my moon," Christian crooned, brushing his thumb over my cheek. "Caiden and I have had this discussion a couple of times already. It's okay."

Tears burned in my eyes. "I'm sorry I couldn't let you be with me first," I hoarsely apologized. I suddenly felt like I'd ripped him of something precious.

Christian softly kissed me. "I understood it, beautiful." He ran his hand over my body. "But don't ever think you're anything less than perfect in my eyes. I love you. I will always love every single part of you."

I reached up and grabbed his face in my hands,

reaching up to press my lips to his. He growled softly, his arms twining around my body. I felt Caiden pulling away from me, and I panicked, reaching back to grab his hand, holding him with me.

He gently squeezed my hand before I felt him press his body to my back. I moaned, warmth surrounding me. Christian kept kissing me as Caiden ran his lips over my back and shoulders, his hands running over my body.

"I want to see you with Caiden," Christian whispered against my lips. "Can you take that right now?"

I snapped my eyes open to stare up at him in shock. I'd had plenty of time for all of that down there to heal, but I was trying to make everything up to Christian—for not allowing him to be with me first.

Panicked tears burned down my cheeks.

He really didn't want me anymore.

"No, no." Christian cupped my cheeks. "Don't go there in your head, my moon. I want you. I'll always fucking want you, and later on, after you've given my brother an opportunity to be with you and to take care of you, then I'll make sweet, slow love to you. But I feel that you need this with Caiden—need the opportunity to allow the person you feel has never looked at you differently to make you feel like the true perfection you are."

"Don't leave," I begged him.

He flashed me that sexy grin that I loved so much, and my anxiety eased. "I told you I want to *see* you with Caiden. I'm not leaving, beautiful."

"Come here, baby," Caiden rumbled into my ear as he tugged me back from his brother, turning me to face him. His dark eyes met mine. "The moment it's too much for you, say the words. I'll stop," he promised. He wrapped his hand around the side of my neck, not hurting me, not even applying pressure. I swallowed thickly. "But I plan to show you that not every man that's a little bit controlling during sex is a monster. Do you trust me?"

I drew in a deep breath and then slowly nodded. He shook his head. "Words, baby. I want words. I can't hear a head nod."

My core clenched at his commanding tone. "Yes," I whispered. "I trust you."

He wrapped his arm around my waist, trapping me against him as his lips took mine in a bruising, claiming kiss. I whimpered, my hands plastering to his chest. Reaching up, I ran my hands over his shoulders, but he quickly grabbed my hands and pinned them in his hold behind my back. My heart thundered against my chest, but then his lips took mine again, this time soothing and slow, giving me a moment to calm back down.

Once I relaxed again, his kiss became rougher, his teeth nipping at my bottom lip. His hand gripped my ass, though I could feel himself holding back due to the bruises still healing on my body.

I squeaked in shock when he suddenly spun me around, turning me to face Christian. His cock was in his hand, and he was giving it light strokes. "Bend over," Caiden ordered from behind me, his voice raspy.

"Trust him, my moon," Christian told me when I hesitated, his voice steadying my nerves.

Drawing in a deep breath, I slowly bent over at the waist, placing my hand on the side of the shower. Caiden gently nudged my legs apart before he leaned over me, his muscular body dwarfing mine. I swallowed thickly, my mouth dry. I was both nervous and extremely turned on.

"Trust me, baby," Caiden coaxed, running his hand over my back. "I'll never do anything to harm you. But I don't want you to fear either of us when you're with us like this."

"Okay," I whispered. I drew in another deep breath, forcing myself to relax for him. Caiden pressed a sweet, gentle kiss to my shoulder blade, letting his lips linger for a moment before he leaned back up. I gasped when I felt him rub his cock along my slit, and my hips pushed back slightly as if they had their own mind.

Christian smirked. "Oh, she fucking wants you, bro."

"I know," Caiden rumbled. "She's fucking *soaked* for me."

My lips formed a silent 'O' as he slowly slid inside of me, his hands sliding over my body as he sank as far in as he could go. He was massive, as big as his brother, and he felt *perfect* inside of me.

Christian stroked himself, his eyes on my face as Caiden slowly began to move in and out of me, giving me a chance to get used to him. His hands never stopped moving over my body, and when he picked his pace up. My eyes closed, my mind completely losing itself in the sensations of being with Caiden like this.

And when I came? I was pretty sure my family downstairs could hear me.

I couldn't find it within me to give a good goddamn about it.

21

SISTER TALK

Christian

Ally whined in her sleep, the sound ripping at my soul. I looked up from the patient folder in front of me to where she was asleep on the bed with Caiden. Caiden had been playing a game on his phone, but he quickly set his phone on the nightstand and rolled onto his side, hugging her tight to him as he whispered soothing words in her ear, coaxing her back into a dreamless sleep.

My brother had always been the wild one—constantly in trouble, never got along with our parents, and rebellious as hell. When he went into the military right after he graduated high school, he was constantly in trouble with his drill sergeants and getting privileges revoked for doing dumb shit.

And he was hot-headed as fuck. He always reacted with his fists, not his brains. But seeing him around Ally from the very beginning? He was completely different with her—almost as if he could sense from the moment he met her how fragile she was.

Growing up, Caiden had taught me how to defend myself, and he always told me "don't ever start something, but you better fucking finish the shit." I never had to fight growing up. I could—Caiden made sure of that. But Caiden allowed me to be the golden boy everyone loved, and it didn't bother him at all.

Caiden ran by his own book. Always had. His rules were the only ones that mattered to him.

Our parents had hated it, but Caiden and I were close as fuck—always had been. Even when he got kicked out of the house on the night of his graduation, he still made plans with me, and I was the first and only person that he told that he was leaving for the Army.

Only now, his career was cut short due to being shot.

"She okay?" I quietly asked him.

He nodded and then brushed his lips to the top of her head. "She's good, bro," he told me quietly. "Go ahead and finish work."

It was quiet between us for a little while, the only

sounds in the room being my pen as I made some side notes, and his grunts of annoyance as he continued dying on his game.

Eventually, I finished looking over my patient files, and I locked them away in my briefcase, setting it aside afterward. I stood and stretched, a soft groan falling from my lips when my back popped. Caiden looked up at me. "I've been offered a position on base," he told me. I arched an eyebrow at him. "They're willing to let me work at the one here in the city."

"I thought you were getting discharged."

He nodded. "I am. But I can still work on base. They have civilian jobs."

"What's the job?" I asked him.

He grunted. "Can't talk about it," he told me. I nodded in understanding. "I just thought I'd let you know." He looked down at Ally. "I don't want to leave her side, bro." He looked back up at me. "I've got some money in savings, enough to help you with half of the down payment on a new house and to also help you do the repairs on the current house so that you can put it on the market."

I shook my head at him. "Caiden, bro, I can't let you do that."

He shrugged. "Not giving you much of a choice." I narrowed my eyes at him. "I plan on staying with you guys. She needs me as much as she needs you, Christian."

I nodded and slid onto the bed behind Ally, wrapping my arms around her, protectively splaying my hand over her belly. Caiden sat up and leaned over, pressing a kiss to her forehead before he got off of the bed completely. He snatched a shirt from the floor and pulled it on. "I need a cup of coffee, and then I'm going to see if Axel and Julian want some help cooking."

"Alright," I told him. "I'm going to get a few minutes of shut-eye."

Caiden snorted. "Few minutes, my ass. Hard to only do a few minutes when someone as soft as her is in your arms."

I opened one of my eyes, looking up at him. He was smirking, laughter shining in his eyes. "Caiden, go fuck off."

He snorted. "Your girl did that for me earlier."

I sighed and shut my eyes again, ignoring him. He snorted. "Get some sleep, Christian, and then, when she wakes up, get some pussy. You obviously need it."

I grunted. "I'm going to kick your ass in a minute."

He laughed and left the room. I tightened my arms around Ally and allowed myself to relax, holding her in my arms.

And Caiden was wrong. She wasn't just *my* girl. She

was his, too. She was going to fight him on it; I could feel it in my gut.

But if there was one thing I knew about Caiden, it was that he fought back for something he gave a fuck about. And he wasn't going to allow her to shut him out.

He'd seen her at her absolute worst. He had held her, taken care of her, and he showed her that not every controlling asshole wanted to destroy her.

She needed him. I wasn't capable of being snappy with her like he was. He kept her on her toes.

He and I? We would balance each other out, and between the two of us, Ally would have everything she had ever wanted and needed.

Ally

My eyes flew open, instantly landing on Christian. He brushed his lips to my jaw, and I relaxed, a soft sigh leaving my lips. Moaning, I opened my legs wider. He growled softly, his hand slipping into my panties.

A whimper spilled from my lips as he slowly slipped his middle finger inside of me, the heel of his hand rubbing against my clit. "So fucking beautiful," Christian rumbled as his lips moved down my neck. "So perfect."

"Christian," I gasped, drawing closer to that sweet ledge.

"Now, baby," he growled.

His lips covered mine, swallowing my sounds as I came hard, my chest heaving, my heart pounding hard against my breastbone.

I pulled him on top of me, angling my head to deepen our kiss. "Make me yours again," I begged him.

"You've always been mine, baby," he promised. He slipped my shirt over my head and tugged my panties down my legs. His lips moved over my body. "And you're going to be ours—mine and Caiden's." His lips closed over my nipple.

I pulled his shirt over his head, my hands running over his muscular body. His lips met mine again as he yanked his sweatpants down his legs. Then, he grabbed my left leg behind my knee and slid deep inside of me.

"Mine," he growled, sounding absolutely feral.

My body trembled beneath his, both of our bodies quickly getting covered in a light sheen of sweat as he took me up to cloud nine over and over again. I was shaking, crying, trembling, but the ecstasy felt so fucking good.

Suddenly, Caiden's lips were on mine, and Christian leaned up, thrusting into me harder and faster. "Ours," Christian told me once Caiden began to kiss and nip at my skin. I sobbed, my hands tangling in Caiden's hair, my eyes locked on Christian. "You belong to both of us now, my moon."

Caiden took my lips in another rough kiss. "Come," he roughly commanded.

Black spots danced in my vision as I came hard around Christian, my name falling from his lips as he came with me.

Meghan dropped onto the couch next to me with a bowl of popcorn. She smiled at me as she set the bowl between us, as was our tradition when we just wanted to talk.

"So, tell me what's going on with Caiden."

I blushed. Straight to the point, as always. "There's nothing going on," I said quietly.

She shot me a deadpan look. "I'm not stupid, Ally. The secretive touches, the sweet little smiles he sends you? That man has it bad for you."

"I, um, he, uh." I swallowed thickly. I knew she wouldn't judge me. It was just so hard to say it out loud. "Caiden has kind of... joined in?" I said, though it came out as more of a question. My cheeks were on fire. "I just—he makes me feel safe, and I trust him." I closed my eyes, drawing in a deep breath as I tugged at the sleeves of my long-sleeved shirt, hiding my scratches, bruises, and the bite mark on my wrist. "He saw me that day, found me on the floor of his room, and he hasn't looked at me like I'm broken, like I'm disgusting."

"Oh, honey," Meghan whispered. She drew me into her arms, and I snuggled close. "You're not broken, and you're not disgusting. You went through something traumatic. A disgusting human being took advantage of you, took you against your will." She cupped my face in her hands and brushed a tear off of my cheek as it fell from my eye. "You are a beautiful, young woman, and you're going to overcome this," she assured me.

I shook my head. "I don't feel like it," I admitted, my voice no more than a whisper. "Meghan, it's so dark. I haven't told them. I'm trying my best to be strong for them, but every time I close my eyes, it's dark, and Randall is the only fucking thing I can see."

She hugged me tighter to her when I started crying. "I know," she crooned. "But I'm telling you from experience that it will get better. It'll get easier to look at yourself in the mirror, and it'll get easier to allow Christian and Caiden to give you all of the love and support that you deserve."

"I'm going to be covered in scars." I whimpered. "Permanent reminders of what happened to me."

Meghan leaned back from me and lifted up her shirt, revealing to me the bite marks covering her torso. I stared at her with wide, shocked eyes. She lowered her shirt. My eyes widened in surprise. "Seems brutal, disgusting men like to leave permanent reminders," she said quietly. "But you know what? Axel and Julian—they still love every single inch of me, and now, every time I think about those dark times, I can easily remember each of my men loving me and taking care of me despite the permanent reminders of that sick fuck on my body."

She gave me a soft, understanding smile. "Those two men, Ally—they will love you even while you feel completely unlovable. And they'll remind you of just how strong you truly are." She shrugged. "Dr. Gresham is going to dig around in your memories, and he's going to peel back every painful layer of that night," I swallowed vomit, "but he's also going to teach you how to cope with it. For right now, though, I just want you to show both Christian and Caiden how lost and broken you feel, and let them love every single, shattered piece. Can you do that for me?"

I drew in a deep breath. "I know Christian can handle it," I whispered. "But can Caiden?"

She nodded at me. "I believe Caiden has gone through his own shit, especially after being in the military. I believe that man is more than capable of taking care of you during your really dark times. Christian wouldn't allow him to be with you otherwise." She hugged me again before she released me and grabbed the throw blanket from the back of the couch. "Now, let's watch this funny ass romance movie and eat our weight in popcorn."

A small smile touched my lips as Meghan covered us both with the blanket. This was the kind of support I needed from Meghan. She was always there to remind me that it was okay to be loved and taken care of when I felt like this.

And after seeing what her body looked like? I knew that if she could get through this, then I could, too.

I might fall a bunch of times, but I would eventually stand back up on my own two feet.

22

THE HOUSE

Ally

D r. Gresham took a seat next to me on the bench across from the late-blooming rose bush that I always found comfort in. It was unnaturally cold today, but we were still outside. I just wished that the air would make my feelings as numb as it was making my fingers.

"So, I understand you had a very traumatic evening a few days ago," he began. I just stared at the rose bush. "Ally, what happened?"

I shook my head. I didn't want to say it out loud. If I said it out loud, I was going to start crying and sobbing, and I was so tired of crying. All I did these days was fucking cry, and it was weak as fuck of me.

"Ally, holding it in isn't going to help you," Dr. Gresham reminded me. I squeezed my eyes shut, Randall's face popping up in my mind in the middle of all that darkness. I shuddered, snapping my eyes back open again.

"He came knocking on the front door," I whispered, not turning to look at Dr. Gresham. I wasn't sure if I could get through telling anyone what happened if I had to look at them. "I tried to lock him out, but he was too strong, and when I slapped him, it set him off. I managed to make it to Caiden's room, and I locked myself in. I was going to try to find something to protect myself with after I dialed 9-1-1. I knew if there was anything in that house that I could use, it would be in his room. But Randall basically tore the door down."

I swallowed past the lump in my throat, tears pouring down my cheeks as I stared at the rose bush in front of me. My chest was aching. I reached up to rub at it, drawing in a deep, shuddering breath. "I fell unconscious for a few minutes, but the pain of him biting me everywhere—it dragged me back awake." My shoulders shook as I sobbed. My skin crawled with disgust.

"I fought back—hard," I choked out. "But he fought back harder. He started beating me." I was going to throw up. "I was going in and out of consciousness. The last time I came to, he was pushing inside of me. When he was done, he just left. Walked out fucking *whistling.*"

I drew my knees up to my chest. "Caiden found me," I whispered. I closed my eyes for a moment, popping them back open before Randall's face had a chance to materialize. "He wrapped me up in the sheet from his bed, and he took me to the hospital."

"What's the hardest thing for you right now about that incident?" Dr. Gresham asked me.

"The visual reminders," I whispered, my voice cracking. "I have bite marks and scratches on my body that will leave scars. I'm forever marked by him— forever marked by reminders of that horrid evening."

"Ally, you are not defined by what happened that night," Dr. Gresham sternly told me, his tone soft and gentle. "You are stronger because of it. Yes, it sucks so much that you had to go through something so traumatic. But you know what? You fought back, Ally, and *that* takes *so much* strength. Fear makes so many people freeze up, but you didn't. You didn't go down without a fight, and that shows just how strong and capable you are." He sighed, reaching over to gently squeeze my hands. "I know it's dark right now, Ally, but you're going to be okay. When you see his face in your mind, though, I want you to fight back, just like you did that evening. Can you do that for me?"

I swallowed thickly. "I can try," I whispered, my voice breaking.

"That's all that I ask, Ally. I want you to *try*. You'll be surprised by how much strength you hold in yourself. You just need to tap into it. You're powerful. Your mind?" He gently tapped my temple. "It holds all of the magic. Tap into all of that magic, that power, that strength, and use it against him. You're stronger than him, Ally. Fight back."

Caiden was waiting for me outside of the center. Christian had dropped me off before heading to work. Julian was supposed to pick me up, so I was surprised to see Caiden standing there.

"Hi," I whispered.

He reached out and drew me into his arms, holding me against him as his muscular arms wrapped around my body. "Hey, baby," he rumbled, dropping a kiss to the top of my head. "You okay?"

I nodded as I looked up at him. He reached up and cupped my cheek, brushing his thumb under my eye. "I can tell you were crying. You sure you're okay?"

I shrugged and sighed. "I'm as good as I'm probably going to get right now," I told him honestly. He frowned. I rested my forehead on his chest. "I just need time."

He pressed his lips to the top of my head again. "I know, baby. I'm here. Christian is here. You're not alone

—never alone." He grabbed my hand in his and led me to his car, opening the passenger door for me so that I could slide in. I watched as he quickly strode around the front of the car and slid into the driver's seat.

We were silent for a moment before I broke it. "Caiden, what's happening between us?" I asked him. I'd been going with the flow, but sitting in the unknown area of our relationship was making me anxious.

He glanced over at me before he focused his attention back on the road. "I want to be with you," he told me bluntly. My breath hitched in my throat at his words. "This isn't a game to me, Ally. I want it all with you. If you'll have me."

"Caiden," I swallowed nervously, "don't you want the opportunity to be the center of someone's world?" I asked him.

He shook his head. "No, because you're the center of mine." A lump formed in my throat at his words. "My feelings for you have been building inside of me since day one, Ally." He blew out a soft breath. "I know I'm bi. I'll still explore relationships with other men, but you— you're it for me. No one will ever be on the level that you are."

My bottom lip trembled as a tear slid down my cheek. I didn't care if he wanted to be with men, too. Just knowing that he cared and was open with me—

that was what mattered. "Even with the way I look?" I asked him, my voice breaking.

He reached over his middle console and lightly gripped my thigh, his warmth seeping into my soul. "You're beautiful—perfect." I swallowed down my sob. "I will love and cherish every single part of you, Ally, even the parts of you that you feel aren't worth loving anymore." He turned down a street, not going back to my brother's. "Christian and I will make you whole again, baby. Just give us time, and don't give up on us."

"I'm more afraid of you giving up on me," I blurted.

He shook his head at me, turning down another street, heading away from town and down a county road. "I could never give up on you, Ally. A woman like you? You're impossible to fucking walk away from. I've been trying to tamp down these feelings for *weeks* now because of my brother's relationship with you, but they won't go away. They just get stronger. I thought I could get over you like I've done everyone in the past, but, like I said, you're a woman impossible to give up on, to walk away from."

I drew in a deep breath, getting ready to bare my soul to him. "Caiden, if we do this, I won't survive the pain of you walking away," I warned him.

"I'm not walking away from you, Ally. I promise. I went through hell and back overseas." He shot me that perfect, cocky, Caiden smile that made my heart flutter in my chest. "You're a walk in the park, baby." He grabbed my hand from my lap and brought it up to his lips, pressing a kiss to my knuckles. "I can handle any shit you throw at me."

Whatever I was going to say to him completely left my mind as he pulled into a driveway. A small, quaint, brick house sat in front of me. There was a good-sized yard, nothing too big or small—just perfect. Trees surrounded the property, giving it a secluded feel.

"Christian doesn't know yet, and he'll kick my ass when I tell him." He shrugged. "But I bought this house a couple of days after what happened at Christian's. I knew you wouldn't ever be able to handle living in that house again. I tried to find something that you would love, something that suited you. It's got top-of-the-line security, and I've set it up so that there's an emergency button in every single room and hallway that will silently notify police as soon as you hit it that you need help." Tears slid down my cheeks at his thoughtfulness. "I want you and my brother to live here with me, Ally. I bought this house for you—*because* of you." He drew in a deep breath. "Please say yes, baby."

"Oh, my God," I choked out. I threw my arms around his neck, my body shaking as I cried. Caiden could be a real asshole, but it was times like this that I knew the man loved and cared deeply. "I can't believe you did this," I blubbered.

"I love you, Ally," he rasped, burying his face in the crook of my neck. I jerked back to stare at him, my eyes wide in shock and disbelief. *He really said that.* "I think I fell for you the very first moment I laid my eyes on you," he confessed. "I want you to feel safe and taken care of, and this is my first step to doing that. Please say you'll stay here, baby. And if you completely hate it, I'll figure out how to sell it and find something else."

I sobbed as I reached up to cup his face in my hands. I couldn't believe this man—this perfect man. "It's beautiful. I'll stay here." I smiled at him, the first real smile I'd had in days, and he grinned at the sight. "But you have to tell Christian."

He laughed. "Baby, as long as you keep smiling at me like this, I'll go through absolute hell and high water with a fucking grin on my face." He brushed his lips lightly with mine. "Besides, my brother will be a walk in the park."

C

Christian dropped his fork to his plate, a look of disbelief passing over his features as he stared at his brother on the other side of me. "You did what?" he incredulously asked.

Julian snickered before he stuffed a bite of chicken

into his mouth, ignoring the glare Christian shot his way for finding the situation amusing.

"I said I bought a house," Caiden repeated. I swallowed nervously. Axel shook his head at me, his silent way of telling me that this wasn't my fault and to let them hash this out.

"I thought we fucking talked about this, Caiden. We decided to go half and half, not for you to just up and buy a fucking house!" Christian exploded, making me jump in my chair. "What the absolute fuck, bro? Why can't you just let me be a fucking adult for once and help with this kind of shit?!"

Caiden sighed and closed his eyes, placing his fork on his plate. He opened them again, staring over my head at Christian. "Because Christian, you're my little brother. You're still in school, still trying to build your career. I don't want you dipping into your savings for this shit. I've got so much fucking money set aside that I don't know what the hell to do with it. So, I bought a house with plenty of land for the three of us."

"I can fucking help, Caiden!" Christian shouted at him. He jerked back from the table. "You always do this shit." He glared at his brother as he stood up. "I get that you feel guilty for the shit that happened with our parents, for the shit that I went through, but I'm grown now. Stop treating me like a kid, and go to fucking therapy for all the shit you're feeling."

With that, he stormed out of the kitchen. Caiden sighed and stood up, shaking his head. He pressed a kiss to my temple. "Eat," he gently ordered. "Let me talk to him."

He quickly walked out of the dining room. I dropped my face into my hands, no longer hungry. I felt Meghan sit beside me, her arm wrapping around my shoulder. "Don't do this, Ally," she told me. "It's clear that the two of them have some of their own problems to work through. This doesn't fall on you, Hun. Let them work out their shit. You need to eat. You have a little one to feed."

"Ally," Axel called, drawing my eyes up to him, "eat. What Caiden did—it wasn't anything Julian or I wouldn't have done for Meghan. I know Christian is feeling differently about this, but Caiden's heart is in the right place, and Christian will come to understand that."

"Do you like the house?" Julian asked me, surprising me with his question.

I nodded. "It's pretty," I told him. "And it's perfect. And Caiden even had a top-of-the-line security system installed that put an alarm button in every single room and hallway of the house. He was so thoughtful about it."

Julian smiled at me. "They're going to be good for

you, Little Sis. Eat your food. They'll work their shit out —trust me."

I drew in a deep breath. I sure hoped so because if they were already stepping on each other's toes, I didn't know how the three of us were expected to live in harmony.

23

BROTHERLY LOVE

Christian

"Caiden, go the fuck away," I snapped at my older brother as I stormed out onto the porch.

I knew Caiden's heart was in the right place with the house he had just purchased. And I knew I seemed unappreciative, but he *always* did this shit. I had busted my ass through college to move off campus and get an apartment, and when I told Caiden my plan, he up and bought a fucking house for me and a goddamn car.

Without even talking to me about it.

And he just basically did the same damn thing again.

I knew it stemmed from all of the shit surrounding

us when we were growing up. Our parents weren't that great of parents. We grew up poor. Some days, our meal would only be a bowl of ramen noodles or a couple of hot dogs. Dad was an abusive fuck, and his kids were his favorite punching bags.

Caiden felt guilty as hell when he was kicked out because he was no longer there to take care of me, though by then, I was old enough to take care of myself. When Caiden had left for basic, he had set me up a bank account, and every time he got paid, money miraculously appeared in my account.

Caiden wouldn't ever just let me figure out things for myself.

"Christian, stop fucking walking away for a fucking minute and turn around and fucking face me!" Caiden barked from behind me.

Clenching my jaw, I spun around to face my dick of a brother, my dark eyes flashing with rage. "What?" I snapped at him. "I don't want to fucking talk right now, Caiden."

"Too fucking bad, asshole," he snapped right back at me. "I know we were supposed to go fifty-fifty on this house. But the house was below market value, and I *knew* it would be perfect for Ally." Some of the fight left me at that information. He had done it for *her*, not for me this time. "If you still want to give me your half of the down payment, fine. I frankly don't give a fuck. But this house is *perfect* for her, bro. I even paid for a fucking security system so she has an alarm button in every single room and hallway that she can press if something happens." He threw his arms up. "If you want to fucking give me half for that, too, then whatever. Fuck it. Give me half. But I didn't do this for *you* this time, Christian. I did it for Ally."

I swallowed thickly. He sighed, shoving his hand through his short strands. "And now she's probably sitting in that dining room, picking at her fucking food, because she feels like she made us fight. I showed her the outside of the house today, Christian, and she's already in love with it. She hasn't even seen the inside yet. And now, I'm going to have to go in there and convince that woman that it's okay to still want it."

"Why the fuck didn't you say that at the dinner table?" I asked him.

"Did you give me a fucking opportunity?" he retorted. I kept my mouth shut because, no, I hadn't given him the opportunity.

"Let's go in there and fucking sit back down at the dinner table. Ally was already drawing into herself when I came out here. We've both got shit to fix with her right now."

"Mostly my fault," I grumbled, and that didn't sit right with me. I didn't like being the reason that she was so upset. I was the one that was supposed to hold her together.

"It falls on both of us, Christian, because honestly, yeah, I should have consulted you. But the realtor told me seven other people were looking at that property, and one was getting ready to possibly close on it. So, I threw down the down payment and signed my name to the papers. I didn't want it slipping away."

I shook my head at him. "You put her first, Caiden, and honestly, I could never really be angry at you about that." I clapped my hand to his shoulder. "I'm sorry for popping off like that." I drew in a deep breath. "Let's go inside and get our woman to finish her dinner."

When we got back in the dining room, Meghan was sitting in my seat next to Ally. She got up without a word, allowing me to sit down. I leaned over and brushed my lips to her temple. "I'm sorry, my moon," I said softly. She looked up at me. I cupped the side of her neck and brushed my thumb over her jaw. "Caiden and I had our own issues to work out." I smiled at her. "I heard you like the house."

She nodded. "It's pretty, and it's the perfect size," she told me, the tiniest of smiles tilting her lips. That light in her eyes flickered for a moment—the smallest of moments—but it was enough. My heart warmed at the sight.

I leaned down and kissed her. "How about we all go

look at it together tomorrow after I get off work?" I asked her. Her eyes brightened, excitement swirling in those pretty brown eyes. My heart squeezed in my chest. *God, she was so beautiful and perfect.*

"Really?"

I nodded. "Really, beautiful." I kissed her again. "Now, eat your food," I told her. "You're pregnant. Skipping meals isn't okay."

She looked over at Caiden. He brushed his thumb over her bottom lip. "Eat," he quietly commanded.

She picked up her fork and began eating again. Julian's phone rang on the bar in the kitchen. He sighed. "I just want one fucking peaceful dinner with my goddamn family," he growled as he got up from the table to go answer it.

"It's his agent," Axel explained at Caiden's confused look. "I don't think that man has a life outside of Julian." He shook his head. "Wish he would give the man some damn breathing room."

Meghan sighed. Axel gently gripped her chin and turned her head to face him. "Easy, sweet girl," he soothed. "You're his priority. Nothing will change that."

Holden suddenly squealed and threw his bowl of food to the floor, clapping his hands together afterward. Julian walked back into the dining room at that moment and threw his hands up to the sky. "Seriously, kid?" he asked Holden. "Aren't you old enough to know that's not okay?"

Ally giggled beside me. Meghan laughed at Julian. "He's your boy. Imagine the hell you put your own mom through, Julian."

He grunted. "I was an angel."

Axel scoffed. "Like hell."

Ally took a bite of her peas and gagged. I jerked my head around to check on her at the same time she shoved back from the table and ran for the nearest bathroom. Caiden and I were both out of our seats in a flash, moving to rush after her. By the time we made it to the bathroom, she was already throwing up.

"Fuck," I swore. I kneeled beside her and pulled her hair out of the way, reaching up with my other hand to rub her back. "I'm here," I crooned.

Caiden grabbed some mouthwash sitting under the sink and a small Dixie cup, pouring some of the mouthwash in it for her. He calmly waited as I took care of her, trying my best to soothe her through her discomfort.

I hated seeing her like this, and I hated that I was the cause of it. I was grown. I shouldn't have solely relied on her birth control to keep her from getting pregnant. Birth control wasn't fully effective. There was always the chance for a slip-up.

And now, she was suffering because of my carelessness.

Once she was finished, I reached forward and flushed the toilet before I eased her back against me. I knew she always felt a little nauseous after throwing up, so I was careful not to jostle her too much.

Caiden kneeled in front of her and silently held out the small cup of mouthwash. She took it from him and swished the liquid inside of her mouth before she spat it back into the cup. Without a word, he took it from her, flushed the mouthwash down the toilet, and threw the small Dixie cup into the trash.

"We'll try to eat something later tonight," he told her. I gently maneuvered her so it was easy for him to lift her into his arms. "I think you and I need a nap. Christian has some work to do, and then he'll join us."

I brushed my lips with hers once I stood up from the floor. "I'll join later, and I'll bring some soup and saltine crackers with me. Sound good?"

"Yeah," she murmured as she rested her head on Caiden's shoulder. "Thank you for always taking care of me."

I smiled at her. "Always, my moon."

Julian was washing dishes when I walked into the kitchen. Meghan was breastfeeding the baby, and Axel was sitting in the rocking chair, gently rocking Holden to sleep.

"She okay?" Julian asked me.

I nodded at him. "Yeah; she'll be fine. Peas didn't agree with the baby," I informed him.

He rolled his shoulders like they were bothering him. "How is she feeling about being pregnant? I haven't had much of a chance to actually talk to her after that fucking incident."

I smiled as I began to help clean up the kitchen by putting leftover food into Tupperware containers. "She's handling it well," I told him honestly. "I think Dr. Gresham helped put some things into perspective for her during one of their sessions. She loves the baby—her words."

"Good," he said with a single nod of his head. "She's going to make an incredible mom. She's good with kids—loves Holden and Lana with every single fiber of her being. And you and Caiden? You guys are good for her." He set a plate on the drying rack on the counter. "You hold her together; you're her source of comfort on her really dark days. Caiden? I can tell he's not all that good at speaking sense into her in a soothing manner like you do. He's more rough edges and bluntness, which she needs in her life as well. Because Ally loses herself in her darkness too much."

"I'm good at coaxing her out of it," I told him.

He nodded. "I agree. And your brother? He puts a fire in her eyes that hasn't been there since she was a kid."

I nodded in agreement. "I've seen it since day one. He gets on her nerves on purpose. It makes her fight back. I think Caiden has known from the very beginning that she was different."

"He knows he can't just walk away from her, right?" Julian asked me. He looked over at me. "Ally won't survive that shit. It took her a long time to come to terms with the fact that she was no longer Axel's first priority. In fact, she became a fucking monster because Meghan became more important to him."

"He knows," I assured him. "He's already said she's it for him."

Julian nodded once. "Good. I'm sure he knows what the fuck he's got coming for him if he breaks her heart. I might have done a hell of a lot of changing for Meghan, but I'm still the asshole that I've always been. That won't change. And I'll fuck someone up for hurting Ally. She's my little sister. I've known her for her entire life."

"Julian, if I hurt her, dig me a grave," Caiden said as he sauntered into the kitchen wearing only a pair of sweatpants—no shirt on. The scar on his side was on prominent display, drawing my eyes to it for a moment.

"Because the only way I'm hurting her that badly is by fucking dying, you got me?"

Julian smirked. "I knew there was a reason I always liked you, Caiden."

Caiden grunted but didn't respond. I rolled my eyes. "Why'd you leave her?" I asked him.

He opened the fridge, cutting his dark eyes to me. "She wants a cold bottle of water and some crackers. Stop being such a fucking worrier, Christian. I'm capable of taking care of her."

I sighed. "I'm always going to worry about her, Caiden."

He clapped a hand to my shoulder after grabbing the water and closing the fridge door. "Christian, bro, she's in good hands with me. Trust me."

I nodded once, but he and I both knew that I wouldn't stop worrying so much about her.

Not until that shine was permanently back in her eyes.

Caiden left the kitchen after grabbing the saltine crackers. Julian gripped my shoulder, letting his blue eyes meet mine. "I know how you're feeling, Christian," he told me. "It gets better; *she* will get better. Just give her time and stand by her side."

"How much time, though, Julian? She was doing good; she was fucking *finally* happy and shining again, and now I'm back at square one with her. I feel lost and helpless."

"You be her strength while she's lost. And you wait for her at the end of that dark tunnel. She'll come back to you—to both of you. Just give her time."

I blew out a harsh breath before I looked up at the ceiling.

Please shine again, my moon.

24

MOVING

Caiden

I looked up as Christian stepped into the bedroom. Ally was passed out beside me, her head on my chest with her leg thrown over mine. I had one arm wrapped around her, my other hand holding my phone as I played a game.

"Do you ever do anything besides play a game?" Christian teased me.

I shrugged. "I'll have more shit to do when we get around to moving," I told him. "And I start work in a week."

Christian closed the bedroom door behind him and unbuttoned his shirt, tossing it into the hamper in the corner of the room. He strode towards the bathroom at the same time that Ally screamed in her sleep, the sound chilling the blood in my veins.

I jerked into a sitting position, quickly pulling her up with me. She was awake, but she was sobbing, her entire body trembling. Christian was already on the bed, both of us holding her between us. Christian was whispering soothing words in her ear, and I just stayed silent, being her steadying force.

It was times like this that I wanted to beat Randall until he was forever eating out of a fucking tube. Prison was too easy of a punishment for him, especially since our judicial system was fucked up, and rapists tended to not serve the sentence that they deserved.

It took a while, but she eventually stopped sobbing. Now, just silent tears slid down her pretty face. Her trembling had eased, but her grip on my hands hadn't loosened. She just leaned against Christian's bare chest with her eyes closed.

"I want to fucking kill him," I gritted.

Ally slowly opened her eyes, locking them on mine. Without a word, she pulled her hand from mine and reached up to cup my cheek. I sighed, closing my eyes, her touch calming me in a way that no amount of medication had ever been able to do.

"Just stay with me," she softly begged me.

I circled my free hand around her wrist and turned

my head to press a kiss to her palm. "For as long as you'll have me, baby," I promised her.

She pulled both of her hands from mine and reached up to swipe at her cheeks. "I want a shower," she said quietly.

Without a word, Christian stood up from the bed with her cradled in his arms against his chest. She looked over his shoulder at me when I continued sitting on the bed. "You coming?" she asked me.

I smiled at her, watching as that light in her eyes flickered the tiniest bit. "Yeah, baby," I assured her, standing up from the bed.

Christian set her on the bathroom counter, and I moved to the shower, turning the water on to let it heat up. After, I turned and leaned my shoulder against the bathroom wall, watching as he took care of her. Her eyes were full of pain and misery, and it broke my heart to see her like this.

But Christian? He was good with her—soothing. He softly spoke sweet things to her, reminding her that she was still beautiful and perfect in his eyes and that nothing would change that, all while he slowly undressed her, taking his time to slide his fingers over her skin.

By the time she was standing in front of him completely naked, all of that pain was gone from her eyes.

It was the reason Christian was probably the best for her.

"Come on," he told her as he grabbed her hand in his. "We'll shower, and then Caiden and I will come to bed with you, and you can sleep between us. You'll be safe. He can't hurt you anymore, my moon."

I stepped into the shower and reached out to grab her hands in mine as she stepped in. Christian stepped in right behind her and closed the shower door. "He *can* hurt me," she said quietly.

I gripped her waist and pulled her a little closer to me. "Close your eyes," I told her.

She swallowed nervously, but she did as I told her to. I brushed my thumbs over the bottom of her rib cage. "Now, I want you to picture that evening in your head." She whined. "Easy, baby," I soothed, rubbing soothing circles into her skin. "Just picture it for me."

Her face scrunched up as she pictured the evening in her mind. I was trying a technique my therapist had tried with me from all of the trauma I faced because of my and Christian's parents, and I was hoping it would work for her, too.

"Now, I want you to picture that Christian and I are there with you," I told her. Her bottom lip trembled. I tightened my hold on her. "Picture it, baby. Randall isn't there anymore. He's not hurting you. We're there, and we're loving you and taking care of you. It's us touching this perfect body." A tear slid down her cheek. "Can you see it?"

She nodded, a very soft, quiet sob falling from her lips. "He doesn't exist at that moment with you anymore, baby. It's just us—your two men who you trust."

She slowly opened her eyes and then she wrapped her arms tight around my waist, resting her head on my shoulder. She softly cried, her shoulders shaking. I just wrapped my arms around her and rested my chin on her head, looking at my brother.

He smiled at me, and that smile? It meant everything. I had always envied my younger brother for being able to accomplish so much. He was a people person, knew how to treat people ninety-nine percent of the time. He was someone you could always rely on.

I had always been the wild card. It was just in my nature.

But his smile? It was encouragement. It meant that I was doing something right.

And with Ally? I was trying my damnest to be perfect for her.

I held Ally's hand in mine as I led her inside of our new house. Christian was walking on the other side of her with his hand on her lower back. Once we were inside, I brought her hand to my lips and pressed a kiss to her fingers before I let her hand go. "Go explore," I told her.

She smiled at me before she leaned up and pressed a quick kiss to Christian's cheek. Then, she walked off from us, looking around the house in amazement. I had gotten all new furniture. I didn't want anything reminding her of that fucking evening.

This was supposed to be a fresh start for her—a fresh start away from all of the bullshit.

"This place is fucking amazing, bro," Christian spoke up. I looked over at him, turning my eyes away from the beautiful woman who was smiling at her new home.

"Thought it would be perfect for her," I told him.

He nodded. "It is." He smiled. "Look at her, Caiden. She's smiling. She fucking needed this. We've still got a long way to go with her, but she's going to be okay. We just need to continue being patient and make sure she receives everything she needs to heal and to get better."

"I think forcing her to go into that night in her mind and replacing Randall with us a few nights ago helped her," I told my brother. He nodded in agreement. "She needed that, Christian. She just needs more proof that we'll always continue to love her."

"And do you?" Christian asked me as he turned his head to meet my eyes. "Do you love her, Caiden?"

I nodded. "With every fucking fiber of my being, Christian. She's my beginning and my end. I'm not walking away from her—never fucking leaving her. She's stuck with me."

"Good," Christian said with a single nod of his head. "Shit with her isn't going to be easy, bro."

I shrugged. "Never said it would be," I reminded him. "But she's worth it. I'm going to light that fire within her," I promised him. "And you'll be there to ground her, keep her together when I do."

Christian laughed softly. "You annoy the fuck out of her when you do that shit."

I grinned. "Fucking good. She needs to be annoyed sometimes. It gives her a reason to come out of her head."

When I walked into the kitchen, Ally was making herself a bowl of ramen noodles. It settled well in her stomach—her words. I frankly didn't care as long as she ate something.

I slid up behind her and placed my hands on the counter on either side of her, pressing my body against her back. Her breath hitched in her throat when I leaned down and pressed a soft kiss to the back of her neck. Her hair was thrown up into a messy bun, giving me perfect access to one of my favorite parts of her body.

"I'm trying to eat, Caiden." She giggled, the sound warming my fucking heart.

"*Mmm*," I moaned right in her ear. Her hands flattened on the countertop, her head leaning back against my shoulder. "I was thinking of having dessert—it's the best part of any meal."

"Dessert sounds fucking fantastic," Christian agreed as he stepped into the kitchen, his voice raspy with sleep from his nap.

Ally squeaked in shock when I pushed her uncooked bowl of ramen noodles aside and lifted her onto the counter. She was wearing a dress today, giving me easy access to what I wanted.

She moaned when I pushed her dress up to her hips, my rough, calloused palms sliding over her smooth thighs. Her body trembled under my touch when I lifted her dress over her head, tossing it down to the kitchen floor.

No bra. *Fucking perfect.*

Christian gripped her chin and covered her lips with his as I pulled her lacy, black panties down her legs, tossing them to the side with her dress.

Today, I was taking care of her. She had been doing

so well the past couple of days by making sure she ate three meals a day, snacking in between. When she was feeling down, she came to either me or Christian and cuddled up next to us, letting us know without ever having to say a word that she was getting lost in her head.

She continued doing her therapy sessions with Dr. Gresham, and every morning and every afternoon, she took her medications like she was supposed to.

I was so fucking proud of her for trying—for pushing forward despite how hard it was.

And I planned to reward her in one of the best ways I knew how because my tongue game was on fucking point.

I yanked her thighs apart and kneeled down on the floor, burying my face between her thighs. Christian cupped one of her breasts in his hand, pulling at her nipple before switching to the other. His other hand continued gripping her chin, kissing her so deeply that I doubted she knew whose air she was breathing anymore.

When she finally fell apart for us, I got to see one of my favorite sites—Ally fully embracing just how fucking beautiful she was, her eyes glowing just as my brother had always talked about.

Perfection.

25

UNEXPECTED CALLS

Ally

I looked up at Dr. Gresham as he walked toward where I was sitting in the waiting room. He gave me a warm smile as I stood up, walking towards him. "How have you been feeling, Ally?" he asked me.

I shrugged. "I've been better," I admitted. "But it's not the worst it's been."

His smile widened. "That's good—it means you're making progress."

I pressed my hand to my stomach, swallowing down bile. "Do you mind if we just do our session in your office today?" I asked him. I drew in a deep breath. "I'm not feeling all that good." I'd been feeling nauseous all morning, but I wouldn't miss this appointment.

"Of course, Ally." He assured me. He changed direction, heading to his office instead of the garden, where we normally held our sessions. I knew I was going to throw up before our session was over, and I would prefer not to throw up in front of a bunch of other people if I could help it.

My nausea hadn't been that bad lately. But this morning? It was kicking my ass.

I dropped onto the comfortable couch in Dr. Gresham's office and closed my eyes, taking deep, even breaths to try to calm the churning in my stomach.

If Christian or Caiden had known about how bad I was feeling this morning, they would have made me do my session with Dr. Gresham virtually, but I knew he was going to want to dive into the deeper, scarier parts of that evening, and I really didn't want to do that through a computer screen.

"Are you going to be okay to get through this session, Ally?" Dr. Gresham asked me, concern flooding his voice. I opened my eyes and looked up at him. He was sitting behind his desk, and his face was etched with concern. "You're looking extremely pale, dear."

I sighed. "It's just morning sickness," I told him. I grabbed his trashcan and settled it on the floor beside my feet, giving him a small smile. "Just in case," I told him when his frown deepened.

"Are you sure you're okay with doing this today?" he repeated.

I nodded at him. "I'm sure, Dr. Gresham." I drew in a small breath. "Caiden actually did something that helped me." I swallowed thickly. Dr. Gresham stayed silent, allowing me to finish speaking. "He had me close my eyes and picture that he and Christian were there with me, that they were taking care of me." Tears burned in my eyes. "It helped," I croaked.

"That's good," Dr. Gresham praised. "And I'm proud of you for leaning on them when you need to, Ally. There's nothing wrong with getting support after a traumatic experience. You're so much stronger than you were a few years ago, and it makes me so happy to see how much you've grown—how much you're *continuing* to grow."

I gagged and grabbed the trashcan, throwing up into it. Dr. Gresham waited patiently, and once I was finished, he picked up his desk phone and called for someone to come change his trash. Without a word, he then took the trashcan from me and set it outside of his room, shutting the door afterward.

"Okay. Let's talk about that night. And we need to go into detail, Ally. Not just the basics. We need to really dig into those memories."

I rubbed my suddenly sweaty palms over my leggings. I knew this was coming, and I still wasn't ready to face it. Then again, I knew if no one forced me to open up, I would bottle it all inside so I didn't have to deal with it.

"I was naked," I told him, my voice quiet. "He had already gotten my clothes off of me." I rubbed at my chest where one of the worst bite marks was located. "And he was biting me—biting me so hard that I was actually bleeding. And it only seemed to turn him on more."

My hands were shaking. I twisted them together, trying my best to keep them still. It still felt as if I could feel Randall fucking biting me.

"It hurt so badly. I remember screaming at him and trying to hit him—anything to get him to stop, but he just pinned my wrists down and continued biting me, saying he would make sure I forever remembered our night together." I shook my head. "God, he must have been biting me for hours. It felt like forever. And then, he started hitting me. I faded in and out of consciousness a lot. My head was hurting a lot —pounding."

I wanted to throw up. My skin was crawling. "The last time I came to, he was—he was pushing inside of me." I began to bounce my knee, getting antsy. Tears poured down my face. "I begged to succumb to that darkness again, but I was awake. God, he was enjoying himself so much. I was bleeding. My entire body was hurting, and Randall was violating me in the worst fucking way possible."

"What happened when he was finished?" Dr. Gresham quietly asked me.

"He just left," I whispered, my voice cracking. "He didn't touch me again. He was done. He got what he wanted."

Dr. Gresham took a seat beside me on the couch. "You're very, very strong for getting through that, for surviving that. It takes real strength to come out on the other side like you have, Ally."

I didn't feel too strong.

"I want you to do something for me," Dr. Gresham requested.

I drew in a slow, deep breath, trying to calm my racing heart. "What's that?" I asked him.

"I want you to write about that evening every single day until you can finally write about it without crying and throwing up. I want you to write about it until you can willingly go to Christian and Caiden again and take control of what you want with them. Right now, they're leading you until you find yourself again. But that's okay."

Write about it. Just the thought of writing about it over and over made me want to throw up again.

"Dr. Gresham?" I asked after we sat in silence for a few moments.

"Yes, Ally?"

"Is it normal for me to have sex so soon after being raped?" I quietly asked him.

"The most important thing to remember about traumatic experiences is that everyone recovers from them differently. Some people draw into themselves and can't stand to be touched after being raped. Some people find that they feel in control again when they decide to have sex. I've had patients who go *years* without doing anything sexual, Ally, and I have patients who literally have sex with as many people as they can. Everyone has different responses to trauma."

"So, I'm not fucked up for still having sex?"

Dr. Gresham shook his head. "Not at all, Ally. If it makes you feel in control and gives you some of your own power back, there's nothing wrong with it," he assured me.

C

My phone rang in my pocket as I was striding toward my car. After eating some blueberry muffins made by Mrs. Evelyn and calming down, Dr. Gresham finally released me from our session with strict instructions to call him if I needed an extra session, but we would keep to our schedule as planned otherwise and do our virtual session on Wednesday.

I pulled my phone out, frowning at my dad's number on the screen. I had deleted his number from my phone, but that didn't mean that I didn't remember his number. It had been the same for most of my life.

Swallowing thickly, I made a dumb decision.

I answered the call.

"Hello?" I asked, hating that my voice broke on the simple word.

"Ally, my little girl, I've missed you," my dad said softly into the line. I quickly unlocked my car and dropped into the driver's seat, my heart thudding hard in my chest at the sound of his voice.

How long had I wished for him to call me—for him to want to repair our relationship?

"Dad?" I croaked, my eyes burning with unshed tears.

"Oh, honey," he said, his own voice thick with emotion. My tears fell down my cheeks. "I'm so sorry. I know that doesn't mean shit. I abandoned you, and I'm so damn sorry. I'll never be able to make up for that."

"I missed you," I cried as I closed my eyes, my shoulders shaking.

"I missed you, too, darling," he rasped, his voice cracking. "I want to see you—dinner or something. Whatever you would be comfortable with. Would that be okay? I want to fix things between us."

He really wanted to see me? He really wanted to repair everything that was broken between us?

"Not without Axel," I instantly blurted. If I agreed to this without bringing Axel with me, my older brother would lose his shit, especially after everything Dad and Mom had done to me—to us.

"He won't answer my calls," Dad said quietly. "If you can get him to come with you, that would be even better. I miss both of you."

"I'll try," I told him, my voice sounding weak to my own ears.

"I love you, sweetheart."

I sobbed and hung up the phone without saying it back.

⸻

I barely cast Axel's receptionist a glance as I pushed through the door that separated the lobby from the counseling rooms. She tried to stop me, but I knocked on Axel's door before she could.

He swung open the door, his eyes widening when he saw how hard I was crying. "Jesus, Sis," he breathed as he pulled me into his arms, holding me tightly. He led me into the room and shut the door behind him. "How the fuck did you even make it here safely?" he demanded.

"Dad called me," I blubbered, crying so hard I could barely speak.

"Oh, fuck," Axel whispered. He sat on the couch in his office and pulled me down to sit beside him. "I was hoping he wouldn't reach out to you."

"He wants to do dinner," I told him. I swiped at my cheeks, but I couldn't seem to stop crying. "I want to see him, Axel, but I told him not without you."

Axel's eyes widened the slightest bit. "He was okay with that?" Axel asked me.

I nodded. "He wants to see you, too." I rubbed my eyes. "He wants to work things out, Axel, and I'm stupid enough to want it."

"Oh, Sis, that doesn't mean you're stupid," he said softly. "It just means that you love our parents, and you crave to have that love and care reciprocated," he assured me. "There's nothing wrong with that." He drew in a deep breath. "If you want to see him and talk to him, then I'll reach out to Dad myself and set up a place and time."

"Thank you," I croaked.

He drew in a deep breath, relaxing back into the couch and pulling me with him. "You just scared the shit out of me."

"Sorry," I mumbled as I rested my head on his shoulder and closed my eyes, sleep tugging at me. He laughed softly. "Do you have any more patients to see today?"

"No. I was just going to catch up on some paperwork and patient files. Get some rest," he told me. "You need it."

"Thank you for always being here when I need you."

He pressed a kiss to the top of my head. "You're my sister, Ally. I'll always be the one person you can count on," he promised.

26

HER PAST

Christian

Axel knocked on my open office door. With a tired sigh, I looked up at him. Today had been exhausting, and after having two crying patients and then one that had a small nervous breakdown in my office, I really just wanted to go home, curl up with Ally, and go to sleep for a couple of hours.

"Ally is here," he announced. I arched an eyebrow at him. "I already talked to Caiden. You were with a patient when she showed up."

I stood up from my chair. "Is she okay?" I asked him.

He shrugged. "She will be. Our dad called her." I stopped. I didn't know much about her shit with her parents, but obviously if she came here, it was something pretty rough. "Sit down," he told me as he dropped onto my couch. "I want to tell you a little bit about our background with our parents so you understand why this phone call upset her so much."

Without a word, I dropped back into my chair, giving him my undivided attention. He reached up and rubbed his temples with a tired sigh. "Ally was always a daddy's girl when we were growing up. Mom was always kind of cold and indifferent with us—always worried about her perfect image and what everyone thought about her." He shrugged. "Mom has an issue with needing everything to be perfect. Ally and I—we were far from perfect, but she did a good enough job hiding that from people she associated with."

He blew out a soft breath. "But Ally got older, and her mind began to develop more, which also meant that Dad began to notice the signs of bipolar depression. I remember Mom and Dad having so many fucking arguments about getting her help, and Mom would always win, so Ally went years without being properly taken care of."

"And it hindered her," I said quietly.

Axel nodded. "A lot. By the time it got bad enough that Mom and Dad finally went and got her professional help, it was so hard for the doctor to figure out where to begin. And by that time, I was already starting my senior year of high school." He shook his head, his lips flattening. "Ally never went out with friends anymore. Mom forbade it. She didn't want everyone knowing how much of a fuck up Ally was. So, she and I grew a lot closer, and she kind of became one of the guys. Whenever Julian and some of the other guys we hung out with came over, she was always included."

"Let me guess," I quietly mused, "that pissed your mom off even more."

Axel nodded. "Now her daughter was turning into a tomboy—playing video games, playing football—it was practically a disaster in her eyes." Axel smiled a little. "But Christian, my sister was finally smiling." He frowned again. "And then college came, and we had to leave." He drew in a deep breath. "I didn't know it then, but Julian found her cutting herself. She was panicking. She was going to be alone. She thought we were all abandoning her."

That was why she freaked out so much about her promise to Julian. She had promised him she would never cut again.

"Julian kept her secret for *years*, Christian. Never told me what she had done." He sighed. "I hate to say it, but I grew distant when I got to college. My parents and I were always fighting. I wasn't following the career path they wanted for me, which was football. Because of my differences with my parents, I ended up separating myself from Ally, too. And she stopped reaching out to me as well."

I stayed silent. He was quiet for a moment, almost as if he were trying to figure out how to word what he was going to say next. "I was already in a committed relationship with Meghan when my mom called me and told me that Ally had locked herself in her room and that she wouldn't come out. So, I went over there to go check on her." He swallowed thickly, pain flashing in his eyes. "She had taken all of her antidepressants." He shook his head. "And her stupid ass ex—that bastard—fucking told *everyone* about the baby and about what she had done. My parents tried covering it up, but when Ally had to be admitted into Dr. Gresham's facility, and then attacked Meghan, my parents took the first opportunity they could to get rid of her."

My heart ached for Ally and everything she'd gone through because of her neglectful parents.

"And when my parents found out that I was with Meghan, but she was also with Julian—that we were basically sharing her—they cut me off, too." He shrugged. "It doesn't really affect me. I'd been so detached from their shit for so long that it literally was just kind of like an 'okay, and?' kind of thing." He blew out a soft breath. "But not for Ally because she was always Dad's little girl. And he abandoned her."

"So, why did he contact her today?" I asked him.

Axel shrugged. "Apparently, he wants to work things out." He leaned his head back and closed his eyes. "At least she was smart enough to tell him she wouldn't come without me."

I clenched my jaw. "She's not going without me and Caiden, either," I corrected him. "She's come too goddamn far. I won't let him push her back further by accident." I sighed and scrubbed a hand down my face. "I'm not saying that you can't take care of Ally and that you don't know your boundaries," I instantly spoke up, knowing how protective Axel was of his sister.

"I know, Christian. If it were Meghan, I'd be doing the same damn thing you are. And honestly, I would be kind of pissed if you didn't bring it up. I think you guys need to come. He needs to see that she has an army of people standing around her, ready to defend her and take care of her. He can't just come in and do what he pleases." He shook his head. "And I have a feeling that she would let him just so she could be his little girl again."

I shook my head. "Not if I have anything to do with it," I assured him. I stood up. "I need to get her home. She needs to eat dinner and take her medicine."

Axel stood up as well and clapped me on the back. "Thank you for giving her a chance, Christian."

I laughed. "I think it's her who gave me a chance." I grinned. "She was trying to stand strong against me, but she couldn't." I rolled my neck around, a yawn falling from my lips. "I'll talk to Caiden this evening about what happened, let him know to be expecting a dinner date with your dad sometime soon."

Axel nodded. "Drive safe. I'm going to go ahead and start locking up. She's asleep on the couch in my office."

I strode down the hall to his office, and sure enough, Ally was passed out on the couch. Her eyes were kind of swollen and puffy, but she seemed to otherwise be sleeping peacefully, which I was thankful for.

Every once in a while, she would jerk awake because she dreamed of what had happened with Randall, but for the most part, she was beginning to sleep normally again, though it always did help for her to have either me or Caiden sleeping with her.

I eased my arms beneath her and slowly lifted her from the couch. She moaned in protest, her eyes slitting open before she rested her head on my shoulder, falling back asleep.

So fucking adorable.

Axel held the front door open for me, and he gave me a single nod before he closed it behind me, locking the building up. He then opened my car door and leaned my seat back so that I could place Ally in the passenger seat.

"Has she been to see a doctor yet for her pregnancy?" Axel asked me out of the blue once I had her deposited into the car, buckled, and had shut the car door.

I grimaced and shook my head. "No—not recently," I admitted. "With everything that's happened, it's just kind of escaped my mind."

He pulled his phone out of his pocket. "I'll shoot you the phone number for the doctor Meghan uses. She's fantastic. Ally will like her." He stepped back from me. "Go on and get her home. Caiden is texting me wondering when the fuck I'm sending her home." He narrowed his eyes at me. "Your brother can be over-bearing."

I barked out a laugh. "He's just worried about her," I reminded him. "We'll come out later tonight and come pick up her car."

He shrugged. "Don't worry about it. If you can't get it until tomorrow, it's fine. Drive safe."

I slid into the driver's seat of my car and smoothly backed out of the parking lot, heading home.

Caiden was waiting on the porch when I pulled into the driveway. Without a word, he walked down the steps and opened the passenger door. I slid out of the car, watching as he gently lifted Ally into his arms.

"Caiden?" she mumbled.

"I'm here, darlin'," he whispered.

"Sorry I didn't come home." She yawned. "I went to see Axel."

He brushed his lips to her forehead. "I know. He called me." He nodded once at me. "How was work, bro?" he asked as we walked into the house.

"Exhausting," I admitted. I dropped onto the couch, smiling at Ally when Caiden set her down beside me. "It was a bit of a rougher day than usual." I looked up at him. "What's for dinner?"

He walked into the kitchen without answering. I scowled at his back. Ally giggled before she leaned up to press her lips to mine. "Stop being such a sourpuss," she whispered as she rested her head on my shoulder.

I wrapped my arm around her shoulders. "You need to eat so you can take your medicine," I told her. "Come on—up. You can sleep after you've taken your meds."

She pouted. I gently gripped her chin and turned her head to face me. "I know why you're sleeping." She frowned, her eyes flickering over my face, worry and fear residing in the depths of her pretty eyes. "We'll talk about it later, okay? But just know that it's okay to be conflicted."

"I'm scared," she blurted. Tears suddenly glistened in her eyes. I pulled her close to me, holding her tightly. "Christian, what if he turns his back on me again?"

"Then he's a cold, selfish bastard that doesn't

deserve your time and your energy, baby girl," I told her honestly. "But when you go see him with Axel, Caiden and I will be with you as well. We'll make sure it's not easy for him to turn your back on you again if he decides to."

She sniffled. "Am I stupid for wanting him to love me again?" she asked, her voice breaking.

I brushed my lips to the top of her head. "No, baby, you're not," I assured her. "What it does show is how sweet and loving you are." I pressed my hand over her chest. "You have a heart of gold, beautiful. The fact that you can still love someone so much after how badly they've hurt you just shows how amazing you are. There's nothing wrong with being the good one, Ally."

Caiden set a plate of food on the table. "Darlin'," he called, drawing her teary eyes to his, "if another man makes you cry, I'll fucking hospitalize him," he promised.

She laughed and swiped at her cheeks. "He's my dad, Caiden."

He shrugged. "And I don't give a fuck, baby." I snorted. *Classic Caiden.* "If he hurts you, he has me to answer to." He leaned forward and pressed his lips to hers. "Now, eat so you can take your medicine," he ordered.

"You're so bossy," she griped.

I watched with a smirk on my face as he lightly

wrapped his hand around her throat. Her eyes sparked with that fire—just for a split second, but it was there. "You like it, baby." He pressed his lips to hers. "Eat."

I brushed my lips to her temple, loving the way her cheeks burned with a blush at what he had just done. "Eat, beautiful," I coaxed.

With a small, tired sigh, she grabbed her plate of food. I smiled at her. "That's my girl."

And her beautiful eyes brightened for me.

27

DINNER

Ally

Caiden cupped my face in his hands once I stepped out of the car. Swallowing nervously, I locked my eyes on his. "Remember, if you get overwhelmed, all you have to do is let one of us know. We'll get you out of there," he reminded me. "Your dad is the one that fucked up, Ally, *not you*," he stressed. "I know you want to rebuild your relationship with him, but make sure you rebuild it on *your* terms."

Drawing in a deep breath, I nodded my head. "Okay," I whispered. "I think I can do this."

"Not think," Christian corrected as he grabbed my hand in his. I looked over at my other rock, the man who had been trying his best to hold me together since day one of us meeting. "You *can* do this, baby. Just take a deep breath. You're not alone."

I looked over at Axel as he made his way over to us. He had Meghan's hand in his own, and Julian was trailing along behind them, talking to someone on his phone—most likely his agent, judging by the scowl on his face.

"Who has Holden and Lana?" I asked, thankful for the distraction from what I was trying to prepare myself to walk into that restaurant and face.

"The neighbor," Meghan answered. She wrapped me up in a hug. "It's going to be okay, Ally. We're all here for you."

"You ready, Little Sis?" Julian asked as he walked up, pocketing his phone. "Just remember that we're all standing behind you, ready to defend you if something happens."

"I'll be okay." Caiden's hand found mine, and he laced our fingers together, giving my hand a reassuring squeeze as Christian placed his hand on my lower back, leading me toward the restaurant.

We were immediately led back to a private room, and my blood drained from my face, my steps faltering. I stared at my mother who was sitting next to my dad— the woman who had always hated me for being so different.

"What the fuck?" Axel seethed once the door was

shut behind us, giving us privacy. "I thought it was just going to be you, Dad—not her."

Mom stood up from the table. "Your father told me he was having dinner with you and Ally, so I thought that I would join as well."

"I didn't want you to come," I blurted, drawing her eyes to me. She narrowed them at me in a warning to shut my mouth, but I steeled myself, remembering that I had both Caiden and Christian backing me. I knew neither of them would let her do something stupid. "I wanted to see Dad."

"I am your mother, Ally. Sit down and stop acting like a petulant child," she reprimanded.

Caiden wrapped an arm around my waist, tugging me against his powerful frame as he glared at my mother. "You sit the fuck down," he snapped at her. Her eyes widened in shock. I honestly couldn't remember a time anyone had spoken to her like he just had—not even my dad. "You intruded on *their* dinner. Frankly, I don't think Axel wanted to see you, either. So, sit down like a good wife and shut your mouth unless you're directly asked a question."

She glared at him. "Do you have any idea—"

"Sit down, Mom," Axel snarled as he pulled out a chair for Meghan and gestured for her to take a seat. "Caiden is right. I didn't want you here, either. So, you can sit there and be silent, or you can leave. I frankly don't give a fuck as long as I don't have to listen to you."

She moved back from the table and snatched her clutch up. "I thought that perhaps your little sister's ex-boyfriend had been lying, but since she nor you have apparently changed, I'm safe to assume that he's telling the truth. I'll be paying for Randall's attorney, and we will be fighting tooth and nail for him to be released."

My mother spat on me, and Julian physically restrained Caiden from lunging across the table at her. I closed my eyes, my hands trembling in my lap as tears slid down my cheeks. I could feel Christian cleaning the spit off of my face. "Three years later, and she *still* can't get her act together."

I heard her storm out of the room. I sobbed, my entire body trembling with fear. Christian wrapped his arms tightly around me, holding me against him.

"Dad, is this true?" Axel asked.

"I had no idea about her talk with him," my dad answered, and I could hear the sincerity in his voice. "I have no idea what she's even talking about."

"I want to go home," I cried. I looked up at Christian through my tears. "Please, Christian, take me home."

He grabbed my hand in his and looked at his brother. "Caiden, let's go. She doesn't need to be here, and you need to get the fuck out of here before you get your stupid ass thrown in jail."

Caiden grabbed my other hand in his, and I kept my head bent, allowing my hair to shield my tear-stained face as my men led me out of the restaurant.

I'd known my mother was cruel, but I never knew she hated me enough to do something like this.

I slowly lifted my head from Christian's shoulder when two cars pulled up in front of the house. Caiden gently squeezed my thigh, and my hand instantly found his under the blanket so I could lace our fingers together.

My dad got out of one car, and Axel and Julian got out of the other. "Meghan had to go home to take care of the kids," Julian said as he strode up the porch.

"Why are you guys here?" I asked quietly as I looked up at my older brother.

Axel sighed. "I think you need to hear what Dad has to say."

I slowly looked over at my dad. I was exhausted. I'd done nothing but cry for the past couple of hours, and now that I was finally done crying, I just wanted to sleep with my two men wrapped around me, keeping me safe from all of the monsters in my life.

"I am divorcing your mother," Dad said, shocking me. My eyes widened in disbelief. "We've been in divorce hearings for about two months now. She's fighting tooth and nail to remain married since she loses all of my money if we divorce. She signed a prenup before we got married," he explained at my confused look.

"If she loses all of the money, then she has nothing to hire this bullshit-ass attorney with for Randall," Julian explained. "In the meantime, I've already contacted my attorney, and he's taking your case." I gaped at Julian. "He's prepared to fight if it comes to that, but he's also still prepared to defend your side of the case in court against a public defender that is assigned to Randall."

"I just want this all to be over with," I whispered. I closed my eyes, just wishing none of this had happened. "This is so fucking exhausting."

Christian pulled me onto his lap and gently rocked the swing back and forth. "I know it is, baby. But unfortunately, shit like this goes through a trial because knowing Randall, he's going to plead not guilty at his court case."

"I have proof of your mother having an affair last year," Dad told me. I looked over at him in astonishment. "I'm taking that to court next week, and I'm hoping that the divorce will finally be granted. When it is, she won't get a penny, Ally, and Randall won't stand a chance. His parents nor his wife's family are backing him on this. He's been cut off from them."

"How do you know all of this so quickly?" I asked. "Just a couple of hours ago, you hadn't even heard of what happened."

"I called—asked around," Julian told me. "I wanted to know who and what we might be going up against with this son of a bitch. He doesn't have a leg to stand on, Ally. He's going to prison for a long time. You fought. His blood was under your fingernails. Everything matches him."

I swiped at my cheeks. Caiden grabbed my hand in his, bringing it up to his lips. "I don't understand why it even has to go to court then," I whimpered. "Why do I have to be forced through this shit?"

"Because every man has a right to a trial by jury," Axel gently explained. "If Randall pleads not guilty, it'll, unfortunately, go to trial."

"They're going to bring everything from that night up," Christian gently warned me. I squeezed my eyes shut, my heart thundering in my chest. Caiden gently squeezed my hand, reminding me that he was still here with me. "They're going to pull out the court records. You're going to be called on as a witness to explain what happened, as is my brother since he was the one that found you. There's going to be photographs of the house shown, as well as photographs of your skin."

"No," I whispered in horror. I stared up at Christian, beginning to panic. "No!" I shouted.

I moved to get up, but Caiden stopped me as I lurched forward, his arms banding around my waist. He tugged me against him, holding my body immobile on his lap. I broke down, sobs wracking my chest. I felt Christian run his fingers through my hair, and his other hand ran up and down my arm.

"This can't be happening," I whimpered. "I don't want anyone else to see."

"I'm sorry, baby," Caiden whispered, his voice hoarse and thick with the emotions he was trying to bury. "I'm so fucking sorry that you're going to have to go through this. But you're not alone."

"Never fucking alone," Christian swore.

"Ally," my brother called, drawing my bleary eyes up to him, "we're all going to be in that courtroom with you. You're going to have all of us standing behind you and supporting you."

Christian gripped my chin and turned my eyes to his. "And you know what, beautiful?" he asked. "I know when you sit at that podium, and you tell your story, I know you're going to cry. I know it's going to hurt like hell, but just remember at the end of it all, *you* are going to be able to watch him get hauled away in handcuffs to get carted off to prison."

"Promise?" I croaked.

Christian nodded. "There's no fucking way he's getting away with this, beautiful."

I rested my head back on Caiden's shoulder. "Life sucks," I brokenly whispered, my throat feeling raw and scratchy.

Caiden pressed his lips to the top of my head. "It may right now, but remember, it's going to get better, and when it does, baby girl, you're going to shine again," he swore, repeating to me what Christian always said.

I'd been waiting so long to begin glowing for him again that I was beginning to think it was never going to happen.

28

GOOD DAY

Ally

My eyes snapped open in alarm when I felt someone pushing the shirt I had slept in up, exposing my breasts, their lips following the path of my shirt. Caiden's face was the first I saw, which meant Christian was the one placing soft, sensual kisses on my belly.

"Good morning, baby," Caiden greeted. He lightly wrapped his hand around my throat and leaned down, smoothing his lips over mine. He started out slow and slowly increased the pace of our kiss. I moaned when he nipped at my bottom lip, gently sucking on it before he coaxed my lips apart, his tongue tangling with mine as he erotically kissed me.

Caiden pulled back from me, and he and Christian switched positions. Christian grinned down at me. "Hey, beautiful." He leaned down and softly kissed me, soothing his lips over my swollen bottom lip.

He pulled my shirt completely off of me as Caiden pulled my panties down my legs, both items of clothing getting tossed somewhere across the room. Caiden lifted my hips up to his lips and flicked his tongue between my folds right as Christian's lips aggressively met mine, kissing me hard, somehow keeping the same pace as his brother as they both took me as their own. I was a helpless, whimpering, moaning mess. Caiden hummed against my clit, and I cried out, coming undone. I ripped my lips from Christian's, my back arching as black spots momentarily danced in my vision.

I squeaked in alarm when Caiden suddenly flipped me over onto my stomach and yanked my hips up into the air. He leaned over my body, and I moaned at the sensation of his body over mine—trapping me, yet I'd never felt safer. "Open those pretty ass lips for him," Caiden growled in my ear as Christian dropped his boxers and grabbed his cock in his hand, slowly stroking it as he watched me lick my lips.

I obediently opened my lips, taking Christian's thick cock in my mouth. Caiden slid in me from behind, his hands gripping my hips. I moaned around Christian's dick, my eyes locking on his. He softly growled as he wrapped my hair around his fist and slowly began to fuck my mouth, making sure I was okay with him taking charge before he finally took my mouth as his own.

My hands twisted the blanket in my fists, my eyes closing as I got lost in both of my men. "Open your eyes," Christian snapped.

I quickly opened my eyes, locking them on his again. I hollowed out my cheeks and swirled my tongue around his cock. He growled and tightened his hand in my hair. Caiden suddenly smacked my ass before he squeezed both of my ass cheeks in his hands, driving up into me harder and faster. "Christian?" Caiden asked.

Christian nodded once and released into my mouth with a growl of my name, his cum hitting the back of my throat. I swallowed at the same time Caiden came inside of me, triggering my own orgasm. I tried to pull back from Christian, but he only smirked down at me and held me in place. My arms shook with the effort to hold myself up. When Caiden pulled out, Christian did as well. I collapsed to the bed, licking my lips as my breaths sawed in and out of my lungs, my eyes sliding closed.

"Babe?" Caiden asked. I slowly opened my eyes to

find both him and Christian kneeling in front of me. "You good?"

"*Mhm*," I mumbled.

"Come on, beautiful," Christian coaxed. He stood up and slid his arms beneath me, lifting me from the bed. "Caiden and I both need showers before we head into work. You need to shower as well and take your medicine."

I groaned in protest. Caiden laughed. "I've never seen someone who gets so damn tired after sex." He shook his head and took me from Christian's arms once he stepped into the shower so Christian could step in. "Woman, if I did everything I wanted to do to you, I'm almost fairly certain I'd put you into a fucking coma."

My cheeks darkened at his words. He pressed a quick kiss to my lips before he eased me onto my feet, keeping his hands on my waist until he was sure I was steady and wouldn't fall. I yawned and leaned my head against his chest. He wrapped an arm around my shoulders and pressed a kiss to the top of my head.

I slowly opened my eyes, watching as Christian lathered my poof with some of my body wash. He smiled at me as he began running it over my skin. "You're so fucking adorable, my moon. You know that?"

"I love you," I told him.

His eyes softened, and he paused in bathing me. He

cupped my cheek, pulling my head off of Caiden's chest. Leaning forward, he pressed his lips to mine. "And I love you, baby girl. Always," he promised.

Caiden turned me so Christian could wash the front of my body. He pressed a tender kiss to my belly. "You're going to really start showing soon," he commented.

I looked down at my belly and placed my hand over it. Caiden's hand covered mine, a silent offer of support. "I can't wait," I admitted. I looked up at Christian. "Do you want a boy or a girl?" I asked him.

He shrugged. "I don't care as long as they're healthy."

Tears burned in my eyes. He pressed a sweet kiss to my lips.

I was so unbelievably lucky to have both of these men in my life.

I smiled at my brother when I stepped inside his office building. He was waiting on his patient to walk over to him. He quietly instructed her to go on to his office down the hall before he walked over to me, concern in his eyes. "You okay, Little Sis?"

I nodded, holding up a bag that contained two subs. "I brought Christian lunch, and I thought I could eat it with him." I frowned, suddenly second-guessing myself. "That is okay, right?" I asked Axel.

He laughed and nodded. "Yeah, Sis. He doesn't have any appointments until after lunch, so go on back there and surprise him." He squeezed my shoulder. "Glad to see you coming back out of your shell, Ally. Just continue leaning on them, yeah?"

I smiled at him, my chest loosening some. "I'm trying."

His smile widened. "That's all I ask for. Just don't ever stop trying."

He walked down the hall, leaving the door open for me. I stepped inside and closed it behind me, heading down the hall to the end where Christian's office was. I admired his nameplate that had been hung up on his door.

How did I manage to make a man who was so successful fall in love with someone as broken as me?

The door suddenly opened. Christian's eyes widened in surprise, but he smiled. "Hey, baby." He leaned forward and kissed me. "I didn't know you were coming."

"It was a surprise." He led me inside and shut his office door behind him. "This is okay, right?"

He shot me a deadpan look, and I blushed. "Babe, of course, it's okay. I always crave your company." He gestured to the couch, a smirk playing on his lips when my cheeks instantly burned redder. "Remember this couch, beautiful?"

"How could I forget?" I sat down. "You kissed me for the fist time here, and you—" I drew in a deep breath, "you told me I deserve to glow—just like the moon."

He nodded. "You're slowly beginning to glow again," he said quietly. "I know shit is terrifying for you right now, but Caiden and I—baby, we're never leaving your side. You've always got us," he promised. "No matter how rough shit gets or how dark it becomes for you, we're always going to be two people you can rely on."

My bottom lip trembled. I closed my eyes, drawing in a deep breath. He pulled me into his arms, holding me until I could bring myself back together. Once I was okay again, I grabbed the bag. "I got you a sub," I told him. "I'm hoping I got it made correctly."

He unwrapped the sub and took a bite, groaning after. "Fuck yes. I think this is honestly the best fucking sub I've ever had." He looked over at me. "What sauce did you have them put on it?"

"Your normal ranch, but I had them add oil and vinegar and toast the veggies with the meat."

"Fuck, this is like Heaven." He pecked my lips. "Thanks, beautiful. I was fucking starving, so right now, you're a fucking Godsend."

I giggled before I grabbed my own sandwich and took a bite. Once I was finished eating, Christian took our trash and threw it away before he grabbed me a bottle of water. I greedily drank the cool liquid down before I curled up against his side on the couch and closed my eyes. "Wake me up when you need to begin getting ready for your next appointment," I whispered.

He pressed his lips to the top of my head before he wrapped his arm around my shoulder, his other hand resting on my thigh. "You're lucky your Axel's sister. Pretty sure he wouldn't allow this if it were anyone else." He laughed.

I smiled. "Family privileges." I snuggled closer to him. "Now, *shh*. I really need a nap."

He trailed the tips of his fingers up and down my arm, slowly lulling me to sleep.

☾

I looked up from the book I was reading when I heard the front door open. My heart picked up speed in my chest, but Caiden quickly emerged around the corner, easing my fears. "Easy, baby." He walked over to me and cupped my face in his hands, pressing his lips to mine. "It's just me. How was your day?" he asked as he dropped onto the couch next to me.

I dog-eared my spot in the book and closed it,

leaning forward to set the book on the coffee table. "Fine," I told him. "I slept for a couple of more hours after you guys left for work, and then I got up and ate lunch with Christian." I gestured to my book. "I came home after taking a nap in Christian's office, and I've been reading that since I got home."

Caiden suddenly got up. I watched him as he moved to the bedroom that he, Christian, and I now shared. "Let me get changed, and then I want to take you somewhere."

Excitement filled my veins. "Where?" I called after him.

He laughed as he disappeared into our room. "You'll see, baby."

I pouted. I hated that answer. He knew I would fret over it until I figured it out, but Caiden liked to do things to remind me to trust him, and this was one of those things. He wasn't as soothing and calming as Christian was. Christian was the person who smoothed out my rougher edges, keeping me calm when I felt like things were spinning out of control.

Caiden was the one that kept me on edge, pushing my boundaries but never pushing them too far. He just forced me to maintain my trust and security in both him and his brother.

And somehow, the two of them balanced each other out, keeping me grounded.

I walked over to the shoe closet and grabbed my slip-on shoes, pulling them on my feet. Caiden unexpectedly smacked my ass, and I squeaked in alarm, swinging around to face him. The man had a weird obsession with my ass.

"One of these days, I'm going to claim that ass," he warned me.

My cheeks burned, desire curling low in my belly at the thought of Caiden doing what he was insinuating. He smirked and gripped the side of my neck, yanking my lips up to his. "Soon," was all he promised.

I pouted. He pecked my lips. "My brother is right. You really are fucking adorable."

Just when my cheeks had started cooling, they flamed up again. He laughed and grabbed my hand in his, gently tugging me behind him toward the front door. He typed in the passcode to set the alarm before he shut and locked the front door behind us.

I ran my eyes over him. He had pulled on a pair of snug-fitting skinny jeans and high-tops with a plain black t-shirt that clung to the muscles in his arms and chest.

"Jesus," I whispered.

Caiden smirked at me. "You really have no filter, do you?"

I covered my face with my hands. "I normally do, I swear."

He laughed. "Come on, baby. It's going to get dark in a couple of hours, and I want you to enjoy this."

Caiden led me away from the park he drove us to, my hand in his. "You like nature, right?" he asked me.

"Yeah." I looked up at him in confusion. "Caiden, what in the hell do you have planned?"

He pressed his finger to my lips as he led me on a paved trail. He then pointed straight ahead. My eyes widened in amazement as I stared at the deer in front of me. He grinned down at me before he pressed a kiss to my temple. "Come on. I come out here all of the time. There's plenty more," he whispered.

"This is so exciting." I squeezed his hand in mine and beamed up at him. His eyes softened, warming my heart. He really could be as sweet as his brother if he wanted to be. "Thank you for this."

He shook his head and brought my hand up to his lips, pressing a kiss to the back of it. "Don't thank me, baby. Just enjoy this. That's all the thanks that I need," he promised.

I leaned up on my tiptoes and pressed my lips to his. "I love you," I whispered, my lips brushing his.

He laced his fingers in my hair and deepened the kiss. It was the first time I'd ever said the words to him.

"Always, baby," he told me. "You're never getting rid of me."

My smile widened. "I don't mind," I assured him.

He laughed and pressed a quick kiss to the tip of my nose before he led me further down the paved trail.

29

BABY APPOINTMENT

Ally

My doctor stepped into the room, smiling warmly at me as she closed the door behind us. Apparently, she was Meghan's doctor throughout both of Meghan's pregnancies, and Meghan highly recommended her.

She held her hand out to me. "Hi, Ally. I'm Stacie. I'll be your doctor." She took a seat on the stool, looking at Christian and Caiden. "Boyfriends?" she asked.

My cheeks burned as I nodded. Christian held his hand out to her. "I'm Christian—the father of the baby." He gestured to Caiden. "This is my brother, Caiden."

She smiled at both of them. "It's great to meet you both."

Caiden grabbed my hand in his, sensing my nervousness, and gave it a gentle squeeze. I looked up at him, his dark eyes clashing with mine. He silently released my hand and reached up, trailing his fingers along my jaw before he lightly tapped my chin with his knuckles. "Chin up, baby."

A smile tilted my lips. He leaned down and pressed a kiss to the top of my head. I turned my attention back to the doctor, my cheeks instantly lighting on fire at the smile on her face as she ran her eyes between me and Caiden.

She grabbed her folder. "Okay. First things first, I need a list of medications that you're taking," she told me.

I swallowed thickly, my face paling a little. Christian turned my head to face him. "Easy, baby," he soothed. "She's a doctor; she's not going to judge you."

I ran my eyes over his face before I nodded and drew in a slow, deep breath. I looked back at Stacie and quickly listed off all seven medications I took. There was no hint of judgment in her eyes as she ran her eyes over the list she created. "Do you see your therapist regularly?" she asked me.

I nodded. "I see Dr. Gresham in person every Monday and Friday, and we do virtual sessions every Wednesday."

She smiled. "Dr. Gresham is an excellent doctor.

You're in great hands with him. And all of these medications are safe to take while you're pregnant, so you're okay there." She stood up. "I want to do a breast exam and a pap smear as well as check your cervix. Then, I want to do an ultrasound, pinpoint your due date, and get you set up for regular check-ups."

The thought of her feeling the scars on my chest and my breasts made me sick to my stomach. I shot my panicked gaze to Christian. He grabbed my hand. "Easy, beautiful. Remember, she's a medical professional. She's here to make sure you're healthy and that our baby is healthy—nothing more."

"Is there something I should be made aware of?" Stacie asked.

Caiden trailed his fingers along my spine as Christian brushed his thumb over the back of my hand. "She was in a bad accident a few weeks ago," Caiden informed her. "It left behind some scars."

Stacie shot me an understanding smile, and somehow, I knew she'd known what I'd gone through. I wanted to cry, and it took everything in me to hold my tears in. "Honey, I'm here to make sure you and your baby are well and healthy, just as Christian told you," she assured me. "I'm not here to pass judgment. I'm here to be supportive." She grabbed my folder. "Now, I'm going to step out of the room. I'll come back in a few minutes. I need you to take your clothes off and cover yourself with these paper sheets," she said, grabbing two out of the closet in the room.

Christian took them from her. She nodded once at me and slipped out of the room, closing the door behind her. Caiden gripped the hem of my shirt and pulled it over my head, and Christian unclasped my bra, taking my shirt from Caiden afterward.

Caiden leaned down and pressed his lips to the scars covering my chest. "Still so perfect," he whispered. He pressed his lips to mine. "Be strong, Ally."

Drawing in a deep breath, I nodded and stood up, shimmying out of my leggings and panties, handing them over to Christian to put with the rest of my clothes. I laid back down on the exam room cot. Christian draped the paper sheets over me, making sure my body was covered.

He lifted my scarred arm up to his lips and pressed a kiss to each healed cut. "You've come so far, my moon. Just draw in a deep breath and remember that we're here with you," he told me. "Caiden and I are never going anywhere, beautiful, and this doctor doesn't care about your scars."

A light knock came on the door. Christian released my wrist and walked over to open it. Stacie stepped into the room. "Ready?" she asked as she grabbed a pair of gloves and slid them on.

"As ready as I'll ever be," I admitted. I drew in a deep breath. "I'm really nervous," I blurted.

"That's understandable. Just remember that there's no judgment in this room." She grabbed the bottle of lube and sat on her stool. I placed my feet on the edge of the bed, spreading my legs for her. I gripped Caiden's hand when she began to do the pap smear, and I winced when she began checking my cervix.

"Everything looks good there," she said as she slid back on her stool and pulled her gloves off. I dropped my legs, easing my grip on Caiden's hand. He kept his hand linked with mine, brushing his thumb over the back of it.

After doing my breast exam, and not saying a single word about my scars, she let me get dressed and then led us to the ultrasound room on the other side of the building.

"Hi, sweetheart," the ultrasound tech greeted. She patted the cot. "Go ahead and lay back on here and pull your shirt up to just under your breasts and pull your leggings down for me some."

I did as she instructed, forcing my breathing to stay steady. I was extremely nervous. This ultrasound would decide if I'd somehow fucked up again.

She squeezed warm gel on my skin and pressed her wand to my belly. Tears instantly sprang to my eyes and spilled over onto my cheeks as I stared at my baby on the screen. I sobbed, my hands coming up to cover my mouth.

"It's still just a little too early for me to tell what you're having, but the baby is extremely healthy. It's a little over its normal range in terms of growth, which is just fine. You might just give birth to a chunky baby." She smiled at me.

My little baby kicked its legs and swung its arms around. Christian grabbed my hands in his, drawing my eyes to him. He smiled at me. "Told you," he whispered. "You're going to be an amazing mom."

"It's not like last time," I choked out.

He shook his head. "No, baby, it's not. You're going to give birth to a beautiful, healthy baby."

I began crying uncontrollably. I was pretty sure the ultrasound technician was alarmed, but I couldn't help it. My baby was alive and healthy.

I was finally being the mom I should have been to my first baby.

The ultrasound tech whispered something about leaving the room and giving us some privacy. Caiden instantly sat on the bed and pulled me onto his lap, holding me tight in his arms, and Christian held my hands in his. "I'm a bit confused," Caiden admitted.

"She lost her first baby," Christian quietly explained. "Her ex—the one you know about—" he said, not mentioning Randall's name, "was the dad.

Long story short, she caught him cheating, and she spiraled—went home and took almost all of her antidepressants. It caused her to miscarry."

"Fuck, baby," Caiden rasped. He pressed his lips to the top of my head and gently rocked me. "You're not losing this one, you got me? You're *never* going to hit that point in your life again. I swear to you, I will hold up every bit of you by myself if I have to, but you will get to be the mom that you should have been able to be from the very beginning."

"I'm sorry," I croaked. "Seeing the baby—it was—" I couldn't finish speaking.

"I know, beautiful," Christian soothed.

I pressed my hand to my belly. Caiden and Christian covered my hand with theirs. I closed my eyes and flipped my hand over, wrapping my fingers around theirs.

I wasn't alone, and my men were never going to let me be alone again.

☾

I giggled as Caiden tried feeding me yet another fry. We were out eating at a casual burger joint per Caiden's request since he was craving something greasy. I swear, this man had more cravings than I did, and I was the one pregnant.

"Caiden, stop." I laughed. "I seriously cannot eat anymore."

He chuckled. Christian arched an eyebrow at me. "So, you're telling me if I ordered you a brownie sundae with extra cherries on top, you wouldn't be able to eat it?"

I paused. "Well, I mean..."

Caiden barked out a laugh. "I swear you're going to have a girl." He shook his head. "Your cravings for sweets are fucking insane."

I shrugged and gave Christian puppy dog eyes. "Please?"

He rolled his eyes. "I already ordered it for you, beautiful." He grinned at me. "I knew you would want it. My brother is right. You can't resist sweets these days."

I shrugged as a blush tinted my cheeks. He grabbed my hand and pressed a kiss to my palm. Caiden wrapped an arm around my shoulders and pressed a kiss to my temple. "I'm going to start looking at nursery furniture here soon," Caiden spoke up. He looked down at me. "I need you to send me some ideas you have in mind."

I furrowed my eyebrows at him in confusion. "I don't even know what I'm having yet."

He shrugged. "I didn't say I was buying clothes, babe—just the furniture. We can go ahead and buy the crib, dressers, and all that other furniture shit." I laughed. He rolled his eyes, but a smirk twitched at his lips. "Do you have anything in mind?"

I shook my head. "I just want the changing table attached to the crib," I told him. "That's my only request." I looked at Christian. "You have any ideas?" I asked him.

He shook his head. "I'm shit at buying furniture— ask Caiden. I left furniture buying up to him for the house. Otherwise, I would have forgotten half the shit that was needed."

I giggled. Caiden gently squeezed my shoulders. "Are you wanting the nursery painted?"

I shook my head. The walls in our house were a light gray, and I liked them. It reminded me of a dark, rainy day, when the rain was just steadily falling. "The walls can stay as they are," I told him. I leaned up and pressed a quick kiss to his lips. "Thank you."

He hooked his index finger under my chin and pulled my lips up to his again. "You're welcome, baby." He nodded his head at something behind me. I turned around and let out a small squeal at the sight of my brownie sundae with extra cherries. Christian laughed and smirked at his brother as the waiter set it down in front of me. "You might be able to kiss her right now, bro, but I'm the one that just made her fucking day."

Caiden rolled his eyes. I had gotten used to the

banter between them. I used to think that they were really in competition with each other, but turned out, they were really just teasing each other.

"You have to go back to work after this," Caiden reminded him. "I'm the one that gets to make her scream my name later while you're sitting behind your boring-ass desk."

I almost dropped my spoon as I stared up at Caiden, my entire face and neck flaming. Christian began laughing. Caiden only smirked at me. "Eat your sundae, babe. You're going to need every bit of energy that sugar gives you."

As soon as the alarm was off, Caiden swept me up into his arms and carried me to our bedroom. He laid me down on the bed before he crawled over me, his lips hungrily devouring mine. I moaned, quickly losing myself in him. I tangled my fingers in his hair and spread my thighs, cradling his muscular body between them.

He lightly thrust against me, and I whimpered, lifting my hips to meet his next thrust. He shoved my shirt over my head and pulled my bra off. Sitting up, I yanked his shirt over his head, pressing my body closer to his as I kissed him again. With a low growl, he gripped a handful of my hair and took control of the kiss, forcing me to submit to him.

We laid back down, and he shoved a knee between my legs. I moaned into the kiss, rubbing myself over his jean-clad thigh, soft moans and whimpers falling from my lips. "There you go, baby," he growled in my ear. He reached down and yanked my leggings and panties off of me, leaving me completely naked beneath him. He kissed me again, his leg moving back to its previous position.

I snapped my eyes up to his when he suddenly gripped my chin. "I want to watch your face and those pretty fucking eyes as you get yourself off," he rasped. He lightly applied pressure between my legs with his thigh. I moaned at the sensation of his jeans rubbing my clit.

"Yes, baby. There you go," he praised when I began to rub my clit over his jeans, so fucking lost in him that I couldn't even be embarrassed. "So fucking sexy, baby."

"Caiden," I whimpered, getting so close.

"Come for me," he ordered. He lightly wrapped his hand around my throat, applying the slightest bit of pressure as he did so. I cried out his name, my back arching as I came, my hands twisting into the sheets of the bed.

He unfastened his jeans and pulled his cock out. With no warning, he pushed inside of me, my walls still pulsing with my orgasm. I shot up into a semi-sitting position, my eyes snapping to his. Gripping the back of my neck, he pulled my lips up to his, proceeding to fuck me and claim me. He followed me back down to the bed, and gripped my right leg behind my knee, yanking it up, driving deeper and harder.

I couldn't tell where one orgasm ended and the next one began. All I knew was that I was begging him to never stop, and he didn't. He kept taking me over and over like a man possessed—like a man starved.

And I couldn't get enough of him.

30

CAIDEN'S DATE

Caiden

"Bro, you barely slept a wink last night," Christian commented as he leaned against the spare bathroom doorjamb. Ally was asleep, having passed out right after Christian woke her up to take her medicine this morning. Since she was asleep, I was getting ready in the spare bathroom so I wouldn't wake her up by accident. She was out of her first trimester now and was fourteen weeks pregnant. Her pregnancy was making her exhausted, and I could normally always find her napping when I came home from work.

"Just got some shit on my mind," I told him, thinking about the date I had planned two weeks ago with a guy that I had met at the tire shop when I'd gone to get my tires rotated on my car. The date was coming up in three days, and I still hadn't figured out a way to gently break the news to Ally.

I didn't know how she was going to take it. I'd told her I would still see other people, but telling her and actually having it happen were two very different things.

Would she flip out, or would she just smile at me and tell me okay? It was so hard to figure out. She was currently having a high, her moods under control for now, and I was terrified of ruining that.

"Like what?" Christian asked me. I stayed silent. He sighed. "Caiden, don't close me out, and don't close her out." I scowled. He knew me too damn well. "What in the hell is going on?"

"I have a date in three days," I told him. I stopped talking so I could rinse my face. "I don't know how Ally is going to take it when I tell her."

"How long has this date been planned?" Christian asked.

I clenched my jaw, then forced it to relax. "Two weeks now," I told him. I sighed. "I don't know how to break this to her, Christian."

"You follow your instincts, Caiden." I glanced over at him. "You've always been good with her. Yeah, you're a blunt asshole who works her nerves," I smirked, "but you also know how to handle her when shit is getting bad. Just trust your heart; it'll lead you." He shrugged. "Besides, she knew from the very beginning that you're bi. She also knows that you're not going to stop dating men just because you're in a committed relationship with her." He narrowed his eyes at me. "But you need to make sure that the other person in your life, whoever he may end up being, understands that she is *always* your first priority."

I rolled my eyes at him. "Like fuck is anyone being placed above her," I told him.

He nodded once. "Good. That's how it should be." He looked at his smart watch and sighed. "Fuck. Axel just reminded me I have a meeting with his attorney after work."

"For?" I asked. Christian wasn't one to get in trouble.

He laughed at my face. "Caiden, don't look so constipated." I scowled at him, only serving to make him laugh harder. "It's nothing bad. Axel is just making me a permanent partner at his clinic; that's all."

I grinned at him. "Congrats on it finally getting finalized, brother."

He smiled. "Thanks, Caiden." He looked toward our room through the living room before he looked back at me. "You'll have time with her this evening. This is apparently going to be a while, and I won't get home until late. So, break the news to her, and remind her of where she stands in your life—where she'll always stand. When you go on your date, I'll handle her. She'll be okay. Our woman is a lot stronger than she seems."

I nodded in agreement. That she was. But she was also so fragile at the same time.

She was like bulletproof glass. She was hard as fuck to break and shatter completely, but it could happen with enough force.

Ally was actually up when I got home that afternoon, her nose buried in the pages of a book. She looked up when I stepped into the bedroom, a beautiful smile gracing her lips. "Hi," she greeted.

I smiled at her and leaned over the bed to kiss her. "Hey, baby." I stood back up and sat on the edge of the bed to unlace my boots, pushing them under the bed afterward. I clasped my hands in front of me and leaned forward, bracing my elbows on my knees. "Ally, baby, I need to talk to you."

I watched out of my peripheral as she slowly bookmarked her book and closed it, setting it aside. She put her hands between her thighs, clasping them together. I knew why; she was trying to hide her nervousness from me.

"Okay," she whispered.

I drew in a deep breath. "I have a date in three days —on Friday," I clarified. She cast her eyes to her lap. Fuck, this wasn't how I wanted her to react. She was drawing into herself. "His name is Michael, and he works at Healey's Tire Shop in town."

"Oh," she finally murmured, her voice barely carrying to me. But she still wasn't looking at me, her gaze firmly locked on her thighs.

"Baby," I called, "look at me." She shook her head, swallowing thickly. Fuck, she was on the verge of crying. I moved toward her and gripped her chin, forcing her head up so her eyes locked on mine. Tears swam in her pretty, brown eyes, breaking my heart. "Say the words, Ally, and I'll call him right now and cancel the date," I told her in all honesty. He was just fun, some guy to fuck around with for a little while. Ally? She was my home. She was the beginning and the end for me. No one else would ever be on her level, and anyone that hoped to be was a damn fool.

"No." She drew in a deep breath, blinking to stop from crying, and she frowned when a tear ran down her cheek. Using my other hand, I caught the tear with my thumb, gently brushing it away. "I knew you wouldn't stop dating men just because you're with me, so I don't understand why it hurts," she admitted, her voice breaking on the word 'hurts'.

"You know you don't mean less to me, right?" I

asked her. Her bottom lip trembled. I'd hit the root of why it hurt. She was terrified that I was abandoning her. I leaned forward and lightly brushed my lips over hers. "No one can ever replace you, baby. You're it for me—my beginning and my end." She sobbed and squeezed her eyes shut as tears ran down her cheeks. "I don't care how many dates I end up going on with other men, baby. I will *always* come home to you every night because you're the only person I'll ever want to spend the rest of my life with."

"I'm sorry I'm being such an emotional mess." She sniffled as she slowly opened her eyes. "I got so terrified—"

I cupped her cheeks and covered her lips with mine, silencing her. She moaned as I coaxed her lips apart, letting my tongue tangle with hers. Her hands ran under my shirt and up my abdomen, making my muscles tense and quiver beneath her touch, a soft growl ripping from my chest as I kissed her harder.

I leaned back on my knees and gripped her left leg behind her knee. She squeaked in shock when I yanked her leg, pulling her body so she lay flat on the mattress. I then moved over her, pressing my lips to hers as I hungrily kissed her, drawing those breathless little moans from her throat that I loved hearing. She was so vocal when I was taking care of her like this, and I fucking loved it.

She gripped the hem of my shirt, and I leaned up to grab the back of it, yanking it over my head and tossing it to the floor. She leaned up on her elbows and pressed soft, tantalizing kisses to my chest and shoulders. A low rumble sounded from the depths of my chest as I laced my fingers in her dark hair and yanked her head back, covering her lips with mine again.

It didn't take me long to undress her, and I made sure to press kisses to her soft skin—made sure to touch her in the way she loved to be touched as I removed her clothes. By the time she was laying completely naked beneath me, her skin was flushed, her eyes darkened to a rich, dark chocolate, her breaths softly panting out of her.

"Caiden," she whimpered when I only stared down at her, at every blemish that covered her body, yet only made her even more perfect in my eyes.

I leaned down and began to tenderly press my lips to each of her scars from that tragic evening. Her body trembled beneath my lips, but her hands came up to lace in my hair. I knew her scars bothered her; I knew they always would. But I would always take time to love each imperfect part of her.

Her scars? They didn't make her any less of a woman in my eyes. They made her stronger. She had survived something horrific, and she never gave up.

That took real strength.

I stood up from the bed once I had kissed every scar on her body. Her eyes followed my every movement, and as I unfastened my belt, I watched as the tears that had been in her eyes slowly disappeared, being replaced with that need she always held for me.

Once I was completely undressed, she suddenly moved forward and wrapped her hand around my cock. A flirty smile touched her lips before she wrapped them around me, taking me deep into the back of her throat. I growled and laced my fingers in her hair, gently showing her the perfect way to suck my cock. She moaned, the nails of her free hand digging into my thighs. God, she was basically a master at this.

"Pay special attention to the tip," I ordered. Her eyes snapped up to mine, insecurity shining in their depths. "No, baby. You're fucking perfect, and I'm restraining myself from fucking you to the point you can't talk without your throat hurting." Her cheeks burned at my words. "But if you pay special attention to the tip, I'll come a lot faster, and then I can bury myself deep inside of you."

Her moan vibrated my cock, and my balls tightened. *Fucking hell, this woman was dangerous.*

Doing as I directed, she sucked at my tip, her tongue swirling around, licking up precum. I growled, my head falling back on my shoulders as I resisted the urge to thrust forward, to make this woman deep-throat the hell out of my cock.

My hand tightened in her hair, and she moaned again. That was it. With a curse, I came, and like a good girl, she swallowed every fucking drop.

I pulled out of her mouth and grabbed her under her arms, gently tossing her onto her back on the bed. I easily slid deep inside of her. She was so fucking wet, the inside of her thighs coated with it. I gently wrapped my hand around her throat, placing my other hand on the mattress beside her head, and leaned up, proceeding to make love to her with deep, calculated, even thrusts.

And there was complete trust in her eyes as she submitted to me.

I leaned down into a push-up position and slowly kissed her. "I'm never abandoning you, baby," I promised. "You're stuck with me for life."

Ally

Christian nuzzled my neck from behind as he wrapped his arms around me. Caiden shrugged on his leather jacket and walked over to me, an easy-going smile on his face, his eyes warming as they locked with mine. The tightness in my chest eased.

He cupped my cheeks in his hands. "Let Christian take care of you while I'm gone, baby."

I drew in a deep breath and nodded. "Okay."

"Promise?" he asked me.

I couldn't help it. I smiled up at him. "Yes," I promised.

"Good girl." He leaned down and pressed his lips to mine, softly coaxing them apart before he slowly pulled back. I closed my eyes again as he pressed a tender kiss to my forehead. "I'll be back before eleven," he promised.

"Don't rush." I swallowed thickly. Christian tightened his arms around me. "Take your time; enjoy your date."

Caiden flashed me my favorite grin. "Baby, I'll always rush to come back home to you."

I stepped away from Christian and wrapped my arms around Caiden's waist. He instantly wrapped his arms around me and buried his face in my hair. "I love you," I told him, my voice slightly muffled by his jacket.

His arms flexed around me. "And I love you, baby. I'll be home before you know it."

I slowly released him and stepped back against Christian again. Caiden cupped the side of my neck and leaned down to press a kiss to my cheek. "Call me if you need me." His eyes bore down into mine. "I know you've got Christian with you, but you are still my priority. If you need me, call me," he ordered.

"I will. I promise."

"Good girl." He pressed one more kiss to my cheek before he walked out of the house, pulling his phone from his pocket. Christian gently turned me to face him. "Come on. Let's go eat this pizza Caiden ordered for us, and then we'll take a nice, warm bubble bath." He caressed my belly. "You've got to feed the little one and take your medicine," he reminded me when I opened my mouth to protest about eating. I wasn't hungry.

But Caiden and Christian made sure that I ate three meals a day. One day, I didn't. I even had a whole argument with Caiden about it, and he left work on his lunch break to come home to force me to eat.

Because once I missed one meal, I tended to conveniently miss others, and it was a sign of my moods going on a downward spiral, which my two men did their best to prevent.

"Okay," I said quietly. I grabbed Christian's hand in mine. "Let's go eat this fattening ass pizza." I shook my head. "I'll never understand how you and Caiden keep up with your bodies."

He laughed. "We work out, babe." I arched an eyebrow at him, considering I still had yet to see them use the gym in the basement. "You're always still asleep," he explained. "But we do work out."

I huffed. "Now I feel like a fatty."

Christian scoffed and pulled out a barstool for me. "Sit your cute ass down, woman. You're not fat. Caiden and I both agree that you still need to gain more weight, especially since you're pregnant."

I pouted at him. He smiled. "Fucking adorable." He leaned down and pressed his lips to mine.

Caiden

The house was mostly dark, the light over the stove and a lamp being the only lights on in the main part of the house. I quickly deactivated the alarm before it woke Ally and Christian up, setting it again once I was inside the house with the door locked behind me.

I rolled my shoulders as I toed off my shoes and took my socks off, tossing them into the laundry room as I passed by it on my way to the bedroom.

Christian was awake, but Ally was passed out in front of him with his arm wrapped around her waist, her back pressed to the front of his body. She was uncovered, most likely hot. Her body temperature tended to fluctuate a lot the further she got into her pregnancy.

"Hey," he whispered. "How did it go?"

"Fine," I told him honestly. It had. Michael was funny—a bit nervous, though. I figured that would go away with a little bit of time. He understood I had a serious girlfriend, one I intended to spend the rest of my life with, and he wasn't bothered by it.

"How did she do?" I asked him.

Christian shrugged. "She tried, bro. It'll take some time for her to get used to the fact that you're still dating men, but she'll come around. She's doing her best to be selfless for you."

I smiled at her as I yanked my jeans down my legs so I could tug on my gray sweatpants. Ally woke up when I slid into bed, her sleepy eyes instantly meeting mine. I leaned forward and smoothed my lips over hers.

Her eyes slowly fluttered back open as I leaned back, and I smiled. Her cheeks burned as she smiled back at me. "Hey, baby." I brushed my nose with hers. "I'm home."

I laid on my back and opened my arm. She instantly placed her head on my chest near my shoulder, her eyes falling shut again. I brushed my lips to the top of her head.

She laid like this with us every night. I laid on the side closest to the door, and Christian laid on the side closest to the window. She slept between us with her head on my shoulder and her ass pressed up against Christian with both of our arms wrapped around her.

"Goodnight, baby," I whispered.

Only a soft snore met my ears.

31

ANXIETY

Ally

I folded another baby blanket and placed it on the shelf inside the closet. Yesterday, after Christian and Caiden were both off of work, we all went shopping for necessities like baby blankets, diapers, wipes, bottles, etc. They wanted to put it away last night while I slept, but I begged them to leave it for today so it would give me something productive to do. I got bored sitting around the house all the time, and hell, there were only so many books I could read.

My phone rang on the dresser in the nursery, and I quickly stepped out, frowning at my Dad's name on the screen. Drawing a deep breath, trying to quell the nerves in my stomach, I answered it, pulling the phone up to my ear. "Hello?"

"Hi, sweetheart." I swallowed thickly, waiting to hear what he had to say. I knew he was trying to do right by me, but it would take a while to undo years of damage. "I was wanting to know if you'd like to meet up for lunch?" he asked.

"Um... sure," I stupidly agreed. "It is just going to be you this time, right?" I asked him. "I don't want to see Mom."

"It'll just be me," he assured me. "I haven't seen your mother since the last dinner. We're living separately, and the divorce is in the last process of being finalized."

I gripped the dresser, relief flooding my veins at his words. The divorce meant that she wouldn't have access to money to support Randall in this trial, which meant there was a bigger chance of him going to prison for what he did.

"Where are you wanting to eat at?" I asked him.

"We can try that new Italian restaurant that just opened downtown. Does that sound good to you?"

"That sounds fine. I'll meet you there soon," I told him. "I just need to call Christian and Caiden and inform them of where I'm going to be."

"Okay, honey. I'll see you in a little bit, then. I love you."

My heart squeezed in my chest, tears suddenly

springing to my eyes. I blinked them back. "I love you, too, Dad."

I hung up, calling Christian and Caiden right after, putting us into a three-way conference call on my phone. "Yeah, babe?" Caiden asked. "You good?"

"I'm okay," I assured him.

"What's going on, beautiful?" Christian asked me.

"Dad called me," Caiden grunted in displeasure. "He wants to have lunch. He said Mom won't be there— that they haven't seen each other since the last dinner we were all supposed to have together. Their divorce is also in the last stage of being finalized."

"Well, thank fuck for that," Caiden grunted.

"Go. Be safe. Call one of us if you need us," Christian ordered. "Make sure you take your anxiety medication with you so you can take one if you feel an attack coming on."

"I will," I promised. "I love you both."

"I love you," they both responded at the same time.

"Be careful," Caiden added. "Let us know when you make it there so we know you made it safely."

"I will."

"Good girl," he praised, making my cheeks burn, but I had to admit that I loved it when I did something that pleased him like this.

"I've got to go," Christian told me. "Be safe. I love you. Make sure you eat while you're there."

I sighed. I really wasn't all that hungry, but I knew I needed to eat. "Okay. I love you, too."

Caiden also hung up a moment after Christian. Drawing in a deep, steadying breath, I stood up and walked to our bedroom to get a quick shower and get dressed in something a bit more suitable than my booty shorts and tank top.

Dad was sitting at a table near the front when I walked in, and he stood and smiled as soon as his eyes landed on me. It was a casual restaurant, which I was thankful for. We hadn't yet gone shopping for maternity clothes for me, so I was stuck living in leggings and one of Christian's t-shirts.

He wrapped his arms around me in a hug. I couldn't help but sink into his warm, fatherly embrace, my own arms wrapping around his midsection. He pressed a kiss to the top of my head. "How have you been?" he asked me.

I shrugged as I took a seat. "Tired." I yawned, blushing immediately after. "The baby drains me."

His eyes widened in shock. "Baby?" he asked. I frowned, trying to remember if he had been told of my pregnancy, but judging by his face, I guessed not.

"Um, yeah." My cheeks darkened. "I'm almost

fifteen weeks pregnant," I informed him. "Wednesday will mark fifteen on the dot. Christian is the dad."

He smiled at me. "You and your two boyfriends seem extremely happy together. As long as you're happy, I don't care." Tears burned in my eyes at his words. It was the love and acceptance I had been seeking from my parents for years.

A waiter came to our table before I could say anything else. I ordered an ice water with a lemon, and Dad ordered a glass of one of their wines. He turned his attention back to me once the waiter walked away. "Axel mentioned that you had to take a break from school due to your, um..."

"My mental disorders," I stated. "That's what it is, Dad. I have multiple chemical imbalances in my brain." I shrugged. "I've mostly gotten used to it."

He frowned. "I don't like calling them disorders," he admitted.

I gave him a small smile. He looked so disturbed by my choice of words. "I have multiple ones, Dad," I gently repeated. "It's just easier to call them disorders. It's not as simple as just saying I have depression, or I have anxiety." I tucked my hair behind my ear. "I suffer from bipolar depression, anxiety, and schizophrenia."

"The schizophrenia is new," he noted.

He'd remembered.

I nodded. "It just popped up a few months ago." I

resisted the urge to rub my wrists, the night Christian
helped save my life flashing into my head. He'd barely
met me, and yet, he was there for me the moment I
needed someone. He hadn't looked at me like he was
disgusted, nor did he freak out. He just wrapped me up
in his arms and got me calm, being the calming,
steadying force I needed.

"Fuck," Dad suddenly cursed. "Ally, I swear to you, I
didn't tell her *anything*," he swore.

I jerked around to see my mother storming towards
our table. Her normally perfectly made-up face and
hair were a mess. She looked stressed—like she hadn't
slept in weeks. She didn't look put-together anymore.

The divorce had taken its toll on her, most likely
because she didn't have all of the money she used to
have to keep up with her appearance.

"You," she seethed as she stepped up to our table,
drawing the eyes of everyone in the restaurant. The
building went eerily silent. "You ruined everything!" she
yelled at me. "You just can't admit that you *begged*
Randall to fuck you! He told me all about how you
begged him to be rougher!" My face paled, tears pooling
in my eyes. Panic clawed at my throat. She couldn't be
doing this—not in public. Not where everyone knew
who the hell me and my family were. "And you have
dragged *everyone* into your lie with you, just like you did
before!"

I jerked out of my chair and slung my glass of water into her face, rushing out of the restaurant right after, taking off for my car. Once I was sitting in the driver's seat, I locked my doors and flew for the highway, gasping in quick breaths of air as I sped toward home. My hands were trembling, my ears ringing, but I had to get home where I knew I would be safe—where Caiden had ensured that I had security while he and Christian weren't home.

I forgot to shut my car door when I got home. I just rushed into the house, slamming the front door behind me and locking it.

She couldn't hurt me here.

I sobbed, hot tears rushing down my cheeks. Once again, everyone was going to know about what happened to me, and once again, rumors were going to spread.

Everyone was going to hate me. Randall had been the town's golden boy, and I was now, once again, tarnishing his reputation.

I swiped at my cheeks and rushed toward the bathroom, turning the shower on. The hot water would ground me, and I was desperately clinging onto something to hold me together. I had no idea where my phone was. It honestly probably got left behind at the restaurant.

My purse. It was in my purse.

Fuck.

I'd left my purse at the restaurant. The only reason I'd had my keys was because they were in my pocket.

I quickly got undressed and stepped into the shower. I closed my eyes, images of that night flashing through my mind. Writing those journal entries Dr. Gresham had ordered me to do—it had helped. But one moment with my mom and all of that progress I'd made was stripped away from me.

I sobbed, dropping to my knees. My skin crawled. I screamed, the present officially washing away, and all around me, all I could see was Randall's face. All I could feel were his teeth and his touch.

I threw up, my vision beginning to darken.

"Caiden," I whimpered. "Someone help me."

"They're not coming to rescue you. You're mine now. I'll make sure you never forget me," Randall promised, his voice ringing through my head.

I screamed.

C

Caiden

I slung my car into park on the edge of the drive and jumped out, slamming the door behind me. Ally's car was parked half on the drive and half on the grass, her door hanging open. Her battery was dead. At a quick glance, it didn't look like she had struggled, but panic still clawed at my throat.

This shit couldn't be happening again.

I rushed up the stairs, thankfully finding the front door locked. I quickly unlocked it and rushed inside, my eyes sliding to the alarm. It wasn't set.

That wasn't like her. She always set the alarm. She was so damn paranoid about it.

I paused, drawing in a deep breath. I needed to focus. Panicking wasn't going to help me. I needed to be strong and calm.

I took a moment to listen, my senses quickly gathering intel from my surroundings.

The shower was running in our bathroom.

I quickly moved to our room, going straight for the bathroom. Water was all over the tiled floor, the shower curtain yanked down. She was unconscious. There was vomit on the floor of the shower, and she was curled in a ball.

I quickly stepped in, hissing out a breath at the iciness of the water's temperature. I quickly turned it off and grabbed a towel, wrapping her unconscious body up in it.

"Fuck, baby, your skin is ice cold," I whispered. And judging by the vomit in the shower, she'd had a *bad* anxiety attack—probably a flashback judging by the shower curtain. I was all too familiar with those.

I stepped out of the shower and trudged into the bedroom. I was going to have to pay someone to come fix our carpet; it was soaked up until about halfway into the room, my boots making disgusting squelching noises as I moved toward the bed.

I quickly kicked them off and pulled off my socks, tossing them into the laundry basket. I covered her up with the blanket, adding two more from the closet. She would sleep for a while—hopefully long enough for me to clean up the bathroom and the bottom of the shower.

I set my boots on the porch to dry as I called Christian.

"Yeah?" he asked.

"She had a fucking anxiety attack," I told him. He cursed. "Judging by the state of the shower curtain, I'm also guessing that she had a flashback. I don't know what the fuck happened at that lunch but get Axel to find out. She's unconscious. I'm letting her rest. No sense in bringing her out of it right now."

"Is she okay?" he asked. Worry tinged his tone, and I knew it took everything in him to trust me to take care of her and not run home to deal with this himself.

I shrugged. "Physically, yes. But I don't know where she's going to be mentally when she wakes up."

"Let me know when she wakes up." He heaved a

breath. "I fucking hate this shit. I'll talk to Axel, and I'll let you know whatever I find out."

I hung up and walked to her car, shutting the door. A silver sports car pulled up to the house, Ally's dad behind the wheel. I crossed my arms over my chest, staring him down as he slid out of the car with Ally's purse in his hands.

"I came to give this back to Ally," he told me, seeming slightly intimidated by me.

Good. He fucking should have been. Because I was feeling goddamn volatile.

I walked down the porch and took her purse from him, opening it up to look inside. Her anxiety medication caught my eye. *Fuck.* We needed to make sure she had some at home and some with her at all times. Her phone was also at the bottom of the purse.

A home phone was next on my list of things to get.

"What the fuck happened?" I snarled at him as I shouldered the bag.

"Her mother showed up." I took a threatening step toward him. I had no fucking idea what game he was playing, but he was swimming in dangerous waters for fucking with my woman. He was nothing more than a tiny little fish, and I was the goddamn Megalodon. He held his hands up. "I swear, I haven't talked to her mother in weeks. I have no idea how she found out where we were at." I took a step back, clenching my jaw.

"Grace basically ended up telling everyone in that damn restaurant about the rape."

I couldn't stop myself, and even if I could, I probably wouldn't have.

I punched him in the face, sending him sprawling on his back in the dirt. I kneeled down and gripped his shirt in my fist, yanking him up so I could glare down at him. "A smart man would know that she probably has a fucking tracking device on you." He swallowed thickly, blood trickling down from his lips onto his neck. "Pretty goddamn convenient that she only pops up when you have a fucking meeting with Ally. Solve that shit and stay the fuck away from my woman until your shit with her bitch of a mother is solved."

I shoved him back onto the ground and stormed inside of the house, slamming the front door shut behind me. I locked it and set the alarm.

He may not have been at fault, but as a business-man, he should have known better, and he should have known what people were capable of if they were looking for information. And in this instance, I knew his wife was looking for a way to hurt Ally.

Fuck with Ally, and you've fucked with me.

32

ATTORNEY

Ally

I nervously applied a light layer of foundation to my face. Today, I was finally meeting with the attorney Julian had hired for me. It was kind of sudden. He had reached out two nights ago asking if I could come in to see him today.

So, here I was, a week after my flashback and anxiety attack in the shower, getting ready to see my attorney for the very first time.

"Babe, you know one of us can take off and go with you," Caiden spoke up as he appeared in the doorway of our bathroom.

I shook my head. "I can do this," I assured him. He frowned. I sighed as I turned to face him. "Caiden, trust me," I begged him. "If something happens or if I get overwhelmed, I promise that I'll call one of you," I assured him.

He arched an eyebrow at me. "Will you?" he asked. A frown pulled at my own lips. He'd been seriously worried about me ever since he found me unconscious in the shower. "You didn't last time, Ally."

My throat closed with tears. I hated being on the receiving end of his disappointment like this. "How many times do I have to say I'm sorry?" I asked him, my voice trembling.

He heaved a tired, worried sigh. "I don't want to hear sorry, Ally," he snapped at me. "I want to see you taking your anxiety seriously. The moment she walked into that restaurant, you should have walked right out, not even sparing her a second of your time. You could have crashed and died on the way home. Do you realize that?" he asked me. "Is that settling into your fucking brain?"

I flinched, a tear running down my cheek.

"Caiden," Christian snapped at his brother. Caiden swung his now angry eyes to Christian. "Go outside and take a fucking breather."

Caiden pushed off the wall and stormed out of the bedroom. I closed my eyes and turned away from Christian, trying not to cry. "I panicked that day," I whispered, knowing Christian would hear me. His arms slid around my waist from behind, and he pulled me back against him. "I wasn't—couldn't—fucking think," I blurted. "All I knew was that I *had to* get the fuck away. I couldn't stay there after she told *everyone* in that restaurant what happened to me—"

"Easy, baby," Christian soothed. He pressed a kiss to my shoulder. "Don't get worked up, okay?" He smoothed his hand over my belly. "Take a deep breath and slowly let it out. You scared the hell out of Caiden that day. I know you've apologized profusely, but see it from his point of view as well. Caiden has his own shit he suffers through. He went through hell overseas, and he came back home a different man because of it. You triggered something in him, too, beautiful." He pressed a kiss to the shell of my ear. "I'll talk to him, too, but what happened wasn't as easy for him as it was for me to move past."

"Okay," I whispered. I really hadn't thought of that. Caiden was never open with me about what he went through, and I respected his privacy enough to not dig. I knew he was on medication just like I was, and I knew that he saw a therapist twice a week. Other than that, no one touched on his mental health.

He pressed a kiss to my temple. "Finish getting ready."

Christian walked out of the bathroom, most likely

in search of his brother. Drawing in a steadying breath, I finished doing my make-up.

C

Caiden was waiting for me in the bedroom when I came out of the bathroom. I hadn't expected him, so I jumped in shock, my hand flying up to my chest to cover my racing heart.

"Um, hi," I squeaked in surprise.

He stood up from the bed and moved over to me. Cupping my face in his hands, he smoothed his lips over mine, taking my lips slowly at first before he deepened it, his tongue dancing with mine so erotically that every part of my body tingled, craving to be touched by him.

"I'm sorry," he told me when he pulled back. His eyes met mine, and he brushed his thumbs over my cheeks. "I shouldn't have been a dick. I should have been open with you from the very beginning about how much that shit scared me. So, I'm sorry." He pressed his lips to the tip of my nose. "I'll do my best to communicate better; I promise."

"Oh, Caiden," I whispered. I wrapped my arms around him. His arms fell around me as he squeezed me to him, burying his face in my hair. "It's okay. I'm sorry, too. I get so lost in my own misery that I forget that other people suffer through shit, too. So, I'm sorry. I didn't think about how badly it would affect you."

"It's alright, baby. Just please remember to call one of us if you have another attack again. Just please, for the love of God, do not fucking drive home."

"I won't. I promise," I assured him.

He tipped my chin up and kissed me again. "I have to go. Christian is waiting on you in the kitchen for breakfast. I love you."

I smiled up at him, the anxiety in my chest easing. "And I love you."

I nervously bounced my leg up and down as the attorney took a seat across from me in his huge conference room. Nerves made it hard to breathe, to think.

I hadn't done anything wrong, so why did I feel like I was the one in trouble?

"Okay. I'm going to break the worst news to you first," Mr. Taylor spoke. I jerkily nodded my head at him. "Randall pleaded not guilty at his court hearing. The trial is in a week. The judge in this town doesn't like sitting on cases like this."

I felt like throwing up. This couldn't be happening. Not only had he pleaded not guilty, but I would be facing him in court a lot sooner than I had been wanting.

"The second bad news is that every picture the police took of you and your old home will be blasted in court. It's the main bit of evidence we have against him."

I squeezed my eyes shut. This couldn't be happening. *Everyone* was now going to see what Randall had done and the damage it left behind on my body.

My throat was closing up, making it hard to breathe. I quickly dug into my purse for my medicine, but my hands were shaking too much. I sobbed, my chest constricting painfully, bringing black spots to my vision.

"Here. Take a deep breath," Mr. Taylor ordered. He had his phone to his ear, and he was holding my bottle of medicine that I kept dropping. He cradled his phone between his ear and shoulder and shook one of my tablets out, handing it to me with an open bottle of water.

"Christian Greene? Hey, this is Mr. Taylor—the attorney Julian hired for Ally. She just had a minor anxiety attack. I think someone should come sit with her while I go over everything that I need to go over."

A moment later, Mr. Taylor held his phone out to me. I shakily took it, holding it up to my ear. "Christian?" I whimpered. I squeezed my eyes shut, sucking in a sharp breath of air.

"Easy, my moon," he soothed. "Breathe. It's going to

be okay. I can't leave work. I have an appointment in ten minutes, and they're already out in the lobby." I sobbed. I wanted him with me. "Caiden just texted me back and said he's on his way. He's only five minutes from you, beautiful. Just keep taking deep breaths."

"I wish you could come," I whispered, my voice breaking.

"I know, baby." He sounded sad, and that tore at my heart. "I wish I could, too, but my patients picked up once Axel made me a permanent partner. I'm flooded right now."

"I know." My voice cracked. I was so happy for him —so happy that he had gotten such an amazing position with Axel. But on days like today, it sucked.

I needed his soothing presence, and I wasn't sure if Caiden and I were back on that level yet.

Caiden suddenly burst into the room, ignoring the receptionist that was shouting at him. "It's okay, Karla!" Mr. Taylor called out.

"Caiden's here," I told Christian.

Christian sighed in a mix of relief and exasperation. "The man has an issue with speeding," he grumbled, but I let out a watery giggle. "Let him take care of you, baby, and I'll take over this evening, okay? Just breathe. I love you."

"I love you, too," I croaked.

I hung up the phone and handed it back to Mr.

Taylor. Caiden kneeled in front of me and reached up to cup my cheeks. "Hey, baby," he soothed, his tone tender and soft. My bottom lip trembled. "It's going to be okay."

"The trial is in a week," I told him. "He pleaded not guilty. And Mr. Taylor said *all* of my pictures have to be shown."

"Breathe," Caiden ordered when I began to hyper-ventilate. "Look at me and just breathe."

I locked my eyes on his, calming my breaths. "Good girl," he praised. "You have to get through this, baby. I know it's hard. I know you don't want to; you just want to bury this in the back of your mind and never think about it again. I get that, and I understand it. But you *have* to do this. If you want to put Randall behind bars like he deserves, then you need to sit through this meeting with Mr. Taylor, and you need to soak in every word of advice that he gives you. *You* are the only person that can make Randall go away."

I nodded, my lips trembling. He leaned up and softly pressed his lips to mine for a moment before he took a seat next to me. Silently, he grabbed my hand in his and gave it a gentle squeeze. He leaned forward and shook hands with Mr. Taylor.

"Caiden Greene," he introduced himself. "I'm Christian's brother and her other boyfriend." My cheeks flamed red.

"Henry Taylor," Mr. Taylor introduced himself. "Thank you for coming. I really need to go over this with her, but I don't want to push her past her limits."

"No problem," Caiden told him. He looked over at me. "You've got this, darlin'. Just be strong."

Mr. Taylor leaned forward, bracing his elbows on his desk. "He has been assigned a state attorney, but unfortunately, this attorney knows his shit, and he's gotten people off scotch-free numerous times." Caiden squeezed my hand. I wanted to throw up. "But, lucky for you, I've gone against him numerous times, and he's always lost. But, my clients *have* to do what I advise them to do."

"Okay," I whispered, nodding my head. I tightened my hand around Caiden's. He lifted my hand to his lips to press a kiss on my knuckles.

"I need you to understand that his attorney is going to rip you apart." I flinched at the mere thought of it. Caiden tensed. "He's going to throw brutal questions at you, and he's going to try to make it seem like you're second-guessing yourself. That's where he trips people up at. Stick with what happened. Don't add unnecessary details. Leave the unnecessary details to me when I'm the one questioning you."

I nodded. My appointment with Mr. Taylor felt like it went on for hours, and more than a few times, we had to stop because the questions he was throwing at me were beginning to make me panic.

But Caiden was there the entire time, grounding me with him to keep me calm.

The day of the trial was going to be absolute hell and torture. And I wasn't ready to deal with it.

Christian

I'd been in a right fucking mood all damn day. I had wanted to be there for Ally at the attorney's office, but I *couldn't get* away from work—not unless it was an emergency, and since Caiden could go to her, I couldn't cancel my appointments.

I kicked my shoes off by the front door and slid my belt off as I walked into the bedroom, tossing it on the floor by the wall. Caiden was spooning Ally from behind, his face buried in her hair, his arms wound tightly around her, holding her to him.

I walked around the bed to my side, quickly pulling off my shirt and tossing it to the floor. Ally blankly stared at me, almost as if she had shut everything off—choosing to feel nothing instead of dealing with what was going on.

I grabbed her hands in mine and gently brushed my

thumbs over her knuckles. She slowly raised her eyes to meet mine, and like a dam suddenly gave in and collapsed, she burst into tears, her entire body shaking.

"You're going to see," she cried.

I quickly sat her up and drew her onto my lap, wrapping my body around hers. Caiden quietly left the room, knowing this was something I needed to do with her. "My moon, I don't give a fuck what those pictures show," I fiercely told her. "All that matters to me is *you*. I will love every scar that was left behind from that evening, and because you endured it and lived, I'll love you even more because you're so fucking strong." I leaned down and covered her lips with mine. "No amount of pictures is ever going to make me love you or crave you any less," I promised.

With that, I slowly began to strip her out of her clothes, pressing kisses to every single scar on her body, including her self-inflicted ones. And when I slid deep inside of her, I slowly and steadily rocked our bodies together, taking my time to remind her of how much she meant to me.

33

TRIAL

Ally

I nervously twisted my hands together as I stared out of the passenger side window at the looming courthouse in front of me. Christian put the car into park and gently hooked his index finger around my chin, pulling my head around to face him. "Remember that you're not alone in that room. He can't hurt you, beautiful. You're going to go in there, and you're going to put him behind bars. You've got this."

"I don't feel like I've got this," I openly admitted to him. His eyes softened. Tears blurred my vision. "I'm terrified."

My passenger door suddenly opened, and Caiden appeared there. I hadn't even realized that he had gotten out of the car. "Baby, I know that today is scary as fuck, but you've got this," he assured me. "After today— after you put that son of a bitch behind bars for a *long* time—Christian and I are going to take you home, and we're going to make sweet fucking love to you. Your brothers and Meghan are here to support you, as well as your dad. Today, you have a whole fucking army of people standing behind you." He tilted my chin up. "I want you to hold this head high and show that mother fucker that he couldn't break you. He fucking tried, but he failed because you, my woman, are a goddamn queen, you got me?"

My heart squeezed in my chest. "Okay," I whispered. I nodded. Christian leaned over and brushed his lips to my neck. "I can do this."

"Good girl," Caiden praised. "Now come on. Get your cute ass out of the car."

I slid out of the car, and he closed the door. He cradled my belly and leaned forward, pressing a soft kiss to my lips. "Chin up."

Christian grabbed my hand in his. "We're with you, beautiful. Remember your breathing techniques. Remember how to ground yourself when you begin feeling anxious."

"I'll do my best," I told him because trying my best was all I could do. "I'm not sure how easy that will be when I'm being questioned left and right."

Christian squeezed my hand. "Then I want you to find me and Caiden in that crowd, and I want you to focus on us. Use us to ground yourself if you can't use grounding techniques, okay?"

"Okay," I agreed. We came to a stop in front of my family and my attorney. Even Julian's parents had shown up to support me. Linda drew me into a warm, motherly hug. My throat closed up with tears, and I squeezed my eyes shut, desperately trying to keep from crying.

She smoothed her hand over my hair. "It's going to be okay, hun," she tried assuring me. "We're all here for you, okay? I know in my gut that this is the very last time you'll ever have to face that bastard."

I slowly drew back from her and sucked in a deep breath, trying to calm myself down so I wouldn't burst into tears. Jaxon hugged me next. "You're a strong girl, Ally. You always have been. I want you to show your strength in that courtroom, but I also want you to show your vulnerability, too. Let the judge and the jury see what that night did to you so they know that fucker is lying—let them see that he's guilty as fuck."

I nodded. The sound of motorcycles riding onto the courthouse lot reached my ears. Julian gently squeezed my shoulders. "Dad called in a couple of favors, and he got the local motorcycle crew to come in to support you." He looked over at Caiden. "He asked me if I had those kinds of connections—thought it might help you to know that you truly did have a small army standing behind you."

I burst into tears, unable to hold them back anymore. They were trying to make this day as easy as possible for me. "They believe me?" I blubbered.

Caiden cupped my damp cheeks in his hands and tilted my head back to look up at him. "Every single man in that MC believes what happened, baby." He drew me into his arms. "It's going to be okay. I need you to tilt your chin up for me."

I swiped at my cheeks. Christian came over and pressed a kiss to my temple. The president of the club walked over to me, holding his hand out for me to shake. I slowly placed my hand in his large, calloused one. He was a huge man with a beard that reached his belly. His hair was tied back into a low ponytail. "Tyler Jenkins," he introduced. "I'm the president. You're Ally, right?"

"Yes." I slowly dropped my hand back to my side. "Thank you for coming."

He nodded at me. "I promise it's not a problem. This is why my club was established."

Mr. Taylor walked over to me. "I want to go over a few more things with you—just last-minute details," he told me. "And I want to do a quick test run of all of the questions. Are you okay with that?"

"Is that really a good idea?" Axel voiced. "She's already going to have to face the questions in the courtroom. I don't think bringing forth an anxiety attack before she has to face him is going to be a good idea, Mr. Taylor. They exhaust her. She needs every bit of her strength to face that son of a bitch in a few minutes."

Mr. Taylor looked down at me. Christian's hand found mine, and he linked our fingers together. "Are you going to be okay with not going over the questions a second time?" he asked me.

I shrugged. "I don't think it's going to matter either way," I admitted. "I'm terrified to face him again."

"Okay. Only if you're sure."

I nodded. I wasn't keen on going through those questions again without it being necessary. I already knew that no matter how many times we went over the questions, I was going to lose my shit on that witness stand.

Meghan wrapped her arms around me. "Just breathe and remember how strong you are," she whispered.

Everyone kept saying that, but right then, I wasn't feeling very strong.

I felt like running.

Caiden and Christian both held my hands in theirs, offering me their strength and support as we stepped into the courtroom. They led me to the seat I was supposed to sit in next to Mr. Taylor. With whispered words of encouragement, they left me alone with Mr. Taylor and walked to their seats directly behind me.

My hands were trembling. Mr. Taylor looked over at me. "They're about to bring Randall into the room," he warned me, his voice low.

I swallowed nervously and nodded my head. A side door opened, and Randall walked into the room in an orange jumpsuit, his arms cuffed in front of him, his ankles shackled together.

He looked up at me, his dark eyes clashing with mine. My heart squeezed in my chest, and I couldn't remember how to breathe anymore. I dropped into the chair behind me, my hand gripping my shirt. Hot tears slid down my cheeks.

"Baby, look at me," Caiden ordered, his hands suddenly grasping my face. I whimpered and slowly opened my eyes, locking them on his. "Breathe," he ordered. "Breathe, baby. He's got a cop on either side of him, and there's two over here by you. He can't hurt you anymore. You're safe."

I slowly nodded my head, dragging air into my lungs again. I hadn't even realized the judge had stepped into the courtroom, but her voice suddenly sounded in my ears. "Someone get Rosco from the back and bring him up here to her. Young man, you stay with that young lady until the support animal is brought up here to her."

"Yes, your honor," Caiden replied.

He gently took my hands in his. My hands were shaking, but he gently squeezed his warm fingers around mine, grounding me and steadying me.

"You did good, baby. I'm proud of you." He brushed his lips to my cheek. "Continue to be strong, okay?"

They brought the dog to me, and Caiden gently placed my left hand in the dog's fur. He pressed a kiss to my forehead before he walked back to his seat.

Mr. Taylor kept me informed of what was happening when I got slightly confused in some parts as the judge spoke. Randall was called to the stand first. I dug my fingers into Rosco's fur, and he settled his head on my lap, the weight and the heat from him settling my nerves some.

"Mr. Farren, can you recount to the court what happened that evening?" Randall's attorney asked.

Randall shrugged. "I came over to her house to apologize for my behavior at the pharmacy. I treated her horribly, and I wanted to apologize for my actions. I've always loved Ally, and I was hurt that she was with another man."

I shut my eyes, my hands beginning to shake. The

dog nudged my other hand, forcing me to pet him. "I didn't even get a chance to apologize. The moment she saw me, she began crying about how much she missed me and how things went so wrong. Before I knew it, we were ripping each other's clothes off."

"So, the sex was consensual."

"Yes," Randall lied. I swallowed vomit as I stared at the wooden table in front of me.

"So, the injuries she sustained—you have no idea what those are from."

"I have no clue," Randall answered, sounding completely sincere.

My attorney questioned him a few minutes later, but Randall's story stayed the same. I hated that he sounded so sincere and truthful. I could feel some of the jury members looking at me as if I were nothing but a liar.

"Your honor, I would like to call Ally Johnson to the stand," Randall's attorney spoke.

The judge looked at me. There was something in her eyes that I couldn't quite identify. She nodded once. I slowly stood up from my chair, and Rosco obediently followed at my side, taking a seat beside me on the witness stand.

"Ms. Johnson, you're claiming that Randall Farren broke into your home and not only beat you but also raped you. Is that correct?"

"Yes," I spoke, my voice shaking.

"But isn't it also true that you and Mr. Farren used to date back when you were in high school?"

I drew in a deep, shaky breath. "Yes."

"Is it not true that you were both deeply in love, but fell apart on a misunderstanding?"

"No," I told him. I tightened my hands on Rosco. "We were not in love, and it was not a misunderstanding when we broke up."

"Please elaborate," his attorney ordered, looking at me like I was a good-for-nothing liar trying to get an "innocent" man into trouble.

I sucked in a deep breath, digging my fingers into Rosco's fur. "I caught him sleeping with my best friend who is also his stepsister. He told everyone I mistook him for his twin brother, but he and his twin do not look alike. I know what I saw that day, and it was also *Randall's* voice that shouted at me to, and I quote, 'get the fuck out and go home.'"

"So, you're claiming that Mr. Farren's story is incorrect."

I nodded. "Yes."

"So, are you also claiming that you did not invite Mr. Farren into your home? That you did not answer the door for him?"

"That's two questions, sir," I responded, just as Mr.

Taylor had instructed me to do. My voice wobbled, but I held strong.

He clenched his jaw, hating he couldn't trick me into answering something wrong. "Did you answer the door for Mr. Farren?"

"Yes."

"Did you invite him into your home?"

I shook my head. "No."

"How did he get inside?"

My hands were beginning to sweat, Randall's enraged face that evening flashing into my mind. "He barged his way into the house."

Pictures suddenly flashed up onto a screen. I stared in horror at my uncovered body, the most important parts of me being covered. Caiden was holding my hand. I was crying, my face beaten and swollen. Blood was smeared all over my skin, and I was bleeding from my bite marks and scratches. Handprints were wrapped around my neck, already bruising to a dark color.

My chest began to get tight. I looked out at Christian, but he was staring at the screen. Caiden shook his head at me, trying to keep me with him, but Christian had already seen the damage.

I was ruined in his eyes.

I whimpered, no air making it into my lungs. I squeezed my eyes shut, the image of Randall's blurry face leaning over me as he smeared his blood-covered hand down my face before roughly biting into my shoulder, drawing blood.

I screamed. Warm hands grabbed mine and arms wrapped around my shoulders. I thrashed, a terrified whimper falling from my lips. "Open your eyes. Goddammit, baby, open your fucking eyes."

I gagged. Then, everything went dark.

Caiden

"Stop!" I shouted at the cop who was trying to barge his way in. "Jesus Christ, she's just having a flashback," I snapped at him. "She's not a threat."

She was unconscious now, her body slumped in Christian's arms. The judge slammed her gavel, silencing the room. She looked down at me and Christian. "Does she need an ambulance?"

I shook my head. "No, your honor. She'll come out of it in a few minutes."

"Your honor, I think the jury and I are ready to go convene," a man announced over the commotion.

She waved her hand. "An hour-long break begins now." She slammed her gavel again and stood up. "Get her into some fresh air and out of this courtroom," she ordered.

Christian swept Ally's unconscious form into his arms and carried her down the steps. I glared at Randall from across the room as his attorney quietly spoke to him.

He clenched his jaw. When he had seen Christian earlier, he had smirked. But I guess I was a bit more intimidating than my brother—not to mention bigger. And I held no qualms about sitting in a jail cell.

Axel gripped my shoulder, drawing my eyes away from Randall. "Come on," he told me. "I know what's running through your head, but this isn't the time nor the place for it. My sister needs us—she needs *you*, Caiden. Don't do dumb shit today."

I drew in a deep breath and followed him out of the door. Christian was sitting on a bench outside. Meghan was holding a fast food cup, and Ally was slowly drinking whatever was in the cup through a straw.

She looked up at me. There was so much pain and sadness in her eyes that it tore at my goddamn soul.

"He still loves you," I told her. Christian tightened his arms around her and pressed his lips to her temple. "That picture didn't change anything for him, baby."

"I know," she croaked, her voice hoarse.

God, the sound that had ripped from her throat when she screamed was still ringing in my mind. It was a sound I would never fucking forget. There had been so much terror, so much pain in that single sound.

And then the cops? They thought she was a fucking threat and were ready to detain her. It took everything in me not to lay one of the mother fuckers flat out on the floor.

I sat down and draped her legs across my lap. Taking the cup from Meghan, I held it up for Ally. "What do you think is going to happen?" Ally asked us.

I gripped her chin, locking her eyes on mine. "One way or the other, baby, justice will get served," I promised her.

She frowned. "How?"

"Because if this court doesn't do it for you," Christian spoke up, drawing her eyes up to him, "I swear to you, Caiden and I will make sure he can *never* touch you again."

34

VERDICT

Caiden

Ally was now sitting on the bench between me and Christian. She was leaning forward, her elbows resting on her knees with the heels of her hands pressed to her forehead. Christian was rubbing her back, giving her a little time to gather herself back together. I knew she was exhausted. Panic attacks and flashbacks sucked the energy out of you.

"What if they find him not guilty? I had an entire anxiety attack in there." She suddenly sat up, her face scrunching up as she closed her eyes. "God, they saw that I really am just a fucking lunatic."

"Hey," I quietly snapped. She turned to look at me. "Don't do that shit, babe."

"What shit?" she retorted, suddenly getting angry. I sighed and closed my eyes, leaning my head back, scrubbing my hands down my face.

"Fucking putting yourself down." I turned my head, narrowing my eyes at her. Her eyes flared with anger. Good. If she needed to be angry to make it through the last little bit of this court session, then I would piss her the fuck off.

I could take care of her when we got home, but the anxiety attacks she'd been having? They were violent, and each one scared the absolute fuck out of me. I literally had to tap back into my military training so that I wouldn't end up in the same damn position she was in.

Christian? He was a natural at this shit with her. He easily went through the motions of getting her out of the triggering situation and calming her down.

I wasn't good at this shit, though I tried my damnest for her.

"You're a dick," she spat at me.

I arched an eyebrow at her. Christian remained silent, and with one glance at his face, I knew he was on the same page that I was. Piss her off—make her angry. Because if she had another anxiety attack, I wasn't sure if she would come out of it unscathed.

"Baby, you haven't seen me be a dick yet," I warned her. "Right now, I'm being honest with you. You don't need to be putting yourself down, especially today of all fucking days. You need every bit of strength that you can find within you because in about," I looked at my watch, "fifteen minutes, you're going to have to go back in that courtroom as they announce whether or not he's guilty." She swallowed thickly, fear flashing in her eyes. I cupped her cheek and brushed my thumb over her cheekbone. "Right now, I need you to remember every single reason you're strong and why you can make it through this."

Christian brushed his lips to her temple. "Give me one reason you're strong," he commanded, his voice gentle and soothing.

She nervously chewed on her bottom lip. I leaned forward and gently pulled her bottom lip from between her teeth. "I never gave up despite how hard it got."

I grabbed her hand in mine. "Good girl," I praised. Her eyes brightened at the pride in my voice.

"Give me another reason," Christian coaxed.

She tightened her hand around mine. "I survived that evening," she whispered. I brushed my lips to her neck. "I didn't let him break me."

"No, you didn't, and *that* is what you need to remember in that courtroom," Christian told her. She looked over at him, her eyes seeking his assurance. He gave her a soft smile. "So, when you step back inside that building, and you see him again, I want you to tilt your chin up and remember that he tried to break you, but you're unbreakable, my moon. I want you to glow despite how terrified you feel. When he's no longer in your presence, you can fall apart. Caiden and I are going to be there to catch you, and I'm going to breathe life back into you as he sparks that fire inside of your soul."

"But while you're in his presence, you show him that fucking strong woman, and I want you to be so fucking strong and resilient that you piss him off," I told her.

She drew in a deep breath—almost as if she were steeling herself against what was to come—and then she nodded at me, that fire burning in her eyes for a split moment.

I gripped her jaw and pulled her lips to mine. Her hand came up to rest on my chest as I coaxed her lips apart, teasing her tongue with mine for a beat before I pulled back. "That's my girl."

Ally

I nervously stood beside Mr. Taylor when the officer in the courtroom announced the judge's arrival back into the room. She took her seat, and once she did, I dropped heavily back into my chair.

I can do this, I reminded myself.

Glow despite how terrified you feel. Christian's words were ringing in my head. I wiped my sweaty palms on my slacks, wishing I could feel as strong as my men thought I was.

Right then, I felt weak and helpless.

What if he walked free? What if they found him innocent after all?

Men walked away from this sort of thing all of the time, and the victim was left living her life in fear all while everyone around her always called her a liar and judged her for having the guts to stand up and speak out.

"Jury?" the judge asked, turning her attention to them.

The man from before stood up. "We find the defendant guilty of all charges," his voice boomed around the room.

Relief flooded my veins. I burst into tears and dropped my face into my hands. He was really going away. He wasn't walking out of this courtroom a free man.

I looked up at the judge, and her kind eyes met mine, understanding residing in their depths. She nodded once at me before she turned her attention to Randall and his attorney. "Mr. Randall Farren, you are being charged with criminal destruction of property to the second degree, rape, assault causing bodily harm, stalking, and harassment." Randall's face turned red with rage, and he clenched his fists on top of the table. I flinched, remembering all too well the damage those hands were capable of doing.

"You are hereby sentenced to thirty years in prison with a chance of parole after twenty. You will see a counselor while you are in prison. I am also placing you on the state's list of sexual offenders." She slammed her gavel. We all stood up from our chairs as she stood, but she walked over to me instead of leaving the courtroom.

She grabbed my hands in hers. They shook in her grasp, but she gave me a warm, kind smile. "So many victims never show up for their court dates against their abusers, and because of that, so many abusers walk free." She gently squeezed my hands. "I want to person-ally thank you for coming in here and facing your fears. He's going away for a long time, and he is one less person that will hurt someone else."

A tear slid down my cheek. "Thank you," I whispered.

She smiled. "No, hun, thank you. Now, you go and you live a happy, fulfilling life. That man can never hurt you again."

She walked away, heading towards the back. I looked over at Randall. His angry eyes met mine. Swal-lowing down my fear, I tilted my chin up at him. Warm, familiar, calloused hands slid over my shoulders.

"There she is," he breathed in my ear. "He may have hurt you physically, baby, but he could never destroy what's inside of you."

I watched as Randall got pulled out of the side door. Only then did I collapse into my chair again and burst into tears, loud sobs wracking my chest. Both of my men wrapped their arms around me.

"You did it, baby," Christian praised. "I'm so fucking proud of you." He cupped my face in his hands and kissed me, my tears tasting salty on my lips. "I knew you could do it. God, I'm *so* fucking proud of you."

I collapsed against his chest all while Caiden held my hands. Christian tightly wound his arms around me, his right hand holding the back of my head. He pressed his lips to my hair. "So goddamn proud of you, my moon."

35

POOL PARTY

Ally

C aiden held my hand in his, slowly bringing me to a stop before we could ascend the porch to my brother's house.

After Randall was sentenced to prison last week, Julian and Axel both decided they wanted to do a small, family get-together to celebrate Randall finally being out of my life for good. So, a week and a half later, here we all were. I could already hear music playing in the backyard and Holden's squeals of laughter.

"What's wrong?" I asked him.

Caiden drew in a deep breath. Christian's arms slid around me from behind, and he rested his chin on my shoulder. "I invited the guy I've been seeing over to meet you," he told me. I frowned, unease filling my gut. He grabbed my other hand and gently squeezed my fingers. "Baby, hear me out," he pleaded. I nodded. "He's sweet, and he's funny. He's eager to meet you." Caiden smiled a little. "I talk about you nonstop." He laughed.

My cheeks burned red. "Does he make you happy?" I asked Caiden.

He nodded. "I haven't put a label on us yet. You're my number one priority—you and this baby." My heart swelled in my chest. I didn't deserve a man like him. "I have to make sure that he can get along with you and that he can deal with me having a family that doesn't include him before I label anything."

I leaned up and softly pressed my lips to his. "Then, I'll meet him," I assured him.

Caiden smiled at me. "Really?" I nodded. He leaned down and kissed me again. "You're glowing, baby, and it's fucking beautiful."

My cheeks darkened again. Christian pressed his lips to my temple. "Just like the moon." I turned my head to catch his lips with my own. He growled softly, deepening it for a beat before he slowly pulled back from me. "Come on. Let's get your pretty ass inside so you can change into your swimsuit and get in the pool."

Meghan instantly wrapped me up in a hug when I stepped into the living room. I laughed and hugged her back, all of the tension in my shoulders leaving now that I was wrapped up in her sisterly, trusting embrace.

"You're getting in the pool, right?" she asked me once she pulled back from the hug. She placed her hands on my belly with a wide smile. "I can't wait to see this cute little belly," she gushed.

I laughed. "I would if I had a swimsuit that still fit," I told her. I frowned. "Besides, I'm not sure how I feel about showing off my skin," I told her honestly, my voice lowering. "Caiden invited the guy he's been seeing over to meet me. I don't want to ruin what they may have together. He'll stare; it's inevitable, and Caiden can't stand it when people stare at my scars."

"Hun, your scars don't define you. And if he can't be a decent enough human being to turn his eyes away from your body, then Caiden deserves better." She shrugged. "Come on. I have a cute, black bikini that you can wear, and it'll look amazing on you."

"I don't know..." I trailed off, completely unsure. My family had seen the worst of it—saw the picture when they put it up in the courtroom. But Caiden's 'boyfriend' hadn't seen me yet.

"You'll look amazing," she tried assuring me as she gently pulled me up the stairs behind her. I sighed, knowing I wasn't getting out of this. "I have scars, too," she gently reminded me. I swallowed thickly. "It still affects me sometimes, but I've learned to ignore everyone's stares. I have two great men standing at my back, ready to protect me if need be. Their opinion of me is all that matters." She turned to look at me over her shoulder. "And Christian's and Caiden's opinions should be all that matters to you, too."

We stepped into her room. She pulled out the bikini she mentioned and handed it to me. Drawing in a calming breath, I walked into her huge bathroom and quickly changed. It fit me perfectly, which I was happy about. And despite the scars covering my skin, I did look really cute, shockingly.

But the scars ruined everything.

I opened the door. "Meghan, I'm not sure—"

Christian and Caiden were both standing in the middle of the bedroom, and their eyes instantly landed on me. My cheeks flamed red as they both ran their eyes over me.

"Jesus Christ," Caiden finally growled.

Christian moved first, his hands sliding over my belly before he leaned down and took my lips in a slow, deep kiss. I moaned, my hands sliding over his biceps and up his shoulders, drawing him closer to me.

"Not now," Caiden warned. I whined when Christian slowly pulled his lips from mine. He pecked my nose. Caiden gently pulled me away from Christian with a shake of his head. "She looks hot as fuck—I know." I covered my face with my hands, making both men laugh. "But Meghan is expecting her downstairs, and she's going to come up here if we don't have her downstairs in the next ten minutes."

"I'm going to be sporting a raging hard-on for the next few hours," Christian grumbled.

"We'll have blue balls together, bro," Caiden told him.

"Oh, my God," I whispered in mortification. "Can you two *not*?"

Caiden and Christian both laughed before Caiden pressed his lips to my temple. "Out," he gently ordered with a tap to my ass. "You look hot as fuck, and it's going to be a fucking task for me and Christian not to take you over and over in that pool." I didn't think it was possible for my cheeks to get any redder. "Go."

Snatching the towel from Christian that he held out to me, I quickly wrapped it around me as I left the room, leaving my two laughing men behind me.

Caiden suddenly spun me around on my float. I squealed, reaching out to grasp onto his upper arms, my eyes wide with shock. He laughed before he leaned down to kiss me. "Michael just texted me—said he's here. I'm going to go meet him out front."

I nodded at him, playfully waving him away. He

grabbed my hand and pressed a kiss to my palm before shooting me a playful wink. I watched, a sigh leaving my mouth, as he lifted himself out of the pool, every muscle in his back and arms flexing.

"He is so fine," I whispered.

Christian barked out a laugh as he appeared in front of me, blocking my view of Caiden. "I'm beginning to think you have a favorite, my moon."

I blushed and grabbed his hand in mine, using it to pull me closer to him. "No favorites," I told him with a smile on my face. "I'd stare at you just as much if you were to flex your muscles like he just did."

Christian rolled his eyes at me before he leaned down to peck my lips. "You're so fucking adorable, beautiful." He jerked his head in the direction of the grill. "Food is done, and you need to eat."

With an annoyed huff of air, I slid off of the float. I squeaked in shock, not realizing that I wasn't where I could touch, but Christian quickly caught me and lifted me up. I wrapped my legs around his waist and pressed a kiss to his cheek, a wide smile on my face.

"My hero," I whispered in his ear.

He playfully nipped at my earlobe. "Keep on, and I'll turn into a fucking villain when I get between those thick ass thighs."

"Christian!" I exclaimed, smacking his arm. He laughed, crouching down to set me on my feet. I stood on the steps and placed my hands on my hips, playfully narrowing my eyes at him. "I'm going to tell Caiden."

He playfully glared at me. "You're going to what?" he asked, daring me to repeat it.

I stuck my tongue out at him. "I'm going to tell Caiden," I retorted. I shoved him, and in his shock, he fell back into the water. I laughed, knowing that if he'd actually been paying attention, I would have never accomplished that.

Caiden shook his head at me as he stepped out onto the back patio with a guy slightly behind him. The guy, who I assumed was Michael, had a lanky kind of build with a light, blonde dusting of hair along his jaw. His hair was the same color as his beard. Caiden easily dwarfed him; he couldn't have been any taller than five-eight or five-nine.

Caiden cupped my face in his hands and leaned down, kissing me softly. "Stop teasing us," he mumbled against my lips.

I giggled when I felt Christian wrapping my towel around my body. "She'll pay when we get her little ass home," Christian told his brother.

I tightened the towel around me as Christian held his hand out to Michael. "Christian Greene. I'm Caiden's little brother."

They shook hands. "Michael Cannon."

Caiden grabbed my hand in his, leading me just a

little bit closer. He gently squeezed my hand in his when I slightly tensed, suddenly acutely aware of the scars that covered me, but Michael's eyes didn't stray beyond my face.

"This is our girlfriend, Ally Johnson," Caiden introduced us. He wrapped his arm around my waist, tugging me against his side, his hand cradling the side of my belly. "She's currently four months pregnant."

"Ally, get your ass over here!" Axel yelled. I looked at him over my shoulder. He was holding up a plate with a burger made to perfection—just how I liked it. "Your burger is going to get cold!"

I leaned up and pressed my lips to Christian's cheek and squeezed Caiden's hand. "My brother is summoning me."

Christian grabbed my hand in his. "Come on, beautiful." He looked at his brother. "Go ahead and spend some time with him."

Caiden looked conflicted, his eyes flickering to me. I grabbed his hand again and gave it a gentle squeeze, shooting him a reassuring smile. "Once I eat, then we can all chill in the pool again," I promised him. "But don't let him feel left out."

He nodded. After pressing a kiss to my forehead, he turned to Michael. My eyes locked on his face, and a shiver of self-disgust crawled down my spine when I found him staring at the self-inflicted scars on my arms.

I quickly turned away, stepping closer to Christian. He softly growled. "He fucking stares at you again, and I'll make sure he knows just how fucking ruthless both Caiden and I can be over you," he quietly warned.

I gently squeezed his hand. "Not today," I begged him. I looked up at him, our eyes locking. "Please, Christian."

He sighed. "I'll do my best," he promised.

That was all I could ask for.

Christian, Axel, and Julian were talking about football, and Caiden and Michael were sitting on the edge of the pool. I was almost asleep, my head resting against Christian's side as he held my float, keeping an eye on me to make sure I didn't fall off.

Calloused hands slid over my belly. I slowly opened my eyes, locking them on Caiden's. He smiled at me before he leaned over and pecked my cheek.

"Hey, sleeping beauty," he greeted. I sleepily smiled at him. "You feeling okay?"

I nodded. "The food just made me tired." I yawned. "Meghan went to go breastfeed, so I decided to take a small nap."

"I swear to fucking God, Caiden, if Michael doesn't stop staring at her every time he thinks none of us are watching, I'm going to fucking hospitalize him," Christian suddenly growled.

I lifted my head, frowning. That time, I hadn't felt him staring, though Christian was right. He'd been staring an awful lot today. "You got a fucking staring problem, kid?" Julian suddenly barked. I sat up on my float, alarmed. Nothing ever went well when Julian got involved.

"Sorry," Michael grumbled, looking away.

"I've told you numerous times not to fucking stare at her," Caiden growled as he moved away from me. I reached out to grab him, but he slipped away too quickly. Nerves began to riot in my belly. "How many fucking times did I tell you before you came here *not* to stare at my fucking woman?"

"Look, it's just—it's hard not to." Michael quickly got up from the ground. "It's not every day that—"

"It's common human decency!" Caiden barked. He shoved him toward the door. Christian settled his hands on my thighs, forcing me to stay on my float. "We're done, you hear me? And you're fucking leaving."

The back door slammed shut after them. I cringed. "I knew it," I whispered. "I knew I would be the one to break them apart."

"No, my moon," Christian soothed. He cupped my cheeks in his hands. "Caiden warned him numerous times that you have scars and not to stare at you. That man is even more protective of you than I am. You did nothing wrong."

I shook my head. "Christian, Caiden actually liked him." I frowned.

Christian shrugged. "So? Caiden *loves* you, beautiful. Every time Michael started staring at you, you tensed up, and you started drawing into yourself. You've been doing so damn good all day. You've been cheerful, and you've been happy. Caiden and I? This has been one of the best fucking days of our lives because you're fucking glowing, baby girl."

I squeaked in shock when Caiden's hand suddenly wrapped around my throat from behind. He tilted my head back, forcing our eyes to lock. "I know I don't hear you doubting yourself again," he rumbled, his chest vibrating against my back.

I swallowed beneath his rough palm. "I'm sorry," I blurted.

"For?" he asked me, not removing his hand from my neck. Christian squeezed my thighs. How the fuck was I getting turned on right now?

"For breaking you two up."

Caiden growled, his hand tightening just a little bit. I bit my lip, barely resisting the urge to moan. His eyes darkened. Christian's hands slid up a little further on my thighs, his thumbs grazing the sensitive areas on the soft, inner flesh of my legs.

"Don't," Caiden warned me. "You are my beginning and my end. No one will ever come before you. Babe, all I want a guy for is some hot anal sex." My breath hitched in my throat. Caiden smirked, a knowing look flashing through his eyes. "But you, baby? I want it all with you. Michael doesn't mean shit to me."

"Anal sex?" I squeaked, still stuck on that.

Caiden huskily laughed before he leaned down and pressed his lips to mine. "One day," he promised.

Oh, boy.

36

TOGETHER

Ally

D r. Gresham met me in the lobby with a warm smile on his face. I returned it before I stood up from my chair, a yawn falling from my lips. I blushed immediately afterward as I walked toward him.

"Sorry if I yawn a lot through our session," I apologized once I reached him. We began walking toward the garden out behind the center. "It's my normal nap time."

He laughed. "You're glowing again, Ally." I tucked my hair behind my ear. "You've come such a long way these last few months, and I'm extremely proud of you as both your doctor and a friend that you've stuck with your treatment plan and continued to stay determined to grow and heal."

"It hasn't been easy," I admitted.

He pushed open the back door, allowing me to slip through. "No, it hasn't," he agreed. The door fell back shut behind him as he walked out onto the brick path. "But you persevered, and you continued to stay strong even on the really dark days." We began to walk down the worn path. "Ally, you've come so far from the very first day you ever came to this center."

"I was a hopeless cause back then," I muttered. And I really was. There was no helping me back then until I wanted the help. And the first time I was put in this center, I wanted nothing to do with doctors, medication, or family.

"No," he disagreed. "Because if you were, you wouldn't be standing here today, preparing to become a mother, and standing strong despite all of the demons in your life that tried to tear you down."

He stopped near a bench, and I eagerly dropped down onto it, my feet already beginning to hurt and swell. My men were going to have my ass later for not drinking enough damn water so the swelling would stay down.

"When I first met you, Ally, you were a self-destructive mess, and you hated everyone that just wanted to help you. You've had your ups and downs since then, but I feel like you're finally on the right track to being healthy again." He looked over at me. "But, we need to talk about the trial and your mother."

I sighed. We hadn't had our normal sessions the week before due to Randall's trial. So, we agreed to resume our normal therapy sessions this week.

"I had some bad anxiety attacks last week," I confessed to Dr. Gresham. I frowned. "They were so bad that I blacked out, and I suffered flashbacks with them. The first time, I was supposed to be eating lunch with my dad, but then my mother showed up." I rubbed my chest when it began to ache. "She blurted to *everyone* in that restaurant that I was lying about being raped."

Dr. Gresham stayed silent, doing what he did best— listening to me. "So, I panicked and rushed out to my car, and I stupidly drove home, but I couldn't stay there. I felt unsafe." A tear slid down my cheek, and I reached up to swipe it away, sucking in a large, deep breath. "I was getting a shower when it got really bad. I had a flashback, and I guess I hyperventilated to the point that I blacked out. Caiden found me in the shower when he got home from work."

"Let's talk about this one first," Dr. Gresham spoke up, stopping me from moving on to my next anxiety attack. "I just want to touch base on your mother for a moment." I nodded, showing him that I was listening.

"One day, your mother is going to reach out to you to mend your relationship. This is inevitable," he warned me when I shook my head. I sighed. He didn't know my mother like I did, but I continued to listen to what Dr. Gresham had to say anyway. "When she does, Ally, I want you to sit on that decision for a while and decide for yourself if it's truly healthy or not, and whether or not you can handle a relationship with your mother."

I nodded. "I don't think I could ever allow her back into my life." I shrugged. "Or, if I do, it won't be anytime soon. It'll be *years* down the road before that happens."

"And that's okay. It's okay to block your parents out for however long you need to, even if that time is forever. You have an obligation to yourself first. You have to take care of yourself before you can start taking care of anyone around you."

"Boundaries," I confirmed.

He nodded, a proud smile tilting his lips. "That's right—boundaries." He gently squeezed my shoulder. "Continue on with what you were telling me."

"I had another anxiety attack on the day that I met with the attorney for the first time." I blew out a shaky breath. That fear that Randall might walk free still slithered through my veins, but I reminded myself that he was locked up—sentenced to thirty years with a chance of parole only after he had served twenty. He was locked up for a long time. He couldn't touch me—not anymore.

"I remembered my medicine that time, though Mr. Taylor had to help me get the bottle open. I was shaking too badly to do it myself."

"You need to talk to your pharmacist about putting your emergency anxiety medication into a non-safety-cap container," Dr. Gresham spoke up.

I nodded. "I'll do that," I told him since I seriously had never thought about requesting that. I'd never had to use them before.

"Continue."

"I got through the rest of that somewhat okay for the most part. Caiden showed up to sit with me for the remainder of the meeting once Mr. Taylor called Christian." I sighed. "Christian couldn't leave work."

"Pause," Dr. Gresham spoke up. I looked over at him. "I imagine you wanted Christian because he has a way of speaking to you when you're in that kind of state, correct?" I nodded. "Let's talk about the difference between Christian and Caiden for a moment, and I'm going to give you my honest opinion."

Wasn't sure if I was ready to hear this, but Dr. Gresham was always helpful, and I trusted him. "Okay."

"Caiden was probably best in that situation." I frowned, not understanding why. "And here's why I think that. Christian is soothing—perfect for a therapist and someone dealing with the aftermath of an episode like you had. But when someone with anxiety drops into a panic attack, they need someone to help snap them out of it, and that's where Caiden steps in for you. He's soothing in his own way, but he's also firm, and he has a different way of making you listen to him when you're having an anxiety attack than Christian does."

"Wow," I breathed. I looked over at Dr. Gresham. "He does," I realized, remembering all those times Caiden had pissed me off or said something I didn't want to hear. Dr. Gresham smiled. "I just—Caiden can be so...blunt." I shrugged. "I don't really know how to put it. He's not a gentle kind of person. I mean, he can be, but it's definitely not in his nature. Even at the court-house, he snapped at me for having so many doubts."

"And where was Christian during that time?"

"Next to me," I informed Dr. Gresham. "But he stayed silent."

"Because Christian knows that sometimes, you need that harshness from Caiden. It keeps you grounded, and it lights a fire in your soul that you're missing during hard times. Caiden just wants to see you continue fighting, Ally. But he loves you. Sometimes, that love isn't always what you want, but it is what you need. Remember that."

I stayed silent for a moment, thinking over all of the times Caiden had been a bit harsher with me than I had wanted, but he had always soothed me at the same time, somehow always clicking my mind back into place where it needed to be.

"Tell me about the trial," Dr. Gresham prompted.

"It was nerve-wracking. But I was mostly okay until I had to get on the witness stand." Vomit rose in my throat, but I swallowed it down. That day still fucked with me sometimes. "When they showed the picture of my body, I lost it. I went straight into a flashback, and all I remember is passing out and waking up on Christian's lap outside on a bench."

"How did you feel when you came to?"

"Like shit," I told him honestly. "My head hurt. I was still shaking a little bit, and I was fucking terrified that Randall would walk free all because I couldn't control my breakdown in the courtroom—that the jury would think I was a nutcase and had made the entire thing up."

"But they had pictures as proof of what happened to you," Dr. Gresham reminded me.

I shrugged. "I wasn't thinking of that," I told him honestly. "I was just terrified that I would forever have to live in fear because I hadn't been enough to get Randall locked away."

"But he is now," Dr. Gresham reminded me. "You did it, Ally. Despite how terrifying it was for you, not to mention draining, you did it. You got him locked away, and he will *never* hurt you or another woman ever again."

I laughed and swatted Caiden's hand away from my plate when he tried to grab one of my fries. He smirked at me before he leaned over and lightly pressed his lips to mine before he sat back up straight in his chair, stuffing one of my fries in his mouth.

"You're a dick," I grumbled.

He laughed. Christian lightly smacked him on the back of his head as he came to the table and sat on the other side of me with his plate of fries and a burger. "Leave her food alone, Caiden."

Caiden smirked. "And miss out on annoying the fuck out of her? Hell no."

He reached for another fry, and I grabbed a fork off the table, narrowing my eyes at him, silently daring him to grab another fry. "I will send you to the hospital," I warned him.

His eyes flashed, darkening to an almost black color. "I've got a thing for pain, baby," he huskily warned me.

My hand loosened around the fork, my breath hitching in my throat. Christian growled and grabbed my chair, yanking it closer to his. "She needs to eat, Caiden. For the love of God, stop turning her on."

My cheeks darkened. Julian barked out a laugh when he stepped into the dining room. Axel pressed a kiss to the top of my head before he passed me on his way to my seat.

"Women's pregnancy hormones are fucking insane," Julian warned Christian. "I don't give a fuck how tired women get—they'll find energy for sex somehow."

"Oh, my God," I whispered in mortification, reaching up to cover my face with my hands.

A round of laughter went up around the table. My dad stepped into the room with Lana on his hip. She was holding a french fry in her hand, making a mushy mess out of it.

Caiden gently squeezed my thigh and put a fry on my plate to replace the one he took. I smiled over at him. "I have an announcement to make," Dad spoke up, drawing everyone's eyes to him. Christian wrapped an arm around my shoulder as he popped a fry in his mouth. Meghan took Lana from him and set her in her high chair with some baby finger foods for her to munch on.

"What's that?" Axel asked, dropping into his seat at the table.

"The divorce has been finalized." My eyes widened in shock. "Your mother and I are now completely divorced, and she has been cut off from all of my money and my accounts."

"Holy shit," Axel blurted, looking as shocked as I felt. "Congrats, Dad."

My dad looked at me. I quickly stood up from my chair and rushed around the table, launching myself into his arms. He hugged me tightly. "She can't hurt you anymore, Ally," my dad promised me. "I'm sorry I wasn't a better father to you growing up, but I'm going to do my best to make up for all of those years I let you down."

I burst into tears, so happy that one of my parents finally gave a damn about me.

Caiden was out on another date later that night, and I was resting with Christian on the couch, the two of us watching a sappy romance movie. His hand was rubbing light circles on my belly, making me drowsy and lulling me to sleep.

Caiden walked in the door at the same time my phone rang on the coffee table in front of me. With a frown, I grabbed it and answered it. "Hello?" Caiden leaned down and pressed a kiss to my forehead before he slipped into our room to change into something more comfortable, though his ass really did look amazing in those tight jeans he was wearing.

"Ally?" my mom's voice rang through the line. I felt the blood rush out of my face.

"What do you want?" I bravely asked. I sat up. Christian did as well, his eyes narrowed at me in concern.

"I want to make amends—" my mother began, but I cut her off.

"Do you, or are you suddenly panicking because you don't have access to money anymore?" I snapped, suddenly angry. Dr. Gresham warned me this would happen; I just didn't think it was going to happen this fast—if at all.

"Ally—"

"No," I snarled, tightening my hand around my phone. "I'm not the one to come crying to about making amends. Do not contact me again."

I hung up the phone, and with an aggravated scream, I threw it across the room, narrowly missing Caiden as he walked back into the living room.

"Woah, my moon." Christian got up and moved in front of me, his hands gripping my face. "What did she say?"

"My mother wanted to suddenly make amends." Tears burned in my eyes, but I forced them to stay back. I would *not cry* over her—not anymore. She made her choices, and now she had to lie in her own bed of misery.

Christian suddenly smiled before he leaned forward

and kissed me. "I'm so, so fucking proud of you, beautiful."

"For?" I asked in confusion, the tears slowly evaporating.

"For enforcing your boundaries."

I squeaked in shock when he suddenly gripped me under my ass and lifted me from the couch. I quickly wrapped my legs around his hips, looking at him in alarm. He wickedly grinned down at me, and my core clenched. "I believe that this is cause for a celebration."

His lips hungrily met mine, drawing a moan from my lips before he laid me down on the bed. Then, Caiden was suddenly there, somehow already naked as his lips covered mine. His muscular body easily dwarfed mine.

But I loved it.

Caiden made quick work of my clothes before he stood up, moving to stand next to his younger brother. My breath hitched in my throat as I openly stared at both of them.

How did I get so lucky to have two, incredibly hot men?

Christian smirked at me. "You're getting both of us at once tonight," he told me.

"At once?" I squeaked, suddenly unsure. Caiden still hadn't made good on his promise to claim my ass, and now that it might be happening, I was extremely nervous and unsure.

Caiden moved towards me and lightly wrapped his hand around my throat as Christian laid back on the bed. "Have either of us ever done anything to hurt you?" he asked me. I instantly shook my head. He tightened his grip the slightest bit. I bit my lip, a soft moan sounding from the back of my throat. "Do you trust us?"

"Yes," I whispered, knowing he wanted a verbal response to that. And I didn't even have to think about my answer. I trusted these two men with my life and the life of our baby.

"Good girl," he praised. He brushed his nose with mine. "Then trust me when I say you'll enjoy this." He smirked, his eyes darkening even further. "I'm the master at anal, baby."

"Oh, fuck," I whispered, suddenly so turned on that it hurt.

He softly kissed me. "Go to Christian," he ordered after he released me.

I sat up before I crawled on my hands and knees toward Christian. He rubbed my belly as I straddled him, then his hands settled on my hips. "Remember, we'll never hurt you," he gently reminded me.

"I know." I grabbed his cock and slid down on him, moaning his name as I did so.

"Christ," Christian growled, his jaw clenching, his hands tightening on my hips.

I squeaked in shock when I felt Caiden suddenly

putting lube on my other hole. I tensed. Christian shook his head at me as he reached up and gripped my chin. "Relax," he ordered. "Caiden knows what's he doing, beautiful."

I drew in a deep breath, trying to relax, but I couldn't. I squeaked in shock when Caiden suddenly leaned his body over mine and began to rub my clit. I cried out, my body trembling as he quickly worked me to an orgasm.

"Now," Caiden ordered Christian, never stopping his fingers.

Christian began to thrust up into me. My eyes almost rolled into the back of my head, and then suddenly, Caiden was sliding inside of me.

But I couldn't even care about the intrusion. It felt so fucking good, even though it burned like hell, and when Caiden was fully seated inside of my ass, I almost collapsed.

It felt so damn good.

"Now, you're going to get fucked properly, baby," Caiden growled in my ear.

My eyes locked on Christian's beneath me. He smirked up at me. "You're glowing, my moon."

Then, my men proceeded to take and claim my body at the same time. All I could do was lay sandwiched between the two of them, taking everything they were giving me, and *fuck*, I never wanted it to end.

37

WELCOME, BABY GIRL

Ally

I blew out a soft breath and focused on the exam in front of me. I was nine months pregnant and finally back in college. It was the day of finals, and though I was nervous, I still felt pretty confident.

Christian and Caiden had both been working with me in the evenings to help me study. So far, I had been holding an A in all of my classes, and I was determined to keep it that way. I had plans to graduate at the top of my class and finally secure my career.

But my body had other plans.

I winced in pain when a contraction tightened my belly. I set my pencil down and drew in a deep breath, reminding myself to breathe and stay calm.

Panicking would *not* help me.

"Ms. Johnson, is something preventing you from taking my exam?" the professor asked, calling me out in front of everyone. I gritted my teeth, unable to think of an answer as I waited for the pain to pass.

I swallowed thickly, the contraction finally easing off. I shook my head at the professor. "No, sir," I grabbed my pencil and resumed taking the test, waiting to see how long it would take the next contraction to show up.

Two minutes.

This one was a bit more painful.

I winced and tightened my grip around the pencil, trying to draw in a deep breath. I was scared. I knew I was excited to have this baby, to finally be a mother, but I wasn't prepared for this part of the process. I had stupidly been hoping that this would happen at home when one of the guys was with me.

Not in the middle of class *in the middle of my final exam*.

"Ms. Johnson, are you okay?" the professor quietly asked me, coming to stand beside my desk.

I shook my head at him. "I need my phone," I quietly told him. "I'm in labor."

He quickly walked back up to the front of the classroom and brought me the basket with everyone's phones. I pulled my phone out of it and quickly turned it back on, impatiently waiting for it to finish powering on.

The professor silently took my exam and folded it, sticking it in his back pocket. He stood next to my desk as I quickly pulled up Caiden's phone number. This was our plan. If I was in school, I had to call Caiden. He was the one closest to me.

"Babe?" he asked. "Are you okay?"

"No," I whimpered, tears suddenly rushing down my cheeks at the sound of his voice. "I'm in labor."

"Fuck," he swore. "Take deep breaths, baby. Can you get out in the hallway for me?"

"*Mhm.*" I slowly slid out of my desk. Another contraction tightened my belly, and I stumbled. The professor gripped my elbow, offering me support as I slowly made my way to the door.

"Breathe, baby," Caiden commanded. "I can hear you panicking. I need you to breathe. I'm in my car. Give me three minutes, and I'll be there with you," he promised.

"Please be careful," I breathlessly begged. The man had a serious issue with speeding.

I slowly sat down on one of the benches. The professor slipped back into the classroom, coming back a moment later with my purse. He set it beside me. "Good luck, and congratulations on your baby," the professor told me with a smile. I nodded, trying to breathe through my contraction. "Send me an email when you're out of the hospital, and we'll schedule a day and time for you to come in and take your exam."

Relief made me slump a little. I would still have a chance to make up this exam. "Thank you."

He nodded and slipped back into the room. I drew in a shaky breath. "Caiden, it hurts," I whimpered.

"I know, baby. Just continue breathing, okay? I'm almost there," he assured me.

Caiden came sprinting up the stairs across from me, not even breaking a sweat or breathing heavily, whereas I felt like passing out just from having contractions.

"I'm here, baby." He grabbed my purse and shouldered it before he lifted me up from the chair and cradled me in his arms, carrying me down the stairs. "Christian is meeting us at the hospital," he informed me.

My face scrunched up in pain when another contraction tightened my belly. "Breathe," Caiden ordered. "Baby, you have to breathe."

"It hurts," I cried, a tear running down my cheek.

He brushed his lips to my forehead after he pushed open the door, walking out into the sunlight. "I know, but breathe. Not breathing is going to make it hurt more," he reminded me.

Caiden somehow speed-walked to his car without jarring me, and as soon as I was in the passenger seat of his still-running car, Christian's voice came through the speakers. I sobbed with relief.

"My moon, I need you to breathe," he calmly stated. "I'm on my way to the hospital. I'll be there when you guys get there, okay? Just breathe, beautiful."

Caiden grabbed my hand in his and brought it up to his lips, holding it there as he pulled out into traffic, heading to the hospital. "I'm not ready for this," I whimpered.

Caiden softly laughed. "Baby, it's a little late to say that." I wrapped my arm around my belly when it began to tighten again. "Just keep breathing, baby. We're almost there," he assured me.

When we got to the hospital, Christian was waiting outside of the emergency room doors for us, and Julian was there beside him. Caiden slid out of the car, and Julian immediately took his place in the driver's seat, most likely to go park it for him.

Christian reached in and slid his arms beneath me, gently lifting me from the car. "You're doing so fucking good, my moon," he praised. I gave him a watery smile. Both of my men smiled back at me. "There you go. Keep smiling, beautiful. It's going to be okay."

"It hurts so bad," I croaked.

Caiden grabbed my hand in his, walking beside us as Christian carried me into the emergency room. "I know, baby. Just breathe and remember that all of this pain is going to be worth it in the end."

Caiden pulled my wallet out of his back pocket once we got up to the desk and slid the receptionist my ID. "She's in active labor," he told her. "Contractions are about a minute and a half apart. They started abruptly. She's forty weeks and three days pregnant."

I gaped at him. "How do you memorize all of that?" I asked him, breathing a little bit easier now that my contraction had passed for a moment.

"Military training, babe," he told me with a cheeky grin. He grabbed my ID back and quickly filled out the form as a nurse brought over a wheelchair to take me up to the labor and delivery floor.

"Oh, God," I cried as soon as I was sitting in the chair, another contraction tightening my belly. Christian grabbed my hand in his, allowing me to squeeze as Caiden quickly filled out my HIPAA paperwork.

"Is it supposed to hurt this bad?" I wheezed.

"Labor pains are different for every woman," Christian gently reminded me. "Breathe, baby. You're not breathing."

Tears slid down my cheeks. "It hurts," I whined.

"I know." He held up my wrist so Caiden could put

the plastic identification bracelet on me. Once that was on, I was wheeled to the elevator, Christian still continuing to hold my hand.

As soon as I was placed into a room, the nurse gave me privacy to get changed into the hospital gown. Christian and Caiden both set to work on getting me undressed. I was sweating by that point, the pain almost unbearable. Both of my men kept reminding me to breathe and to just count back from one hundred through the contractions since it made me focus more on counting than the pain.

It somewhat worked, but fuck, it still hurt like a bitch.

Christian and Caiden were standing on either side of me when the nurse began to check my cervix. I gritted my teeth, clenching their hands, trying to force myself to breathe.

"Hun, you didn't notice any labor contractions before a little while ago?" the nurse asked me. She was trying to hide the alarm in her voice, but I could still hear it, and I was doing my best not to freak out with her. What was going on?

"No," I gasped out.

"You're ten centimeters dilated, honey," she informed me. *What?* "But I need to get the midwife. Your baby is breeched."

"*What?*" I asked, momentarily forgetting the pain.

My heart thumped crazily in my chest. "That's not possible. She was head down at my last appointment."

"I don't know how she turned, honey, but she's definitely breeched. Just hang tight."

Tears poured down my face. "What's going to happen?" I cried.

"Easy, baby," Caiden told me, his voice hard and firm. "Panicking isn't going to do anything but raise your blood pressure, which is bad for the baby. You need to stay calm."

"But—"

"Breathe," he snapped, his harsh tone grounding me. Christian only squeezed my hand in his, pressing soft kisses to my fingers. "You need to breathe, baby. Focus on me and just breathe. We're going to get through this, and you'll still give birth to a very healthy baby girl."

My midwife came into the room at that moment. "Alright, Ally, I'm going to take a look, okay? If I can't safely deliver your baby girl like this, then we're going to immediately get you prepped for a c-section, okay?"

"What happens then?" I asked her, my voice trembling. We hadn't discussed a c-section because the baby had been head down ever since I was thirty-two weeks. We didn't think we would have this problem.

"We'll give you some anesthesia to numb your belly, and we're going to have to cut you open to get your little girl out." I squeezed my eyes shut, my breathing quickening.

"Ally, open your fucking eyes," Caiden barked. I opened them, locking them on his dark ones. "Breathe. Stop panicking. It's going to be okay. We're not leaving your side. C-sections happen all of the time. They're safe."

I winced when my midwife began to check me. She pulled back a moment later and looked up at the nurse. "Let them know we need a c-section room prepped immediately. The baby is under a lot of stress. We need to get this done quickly." She stood up and walked closer to me. "Ally, we're going to have to do a c-section. All of the contractions are stressing the baby out since you can't push. I need you to breathe and relax as much as possible, and listen to both Caiden and Christian as they coax you through each contraction, okay? We're going to get you prepped here in just a few minutes."

"Okay," I whispered. I was terrified, but I would get through this. I had to. My baby was relying on me to safely bring her into this world.

She smiled at me. "You're doing fantastic, Ally. Just breathe."

She quickly left the room, and I burst into tears.

Christian

A few hours later, I was finally able to hold Taya Faith Greene in my arms. She was the spitting image of her beautiful mother, except she had my extremely dark hair and my nose. And somehow, she ended up with my brother's more angular jawline.

Caiden slowly opened one eye as I got up to grab her a bottle since it was time to feed her. He was laying on the hospital bed with Ally as she slept, though I knew he hadn't slept at all.

He wouldn't—not until Ally wasn't in so much pain anymore. That was how my brother operated.

"She okay?" he quietly asked.

I nodded. "She just needs to be fed," I whispered. I grabbed the small bottle of pre-made formula since Ally was still sleeping, and I didn't want to wake her to breastfeed Taya.

We had decided a few months ago to do a combination of both breastfeeding and formula since Ally was going to be in school. Though she would be doing online schooling until Taya was one, it would still be easier for her than to have to stop doing schoolwork and breastfeed, not to mention, it wouldn't overwhelm her either.

I walked back around the bed and sighed when I

noticed blood on the sheets. "Call for a nurse and wake her up," I told Caiden. "She's bleeding through."

He pressed the button on the bed for a nurse before he gently shook Ally awake. She groaned in protest, her sleepy eyes looking up at him. He softly smiled at her. "Come on, baby. You're bleeding through. We need to get you cleaned up."

"Hi, how can I help you?" a woman's voice came through the little speaker in the bed, making Ally jump in shock.

"We need clean sheets," Caiden told her, his hand smoothing over Ally's hair.

"We'll be there in a moment."

Caiden got off of the bed and helped ease Ally to her feet. She winced in pain, but the pain medication she was on was keeping most of her pain away so she could at least somewhat walk, though Caiden walked behind her, keeping his hands on her hips to steady her and held support her.

By the time they came back out of the bathroom, the bed sheets had been changed and the nurse was gone out of the room again. Ally was changed into a pair of Caiden's plain black sweatpants that she had rolled up but riding low on her hips with a belly shirt, her c-section area left open.

"You good, my moon?" I asked her as Caiden helped her back onto the hospital bed.

She winced in pain. "Yeah." She cringed. "For the most part, anyway."

Caiden got back on the bed beside her. I stood up and walked over to her with Taya. She beamed, her eyes brightening, that beautiful glow lighting up the fucking room as she held her arms out for our little girl.

Caiden smiled at her. "You're a beautiful, amazing mother, baby," he praised.

She beamed at him, her cheeks burning red. She maneuvered Taya under her shirt. Our little girl quickly latched on. I leaned down and smoothed my lips over Ally's.

"Thank you for this, baby."

"For what?" she asked me, honest confusion in her voice.

I smiled at her. "For Taya," I told her. Her eyes softened. God, our woman was fucking beautiful. "Today, you made me one of the happiest fucking men in the world."

"Does that mean my name is going on the marriage certificate, then?" Caiden asked. "You got the baby with her first. I want to marry her."

She gaped at him. "Caiden!" she exclaimed. But I couldn't help but laugh. He and I already had this discussion, and I had actually been the one to tell him to marry her. He had TriCare health insurance, and if he married her, both she and our baby would go on his insurance.

Not to mention, she would get a hell of a lot of benefits because he used to serve in the military, and since he got an honorable discharge, he got to keep most of his benefits.

"What?" He grinned at her. "I'll do a better proposal later, but I want to marry you."

"But—"

"We've already talked about this, beautiful," I assured her, deciding to put her out of her misery. She looked up at me. "I want him to marry you. In terms of marriage, you'll benefit more by marrying him, as will Taya. Otherwise, neither of us would give a fuck who you decided to put on the marriage certificate."

"Oh, my God," she whispered. Tears filled her eyes. "You mean you don't want to actually marry me?" she asked, looking at Caiden.

"Fuck," he whispered. He cupped her face in his hands. "That's not what I meant, baby. I want everything with you—marriage, family, a baby of our own a little further down the road—but Christian and I both want you to have everything you may need, and I have government benefits, which would be better for you in the long run. Don't twist it up and get lost in your head, baby girl."

"Sorry," she croaked. She swiped at her eyes with her free hand. "I guess I'm still pretty emotional."

I leaned over the bed and kissed her. "You're always emotional, baby girl, but I love it," I assured her. "Besides, we have time. Fucker needs to propose to you properly."

Caiden rolled his eyes but grinned at her when she blushed. "So fucking cute, babe." He brushed his thumb over her bottom lip.

Her cheeks darkened. I laughed softly.

Her innocence would never grow old for either of us.

EPILOGUE

Ally

My cheeks were on fire as the president of the school called my name to come on stage and grab my diploma. Being the center of attention was never my thing, and it still wasn't.

Two and a half years later, I was finally finished with pharmacy school, and I was now a full-time pharmacist at a hospital I had done one of my internships with. Today, I was finally getting my diploma—finally graduating.

Caiden and Christian had been there for me every step of the way, taking over Taya's care in the evenings so that I could focus on getting my schoolwork done.

Caiden was amazing at math and science, and with his help, I passed all of those courses with flying colors. And with Christian's help, I passed all of my English and Language Arts classes, as well as all of my history classes. Between the two of them, they helped me memorize everything else.

I was graduating with a 4.0 GPA and was at the top of my class.

I had declined doing the speech, and with my medical history, they let it go, instead choosing the next available candidate.

When the ceremony was completely over, I was immediately engulfed into a hug between my two men as they congratulated me, proud smiles on their faces. My heart swelled in my chest.

I really couldn't be happier.

Taya ran up to me with a squeal. "Mommy!" she yelled, launching herself at my legs. I laughed and leaned down, swooping her up into my arms, the motion making me slightly nauseous, but I managed not to throw up everywhere.

"Hi, baby," I greeted.

"You did it!" she yelled. She planted a wet, sloppy kiss on my cheek. I laughed.

I pressed a kiss to her nose. "I did it, baby." Julian walked up to me with Axel and Meghan. Christian reached out and took Taya from me before Axel swooped in and wrapped me up in his arms, spinning me around. He pressed a kiss to the top of my head once he set me back on my feet.

"You have no fucking idea how proud I am of you." Tears sprang to my eyes. Axel had always been my role model and my rock, and to hear those words from his mouth on one of the biggest days of my life made my chest swell with so much happiness that it felt like it was going to burst.

"You're going to make me cry." I quickly fanned my face. I was wearing make-up, and we still had pictures to do. Raccoon eyes were *not* pretty.

He grinned at me. Julian hugged me next. "Always knew you were destined for great things, little sis. You did so good, and you stayed strong despite the odds being against you. I'm so damn proud of you."

Meghan yanked him back before she wrapped me up in a tight hug. Julian laughed at her. My throat closed up with tears as I tightly hugged her back, my heart squeezing in my chest.

"I am so honored to be part of your beautiful journey, Ally," she quietly told me. I sniffled, blinking fast to keep from crying. "You've blossomed into such a beautiful and strong young woman, and I'm so fucking proud of you. Continue pushing through and climbing upward, Ally. You're going to do great, amazing things."

She pulled back from me and reached into her

purse, pulling out a tissue. I took it from her with a grateful smile, and she held up her compact mirror so I could fix my makeup. I laughed. "You're a lifesaver."

She grinned at me. "What are sisters for?"

Her eyes widened at something behind me. I spun around only to see Caiden on one knee, a black, velvet box in his hand opened to reveal a beautiful, diamond ring. My hands flew up to my mouth, tears instantly rushing down my face and ruining my make-up.

But he still smiled at me like I was the most beautiful person in his life.

"Ally Johnson, two and a half years ago, when you gave birth to our beautiful daughter, Christian and I told you that we both wanted you to marry me." He drew in a deep breath. "I've just been waiting for the perfect time. I wanted it to be the perfect day for you— something beautiful and unforgettable—just like you."

I sobbed. "I never wanted to settle down with anyone, much less a woman," he smirked, "before you." I laughed, though it sounded like a mix between a sob and a laugh. "But I've got to admit, babe, anal—"

Christian smacked him on the back of the head, but all of us were laughing. Caiden couldn't be serious for shit.

"What I'm trying to say is, baby, I want to marry you. I want to make you a Greene, and I want to spend the rest of my life loving you and watching you continue to glow between me and my brother."

He drew in a deep breath. "So, Ally, will you marry me?"

I laughed and placed my hand over my belly all while my tears ran down my face. "I guess it's a good thing you popped the question before I told you I'm pregnant," I teased. His eyes widened in shock. "Otherwise, it would make your proposal look horrible."

"You're pregnant?" he asked, not even caring I was poking fun at him.

I smiled at him as I held my hand out to him, a giggle falling past my lips at the stupefied look on his face. "Yes, I'll marry you. Yes, I'm pregnant. And, thank your brother—he helped me plan this. It's your baby."

"Holy shit!" he yelled. I screamed in shock when he suddenly lurched up from the ground and yanked me into his arms, swinging me around in a circle.

He set me on my feet and grabbed my face in his hands, taking my lips in a hard, bruising kiss. I moaned, my hands gripping his shirt in my fists, my lips instantly opening beneath his.

"Bro, I think you're forgetting to put the ring on her finger," Christian teased, breaking through our moment.

"Fuck," Caiden grumbled. He grabbed the ring from

Christian and slipped it on my finger. "I got distracted." I giggled, leaning up on my tiptoes to kiss him again.

Meghan squealed and wrapped me up in her arms as soon as I stepped back from Caiden to look at the rest of my family. I sobbed, completely falling apart.

I was going to get married.

I turned to face Christian. Caiden took Taya from him, and Christian reached up, cupping my face in his hands. "Glow, my moon. Always fucking glow."

Then, his lips covered mine.

ALSO BY T.O. SMITH

Want to stay up to date on new releases, preorders, sales, and freebies?

Join my newsletter and be one of the first to know!

https://www.tosmithbooks.com/newsletter

Facebook

Instagram

Facebook Group

Twitter

Pinterest

Patreon

TikTok

https://tosmithbooks.com

Click here to access my merch store.

ABOUT THE AUTHOR

T.O. Smith believes in one thing - a happily ever after.

Her books are fast-paced and dive straight into the romance and the action. She doesn't do extensively drawn-out plots. Normally, within the first chapter, she's got you - hook, line, and sinker.

As a writer of various different genres of romance, a reader is almost guaranteed to find some kind of romance novel they'll enjoy on her page.

T.O. Smith can be found on Facebook, Instagram, Twitter, and now even TikTok! She loves interacting with all of her readers, so follow her!